D1234770

E-BOOK EDITION

𝔇isenchanted © 2015 by Leigh Goff and Mirror World Publishing

Edited by: Gail Dowsett

All Rights Reserved.

   *This book is a work of fiction. All of the characters, organizations and events portrayed in this novel are either products of the authors' imagination or are used fictitiously. Any resemblance to actual locales, events or persons is entirely coincidental.

Mirror World Publishing

Windsor, Ontario
www.mirrorworldpublishing.com
info@mirrorworldpublishing.com

ISBN: 978-0-9920490-9-6

To Brian, Carson, and Chase for making all my dreams come true.

To Delia,
You have been so kind and generous with your support and I truly appreciate it!

Disenchanted

Leigh Goff

Leigh

June 2015

M|W mirror world publishing

While scooping dried witches wort into sachets at the shop counter, I watched a girl with dark upswept hair, wearing a Puritan cap and dress, emerge from behind a tall display shelf of Aunt Janie's Forbidden Passion Potion. She looked to be a bit older than me, maybe seventeen or eighteen.

"Are you one of the historic foundation's tour guides? If so, you get a discount on the merchandise."

It wasn't unusual for ordinary girls to be touring around Wethersfield, Connecticut, in period costumes, pointing out graves of the seriously self-righteous Puritans who participated in hanging the Wethersfield witches. However, I knew all the ordinaries who had summer jobs with the foundation, and I didn't recognize her, not that she looked like one of them beyond the outfit.

I tightened the strings on the sachets and tossed them into a large decorative basket on the shop floor. I wiped the honey-scented witcheswort dust on my spring green apron.

"Would you be interested in sampling our Tulips to Kiss Stick? The tulip pollen lushifies your lips."

Her dead silence forced my eyes up. As I looked her over, I noticed how her wide blue eyes imparted a look like she was lost and far from interested in lusher lips.

"You are a Greensmith, no?" she asked with a hint of a Puritan accent.

Outside of the coven, no one was aware of my family tree or that I was Rebecca Greensmith's ninth great-granddaughter.

"I'm descended from a Greensmith. Sophie Goodchild, at your service. Who are you?" *Because you're not an ordinary*, I thought. I glanced at her heart-shaped face, luminous without Aunt Janie's Phyto-Glo powder, and her gentle hands, which rested lightly on the counter.

"And this is your family's store?" The way she asked, she seemed to already know.

The four-hundred-year-old shop resembled a whimsical Pottery Barn store for aromatherapy products and the current owner, another Greensmith descendant, Aunt Janie, quaintly renamed it *Scents and Scentsabilities*. I furrowed my eyebrows.

"Uh-huh. What can I help you with?"

The frail-looking girl stared at my red crystal pendant, which had slipped out from beneath my T-shirt. I pressed my warm fingers to the simple stone that once belonged to my mom. As I tucked it away, a crash and thud from the back room snagged my attention. I whirled around.

"Aaah! Sophie!" My best friend, Macey, rushed toward me. Light brown tendrils cascaded into her green eyes. She tucked the curls behind her ears, but they popped forward again as she shook her phone at me.

I caught my breath. "Are you okay?"

"Okay?" she panted. Her glossy lips stretched into a wide smile and she began to bounce into her happy dance as she whirled around. "Daniel sent me the sweetest text." She flashed her phone in the air. "Share time."

I blew a long wisp of wavy sable hair from my eyes, relieved. "I thought you were going cray-postal on a mouse."

She threw a hand up as if she were in class. "Is that Soph-ese for crazy? How do you come up with these Frankenwords?"

"Said the girl who just made up 'Soph-ese' and 'Frankenwords.'" I laughed as I spun back around to apologize to the strange customer and assure her there were really no mice in the shop, but she was gone. I scanned every cream-colored nook. It was as if she had fallen through a crack in the wide planks of the wood floor. "Did you hear the shop bell chime?" I asked Macey, pinching myself to make sure I hadn't hallucinated the girl.

"No. But look at this." She shoved her phone in my face, excitement shivered in her fingertips. "Daniel loves me. Can you believe it? Shout out to your aunt for her Tulips to Kiss Stick followed by the Forever First Love Lip Balm." She tilted her head in a dreamy sort of way.

I smiled, happy for her because she had been crushing on Daniel forever, but at the same time wondering what it was like. Ordinary girls only noticed my oddness and mishaps, but the boys didn't notice me at all. It had been ingrained since birth that getting attention was dangerous and that was—sigh—fine, but the problem was, I wasn't great at blending, either.

"He'd be stupid if he didn't. Did you see the girl who was just here?" I peered around the displays again. When I looked down at the counter, I noticed she left something behind. I slipped the small, inconspicuous book into my apron pocket for safekeeping, but as I grabbed hold of the little painted figure, it warmed too quickly to my touch. *Pure iron*, I thought.

As a half-witch, I could handle the particular metal for only a short amount of time. I lifted the tiny figurine toward the antique chandelier's light for a better look. My eyes narrowed. Could this be?

"What's that?" Macey asked.

Ding-a-ding-ding. I glanced at the door, hoping to catch sight of the girl returning for her stuff so I wouldn't have to lie. Instead, Aunt Janie blew in on the warm evening breeze. I dropped my hand to the counter, covering the mysterious iron object so she wouldn't freak if my guess was right. Her brunette bob blew about her ivory face as she read the fake "everything's okay" look on my face. Hiding my emotions was, regrettably, not a gift I possessed. Her happy-to-see-me smile faded and her face immediately creased with anxiety. "What's going on?"

I said nothing. Although her clairvoyant and herbalist gifts were as sharp as ever, her spirit had been as fragile as untempered glass since my parents died and there was no need to upset her.

Macey pointed. "A customer left something behind."

My jaw jutted out as I restrained to keep my elbow from shifting into her side. Aunt Janie's eyes, warm brown like the center of a delicate black-eyed daisy, focused on mine, willing me to lift my palm. A lifetime of secret-keeping took over. The devil's bit nectar, which helped with lying, tingled on my lips.

"It's nothing. I'm sure."

Her thin movie-star eyebrows arched for a second. "Then let me see."

As I revealed the object, her mouth dropped open, confirming my suspicion while sending a foreboding chill up my spine like the tracing of icy fingers.

"What is it?" Macey asked.

My lips tingled again. "I don't know," I said, wanting to sound clueless. I had to. Although she was my best friend and way nicer than the other girls, she was still an ordinary. I backed away from the counter.

"It's something."

Aunt Janie stood there, speechless, and then glanced at the deceptively innocent-looking woman in the seventeenth century oil painting which hung on the store wall behind me. Everyone assumed the anonymous painting was there to add a historical feel to the old shop, but we knew who she was. A powerful Wethersfield witch and my ancestor, Rebecca Greensmith.

Aunt Janie looked as if she were casting blame on her for the figurine, and then her storytelling talent kicked in. Her voice dropped to a low solemn tone.

"From what I know about the town's history, nearly four hundred years ago witches settled here from Essex, England, and offered their healing and fortune telling services to the locals, but some chose a darker path, like the witch who created this…"

"You mean, black witches?" Macey asked. I heard her swallow a gulp.

Aunt Janie peered over at me with an anxious look as one of her classical Mozart mashups played in the background.

"Yes. This sinister object was created to bring death to the one it resembled." We stared at the iron girl. She was painted with long, dark, wavy hair, wide blue eyes, and a blue gown the color of a cloudless sky. The most striking detail, however, was her nearly severed-through neck.

Goose pimples popped up all over my arms. I shuddered at the thought.

Without taking her eyes off the object, Aunt Janie recalled the history, a story ingrained in our coven's memory.

"Ever heard of the Wethersfield Witch Trials?"

Macey nodded.

"I heard Laney Mayapple say how Judge Mather is related to the minister who hung the witches for crimes of, get this, dancing with the devil and casting curses on the locals. It's like Wethersfield was the *Footloose* town of the sixteen hundreds."

"Yeah, except the minister in *Footloose* didn't hang anyone."

She grimaced. "Yikes. Anyway, the story came up because the Mather boys just moved back from London, and apparently, their return has the Glitterati all abuzz."

I peered over at Aunt Janie, wondering if she knew the Glitterati were the prettiest and most obnoxious witches at Wethersfield High who wanted nothing to do with me.

She turned her focus on Macey.

"More Mathers in town?" A concerned expression gripped her face. "So his three sons moved back?"

"I think Laney said only two, but hey, the more the merrier. Wethersfield High could use a transfusion. We have so many Goth boys. I mean, can't that trend die already?" She meant some of our coven's warlocks who took a little too much pride in their heritage and had been warned to tone it down, not that *they* had to worry about blending in.

"Two? Guess my memory isn't what it used to be," Aunt Janie said.

Macey plucked the iron figure from the counter. "What are you going to do with it?"

Aunt Janie paused, deep in thought. "I'll let Sophie take care of it." As a full-blooded witch, touching iron would cause her great pain so she'd have to let me handle it.

Macey laughed to herself as she examined the relic.

"That's funny. It kind of looks like you, Sophie. Except for your neck not being half-detached. And she's wearing a dress."

I drew back in disbelief. Her comparison of the sculpture to me was beyond ridiculous.

"No, it doesn't, and I wear dresses. Sometimes," I protested, instantly defensive.

She knew me like a sister, prodding in all the right places.

"Like when? You'd rather run barefoot through your garden than wear a dress."

It wasn't an insult, but her persistence with the topic caused the heat to rise up in me. I scrunched my mouth into a knot and snatched it from her hand, stuffing it in my apron pocket next to the book.

"She doesn't look anything like me. Period!"

As I spoke, my lips tingled from the nectar, which only happened when I was lying. But I had no reason to lie about this. The cursed figurine was a witch creation, but it had to be hundreds of years old and crafted with black magic, which Aunt Janie and I had nothing to do with.

"It does, too, look like you. Her dark, wavy hair matches yours and those eyes." Astonished, her mouth dropped open.

"Take it back out and look. It's like your own little bobble-head."

My shoulders tightened as my short-fused temper sparked. Latin bubbled on my tongue. I tried to bite down, but it was too late.

"*Ictus.*"

I cast through my clenched teeth. Without thinking, my fists uncurled and a cyclone of energy whooshed out of my right index finger in a whirling corkscrew of air, tickling as it rushed from me and sending a flurry of fliers and lace doilies from a display table.

Macey's jaw dropped. Aunt Janie flashed her panicked eyes to mine, sending my heart into a flutter.

Crud! I would end up in Kingshill for sure, leaving my poor aunt chewing on anti-anxiety herbs in a corner somewhere. And worse, I'd become a pawn for Laney's mom, the head of our coven. I wiped a dark tendril of hair from my eyes and focused my gaze on Macey. With a subtle pointing of my finger and a whispering of the *deleto* spell, I cast again, this time with laser focus.

The magic swirled out controlled and even, tickling like little granules of sugary sand from an hourglass. Her eyes glazed over, assuring me the spell worked the way I needed it to. I took a deep breath, recouping from the pull of blood from my brain to my hands, leaving me dizzy. Then the guilt from losing my temper and manipulating her memory seeped in, twisting my stomach into a knot.

She shook her head in a daze and looked blank-faced.

"What was I saying?"

I had used the spell before with some accuracy and it didn't seem to have any long-term effects. Laney endured enough of it from me and she was still as mean as a Venus flytrap.

"Girls, stop arguing."

"We were arguing?" Macey met my eyes with a puzzled expression. More guilt. My stomach knot tightened from not feeling like a very good friend.

Aunt Janie glanced at the scattered mess on the floor. She tucked her straight brunette strands of hair behind her ear, her tell when she lied. "A gust must have blown in from under the door and sent those flying," she said. From the back wall, the antique grandfather clock chimed, eerily reminding us of the time.

"Why don't you both straighten up this mess and be quick? Sophie needs to run an errand for me."

I glanced at her quizzically. "It's summer break and Macey and I were planning to hang at Summerfield's Smoothies."

"Not this evening. A special delivery is arriving at the house. Need you to be there when it comes." She winked at me. "Tea leaves."

An excited grin tugged at my cheeks. "Oooh. From the Fujian Province?"

"Where else?" Her eyes glimmered with clairvoyant excitement.

Macey tilted her head, baffled. "You know, they sell tea leaves at Goody's Market. You don't have to import them."

"She's particular about her tea," I said, afraid we had said too much in front of her. "Sorry about the smoothies."

"No probs." We cleaned up and before we left, I slipped the book and figurine into my back pocket for safekeeping, but as I touched the little book, it sent a cool chill across my skin. *Enchanted*, I thought. I tossed my apron under the counter, excited to get home. Macey smiled and waved as she left, her curls blowing all about her face.

"See you tomorrow."

"'Bye," I said, heading in the opposite direction. A rain-scented breeze blew across my face as the black clouds snuffed out the lingering sunlight. It was all so ordinary, working with her for the summer and talking about boys. I couldn't help to wonder if it wouldn't be simpler being an ordinary.

I walked fast, hoping to outrun the rain, but the staccato rhythm of heavy footsteps in the distance drew my attention. I glanced all around at the empty street. The leafy trees lining the sidewalk whooshed back and forth, urging me to get home. My heart raced.

Thunder growled like a hungry lion. I continued walking, even faster than before. Everything in me wanted to turn around, see who he was. I knew I shouldn't. A glimpse would slow me down, but I couldn't stop myself. I tucked my long, wild hair behind my ears and subtly craned my head over my right shoulder. I spied a man of average build wearing a black hoodie, the hood up, obscuring his face. I whipped my head forward. My pulse jumped. The summer heat forced the obvious question to the surface. Why was his hood up?

I picked up my pace. His steps grew louder.

My thoughts raced as fast as my heart. With a boom and a crack, rain dropped like tiny glass beads falling from the sky. I rounded a curve in the sidewalk and broke into a sprint. My feet splashed through fresh puddles. I felt a slithering sensation down my chest, but I couldn't stop. I frantically blinked and blinked to clear my eyes of the trickling raindrops.

He approached closer. His loud breathing was upon me as he breached the gap I was desperate to maintain. Lightning ripped through the black sky. In a violent flash, the stranger's cold, strong arm strapped around my shoulders like a formidable steel vice, his limb mashing against my bones. He wrapped his other arm tightly around my waist to secure my wriggling frame. My heart hammered in my ears. I flailed, hoping to kick myself free. A rush of panic sent adrenaline coursing through my blood, speeding everything up, making it impossible to think through the chaos.

I wanted to scream. I wanted spells to flow and a tree to fall on him, but my voice abandoned me as his forearm crushed violently against my neck, paralyzing my vocal cords. My lungs burned, craving air.He inched his fingers toward my pendant.

"Give me the necklace!" he seethed, his furious words stinging my cheek like sharp tacks.

Rain gushed hard against my body. I clawed at his skin. I wriggled, struggling against the stranger's unrelenting strength. I scanned the area, searching for a way out. His one hand slipped closer to my neck. Under the light of the streetlamp, I noticed a mark, a tattoo staring at me from his wrist. My eyes grew wild, absorbing the details; a roaring lion encircled in a black ring. The realization of who he worked for hit me hard and anger saturated every part of my body.

Then, a sudden and unexpected smack of flesh hitting flesh set me free. The attacker released me to the concrete sidewalk with a jarring thud. I swirled my head around. A tall man grabbed the thief. He twisted him into a choke hold and began shaking him back and forth like a wrestler about to toss an inferior competitor out of the ring. A few seconds later, the attacker submitted to the man's strength, dropping to the ground and clumsily scrambling into a sprint.

I sat, soaking wet, shaking from the adrenaline. Whoever he was, he rescued me from the would-be thief who bore the symbol of the Leos, a breath-saving nickname I gave Judge Mather's Law Enforcement Organization. I strained to see, but the rain drops clinging to my long eyelashes blurred my vision. I wiped them away as my heart settled to an even pace.

With his back to me, he watched the thief disappear into the stormy night. He ran his hands through his thick, wavy, wet hair. His broad shoulders relaxed before he turned to offer me assistance. He extended his long arm to help me to my feet. I hesitated for a second, unsure of him, but as he reached for me, our fingers brushed together. A shock of electricity bolted through my hand. I froze as I caught the surprised reaction on his face, telling me he felt it, too. His fingers clasped firmly around mine and, with no effort, he pulled me to my feet. Unsteady, I pressed my hands against his firm muscled chest that showed through the drenched white shirt. A dizzy, swirly sensation swept through my head as if I were on a merry-go-round spinning around at one hundred miles per hour.

He had to be six feet tall.

"Are you okay?" he asked in a smooth British accent. His deep voice vibrated with tension, sending warm chills inside me.

I balanced myself and brushed my wet hair behind my ears, swallowing hard. A British accent that could make a girl melt if the girl didn't have alarm bells going off in her head. There were no Brits currently living in our small part of Wethersfield, which meant he had to be one of *them*. My wide eyes flitted around, looking for a clue to make sense of why the statuesque Mather boy with his soaking wet shirt and black tailored pants left the comfort of his father's manor house to brave the storm.

He stepped closer, breaching the already slim gap between us and forcing my eyes up. The streetlight illuminated his handsome features. His ivory complexion, dappled with raindrops and a shadow of thick stubble, revealed a hint of blush as if it were wintertime and the cold air had plucked at his cheeks.

I followed the perfect straight line of his nose to his brooding, dark eyes full of mystery. His eyes wandered over the details of my face and settled on my own, waiting for me to reply. A warm, wet breeze swirled up from behind him and wrapped his alluring scent around me; clean, woodsy and thoroughly masculine. I inhaled again and again, unable to exhale. With all the plants and flowers I had smelled in my lifetime, he smelled better than any, alone or in combination. I wavered slightly side to side, feeling dazed. I gulped a mouthful of air, trying not to breathe him in. What was wrong with me? I shook myself out of the stupor.

"Did you know that man?" he asked.

"Did *you*?" I said in an accusatory tone, but at that moment, I didn't care about the attacker.

"I don't know what you're talking about."

He drew back like I was crazy for suggesting anything. He was the enemy. *Say something*, I thought.

"What…what are you doing out here anyway?"

He furrowed his eyebrows inward.

"Saving you, obviously."

I threw my hands on my hips, shocked by the irony. A Mather helping a Greensmith? Hell was freezing over somewhere beneath our feet and every kind of farm animal was sprouting wings to fly.

"That's impossible."

"And why is that?"

"Because…because you're a Mather," I said, not meaning to sound disgusted, but I struggled to contain my feelings. Fact was, the Mathers had Greensmith blood on their hands, as well as my coven's blood. Through Wethersfield's history, they were known as witch-hunters and with each generation, they changed only to appear more politically correct, but their intentions remained unchanged. His eyes tensed at the corners, as if it were possible he didn't hate me.

"And what does that mean?"

Did he really not know or was he messing with me for the fun of it?

"That means someone like you doesn't leave his dad's house to help someone like me."

His head tilted slightly. "Sounds like you're insulting both of us."

I shook my head and said nothing, unsure what to think of him.

"And how is it you know I live with my father? I literally just moved in today. Or back in, I should say."

I stepped back, feeling slightly transparent.

"Small town. Plus your accent gives you away."

"I guess your access to town gossip gives you an advantage over me. It's unfair really, because the only thing I know about you is that you have strong shoulders." Sarcasm drenched his words.

"What does that mean?"

His eyes glinted like a lion's before a fight. "Means they're strong enough to carry that huge chip around. By the way, you're welcome for the help."

I mashed my lips together as the rage settled in. "I don't have a..."

He shook his head with a cool abruptness and turned to leave, as if he hated me now.

Without thinking, I grabbed his hand to argue he was wrong, but the sparks sparked again. I closed my eyes and tried to clear the daze.

"W-Wait. What's your first name?" I asked, immediately wishing I hadn't. I mean, did it matter?

His hand slipped away from mine. He stared at it for a moment and then cleared the dismay from his face.

"Sounds like my last name's enough for you."

"I'm asking. I want to know."

His head dropped as he stared down at nothing in particular, suddenly looking lost. "You don't want to know me."

The dash of humility threw me. I never heard of any Mather expressing anything close to it. Stumped, I crossed my arms against my drenched white shirt. He wasn't at all what I expected. I was curious why he wasn't, and why their return to Wethersfield was such a big, stupid secret.

He glanced around, as if he were checking to make sure the thief was long gone. "You should go home." He pressed his wet lips together and set his penetrating gaze back on me.

The warmth of blood flushed to the surface of my cheeks. My heart beat a little faster as I stood there, thoroughly confused. Without another word between us, he turned away. His footsteps splashed softly through the puddles, heading away from the street where we both lived. I wanted to run after him, make him explain what he meant, but he was gone before I could.

Looking around, I realized I was quite alone and unsettled from the attack. An attack that made no sense since my necklace was only valuable in sentiment, nothing more. I bolted down Alix Street and cut through the grassy path to the back of my property where I squeezed my small frame through the gap in the stone wall.

I raced up the terraced tiers and stood beneath the balcony of my bedroom window, which hid a little secret that Callum, my friend and distant cousin, helped me install years ago when we were kids. I closed my eyes and pointed my finger, recalling the spell for unroll.

"*Expedio?*" I peeked, but the rope ladder remained in place.

"*Sejungo?*" I waited for the splat of the ladder hitting the ground. Nothing. I exhaled my impatience.

"*Vestibulum!*" I commanded.

The magic trickled from my finger and the ladder released. I wobbled up, my head enveloped in a whirly sensation. I reached the balcony and rolled it back up by hand, not wanting to deal with my erratic spellcasting anymore for the night. I gulped a breath, waiting for the dizziness to dissipate, and then I pressed my hands against the wet glass surface of the window, pushing up. Feet first, I landed on my bright pink carpet with a small *thunk*. Through the rain and adrenaline, the tingling sensation from touching the Mather boy still lingered on my fingers like liquid peppermint.

My hand drifted down my cheeks, wiping long wet strands of hair from my face. I wrapped my arms around my stomach. Maybe there was something wrong with me because I didn't care about the attacker anymore. He didn't get what he wanted. However, the Mather boy was a mystery and rules might have to be broken. Ordinaries were forbidden territory to witches, especially the Mather ordinaries, but what would a few more secrets on the pile matter?

I pulled the damp journal from my pocket and left it to dry on my night table and tossed the iron girl in the drawer. It wasn't that late, but I was exhausted. I slipped out of my wet clothes and slid into bed, letting my head sink into the perfumed plushness of the lavender pillow. I took a deep breath, trying to clear the questions that wouldn't go away. Questions I had every intention of finding the answers to.

Disenchanted

Buzzing from the east terrace of our garden caught my attention. Three tiny pollen pixies, courtesy of my eccentric godmother, Mistress Phoebe, flitted about with their chartreuse, Velcro-like wings, providing a little extra pollination for our needier plants. My godmother enchanted her mystical helpers so we never had to worry about ordinaries seeing them. If they got close enough to the pixies or sprites, they only heard the buzz of their delicate wings.

I plucked a devil's bit blossom and pressed the periwinkle petals to my lips, the hush-hush nectar tingling against them like a spray of tiny firework sparks. The nectar made lying an art, a minor but necessary art if one was a witch in Wethersfield because the Mather family was still determined to get rid of us, although in this era they were locking us up at Kingshill. I shivered at the thought of the old haunted psych hospital on the outskirts of town, revamped as a privately run detention center for young witches who were unable to control their emerging magic. The only thing keeping me out of there was my semi-reliable *deleto* spell and help from Aunt Janie's botanical concoctions. I dropped the blossom to the ground, watching it wilt and wither as Aunt Janie's special dark, fertile soil absorbed it.

I looked around to see if I was alone, and then from my pocket I removed the little enchanted book along with a single letter that arrived in the mail earlier and was certain to cause grief. I set that aside and focused on the book's brown leather cover, tracing it with my finger. After a moment, I opened it and saw a name written in the front cover.

Elizabeth.

Nothing more, just that single name written in archaic script. I sat down and lingered over the name as if by touching it I could reach back in time. I fanned out the pages, all blank. I slapped it shut, and twisted my lips to the side. Disappearing girl. Disappearing ink. I opened the cover to the name and traced my index finger over it again.

"Elizabeth, talk to me." Maybe she needed a nudge. My index finger swirled and pointed at the opening page.

"*Revela.*"

The blank pages flipped open as if a breeze took hold of it. Suddenly, the most beautiful script appeared. I watched in awe as the invisible quill scratched its purplish black ink across the parchment.

It was a pleasure to finally meet you, Sophie.

I devoured the writing, my curiosity unleashed.

"Finally? Are you the girl who left this book in the shop?" I asked out loud, sounding a little crazy, but too intrigued to care. She had to be a witch, and I had questions for her. Her elegant script revealed itself, word by word on the page. I sat down, waiting for the dizziness to settle.

June 1662—He is not as I deemed him to be. He has left me inflamed with impatience and vexation. I shall follow the dictates of the Coven Council since I desire nothing more to do with him. After all, I find him thoroughly conceited. The same as his falsely pious family. I should not have allowed the introduction. However, I cannot stop questioning the fire sparks from his touch. Strange, yet pleasant.

A diary entry from 1662? It was strange that I found myself relating to her experience. Sort of. The vexation thing, specifically.

"Are you Elizabeth?" In the purplish-black ink, in the prettiest handwriting, the answer appeared.

Yes.

"It's nice to meet you, Elizabeth."

The writing started again, this time centering on the page so the words stood alone.

Take what I offer you for later.
You will know when.

The book slapped shut on its own, revealing two silver coins. I picked one up to examine it. My brow crinkled as my finger ran over the raised king's crown on one side and a horse on the other.

Ancient Celtic coins? The book remained closed. From what I knew of our coven's history, this was the currency used by the witches in ancient England—and even here in Wethersfield—to purchase rare, magical items or services, but I had never seen one up close.

"Sophie," Aunt Janie's gentle voice sounded from inside the house. "Where are you?" I scrambled to slip the book and coins into my pocket.

"Garden."

As witches, we had an affinity with nature and our garden most of all. It contained plants from the Greensmith list of things to grow, Greensmith being my mother's bloodline. The side yards flaunted exotic jasmine-scented golden hydrangeas and mystical Salem blue roses. The lower terraces contained the butterfly, wilderness, and cutting gardens. With its six-foot tall stone wall in the front and back and tall hedges around the rest, it felt like my own secret garden.

I hummed a haunting melody as I jumped up to water the newly planted wolfsbane seedlings and orange thyme sprouts. Aunt Janie urged me to sow them in the south terrace before sunset or they would be less potent at harvest time. A breeze rustled the skirt of her primrose pink day dress. With the back of her hand she wiped the summer's stifling humidity from her brow and eyed the freshly planted seedlings. She sighed approvingly and turned her attention to the letter resting on the small, round garden table. I gulped, wishing I had thrown it away.

"Are you ready to practice?" She spent her free time quietly inspiring me in our garden, hoping to provide me with some kind of herbalist skills within the next four weeks.

I set the watering can down and wiped my damp hands on my shorts. "So I don't mess up at the Seeking?"

"The ceremony is a big deal. Think of it like the ordinaries' debutante balls. Instead of ascending Connecticut society's ranks, wearing white gowns and gloves, you will be sorted into the coven's hierarchy based on your talent, wearing a black robe around a fire."

I closed my eyes and smirked. "You make it all sound so easy. You know it's not going to be, right?"

Her expression turned stern. "You have to practice more. That's all you need."

I nodded. The weight of performing like an herbalist pressed on me like an elephant sitting on my chest.

"We convinced the Council your magic was heading in the herbalist direction. If they find out what you can really do, they will take you away and use you like a pawn against the judge."

I grimaced, filled with frustration. "Would that really be so bad? None of us like him."

"So you want to leave here? Have Eldress Mayapple train you to be her spellcasting monkey?"

Fear shuddered through my body. The eldress, with her stocky upper body, thick brunette hair, and chalky white skin, was a witch on a wicked mission.

"No. Never." I didn't, and I worried what would happen to Aunt Janie without me.

Aunt Janie's head lifted momentarily as she smelled the air. "Freshly squeezed oranges. Wait." *Sniff, sniff.* "Ohh. Blood oranges."

"How can you smell that from here?" I asked, reaching for the letter, but she yanked it away from my eager fingertips.

"My emotional state may be shaky, but my nose is spectacular."

I laughed with hesitation. "I mixed up fizzy blood orangeade earlier. Want some?"

She nodded, examining the return address on the envelope. She gritted her teeth and ripped the letter to tiny pieces, leaving them in a heap. From the seed chest, she grabbed the antique magnifying glass, setting the sun's blaze upon the paper until a small fire hungrily devoured the pieces. She shook her head, sending her no frills bob into a swing that quickly settled straight like brunette tassel strings.

"Judge Mather's law enforcement bullies," she eked out under her breath. Her head shook as the argument within herself escaped. "He thinks the law gives his men the right to inspect and question everything we do, which seems out of the ordinary. Well, of course what we do is out of the ordinary, but my shop products are organic and safe and not dangerous to the public. They have a better chance of finding toxins in their tea courtesy of Eldress Mayapple than they do of finding them in my holistic store products." She stared at nothing as she fiddled with her black pearls, lost in the stress.

" Aunt Janie?" Why didn't I throw the damn letter away earlier?

She snapped out of the blankness. "Yes?"

I exhaled a quiet breath of relief. "Don't worry about the Leos." I wasn't afraid of them, not even the bumbling thief. "They're desperate if they want to search our garden." Her face flushed red and not from the blazing sun. "At least they aren't hanging our kind anymore."

She released a muted grunt as she looked across the tall hedges toward Judge Mather's house. "Kingshill isn't much better. Our magic is useless against those iron locks on the cell doors and the judge knows it. It is the only reason that dilapidated building wasn't knocked down decades ago."

She was right. The judge knew our weakness, but because we looked the same as the ordinaries and were used to keeping our heritage a secret, he couldn't tell who was a witch and who wasn't unless we slipped up in public.

"You need to calm down."

"You're right." She focused her lost gaze on me. "How far have you come with the pansy seed?"

She had a knack for transferring her angst to me through stress-mosis. "Not far. I've made no progress with sprouting it." My shoulder muscles tensed and tightened into knots.

She gripped her chin. "Hmmm. Have I taught you the hummingbird trick?"

"Does that have something to do with your humm-cay recipe?"

She laughed, not understanding. "My what?"

"Hummingbird cake recipe." The recipe was so delish it was like eating cake-ified nectar.

She shimmied to life with a mischievous grin. "No. This is fun. Watch." She darted around the yard, gathering a handful of blue rose petals and violet pansy petals. Then she plucked sour chokeberries from their shrub, counting aloud to six. In her palms, she smashed the mix into a pulp, tossing the berry pits aside. She scraped the mash into the hummingbird feeder and whispered,

"Come hummingbird to me,
Wings fluttering too fast to see,
Come hummingbird to me,
One taste and altered you shall be."

She stood back. "Wait for it." Within seconds, the scarlet-colored syrup churned into an eddy of brilliant indigo violet. A thick scent of baked cherries and sugared rose petals emanating from the feeder lured two ruby-throated hummingbirds. They delved their needle-like beaks into the sweet purplish water. As they probed and dipped, their green and red bodies phased completely to a sparkly blue.

"Ha! That's a-maz-ing. Is it permanent?" I stared in awe at the hovering birds, their now sapphire-colored wings a blur.

"Oh, no. Temporary. The special dye will wear off at their next feeding."

"Wow! What was in the mix again?"

She laughed. "We'll go over it again tomorrow."

I smiled. "I wish I were an herbalist like you. Life would be less complicated. All I do is make a mess with my magic."

"You should have been able to master your spells by now. I can't help to wonder if your ordinary half is affecting your witch half. But that's not important. You need to focus on mastering one of my lessons and you have a month. Plenty of time. Maybe more studying in the Flower Library. Mistress Katherine will be glad someone is putting the town's collection of gardening and botanical books to good use."

When the judge began burning the town library's flower book collection, Mistress Katherine, the head librarian and a descendant of Mary Johnson, the first Wethersfield Witch to be hung, moved quickly to secretly store the surviving books in our lemon-colored sitting room, which I happily renamed the Flower Library.

She crinkled her lips, thinking. "You know, your mother had talent in casting spells..." Her nerves, probably frayed from the judge's letter, forced her to stop short, not able to delve into the emotional pool of loss.

"Shh. Don't." I didn't know much about my mother and I wished with all my heart she was alive to help me figure out what I could do, but she wasn't and there was nothing I could do to change that. An ache settled in my heart. "We need to focus on the future. What if I can't master your lessons? Look at the time you encouraged me to mix up the bacopin and annatto tea to improve my memory before finals. Huge fail." The memory smacked me in the face. "The Glitterati with their magically straightened hair and unblemished faces, asking me questions. As soon as I opened my Oompa Loompa-tinted mouth, thin unaffected Laney with her icy gaze, pale complexion, and sea of long blonde hair, snapped my pic and posted it on the school's social website." I covered my eyes with my hands, feeling the embarrassment seep back. "And it's not just the other witches who treat me like an outcast, the ordinary girls do, too. They think I'm weird. Not that I blame them when I send papers flying and set things on fire."

She looked me over with a puzzled glance. "Macey is an ordinary."

"She's sooo not like the others."

The subtle twist of her mouth accented her high cheekbones and pointy chin. "What's wrong with you? You're never this pessimistic."

I blew a wisp of hair from my eyes. "Do you want a cold drink?" She nodded.

From the apple green kitchen I grabbed the pitcher of fizzy blood orangeade and poured the bubbly crimson juice into two glasses over crushed ice. I set the glasses outside on the table and plunked into a chair, soaking up the sun. She sat down across from me, looking upon me with affection.

I shrugged my shoulders, unable to contain the questions anymore. "Did you see the Mather boys moving in next door yesterday?"

"No. I've been so busy with harvesting for the shop products."

"Were they living with their mother while they were there? What's she like?"

"I never met the mother. No one has. But we know they have the same blood flowing through their veins as the old reverend who threw a noose around our ancestor's neck."

"You know how Mrs. Dayo likes her gossip? Well, she heard one of them has a criminal record." Mrs. Dayo, a family friend, was the shop manager and was just as interested as Laney Mayapple in the mysterious return of the Mather boys to Wethersfield.

She slapped her hand on the table. "You've been inquiring?"

I looked at her, hoping she couldn't read my face because I couldn't stop wondering about him. "She volunteered it, but isn't it better to know your enemy?"

Her eyes narrowed as she grew suspicious. I wiped fresh beads of perspiration from my brow and felt nervously for the crystal pendant I kept out of sight beneath my collar.

My heart stopped. Where had it gone? I wrapped my hand around my neck, searching for the chain. I looked at her, trying not to look freaked out. She didn't know I had taken the necklace from a box of my mother's possessions she kept hidden in her closet. I felt bad about that, but the stone seemed to sing to me, like it wanted to be with me. I searched the ground around my feet. A hot churning began in my stomach, as if I had lost my mother all over again.

"Sophie?"

I took a breath and focused. It must have fallen off when I was running from the attacker. Find it later, I promised myself. I had to. "Criminal record. Can you imagine with the way the judge goes around looking to punish us for barely real offenses and then his own son is a law breaker? Hashtag hypocrite."

Aunt Janie nodded. "That sort of thing could potentially devastate his chance to be re-elected, which would be great for us, but if there's no proof…what can we do? We have to rely on time to reveal it." She took a sip of her fizzy blood orangeade.

I pictured a slow ice melt finally exposing the remains of a ten-thousand-year-old caveman. "How much time?" My curiosity couldn't wait that long. I felt again for the spot beneath my T-shirt where the pendant always rested, right above my lack of boobage. Gone. I continued to search around me.

Her mouth puckered. "Why are you humming?"

I looked at her, unaware of it. "I was humming?"

Her fingers tapped out a drum rhythm on the tabletop. "All this talk of the Mathers reminds me of a story. Have I ever told you about the creepy thing the judge did a few years ago?"

I shook my head and leaned it into one hand as I waited with curiosity.

Her eyes sparkled with delight. "You like my ghost stories and this one will definitely creep you out. Most of the Mathers are buried in Boston, but there are a few interred in the Village Cemetery near First Church."

"So?"

"So, Judge Mather decided to dig one of them up and have genetic samples taken."

My face crinkled as I processed the icky visual image. "Eww. Talk about tales from the crypt. Gruesome work there, huh?"

"Indeed."

"What was he looking for?"

"Not sure. Told Mr. Chase, the groundskeeper, whom he didn't realize was a warlock, he wanted to get to the root of a family medical problem. Seems rather extreme to me."

"More like freak-adocious."

Aunt Janie patted my hand. "If that means creepy, I agree." The translucent ice cubes tinkled against the pulp-lined glass cylinder as she took another sip. "The sun is melting my ice. Let's go inside."

I followed her into the kitchen, leaning against the counter. "What if these boys are as bad as their father? They live right next door and could be spying on us. Look at what happened to Bess. Five years ago, the judge saw her use an alluring spell on one of his clerks and days later, she was arrested for being a con artist."

"There are enough tall trees, hedges, and property to keep us divided, but I remember. She went through his conversion therapy at Kingshill and when she was finally able to place a call to her mother, she told her she was dropping out of school and going to work for the Leos. Poor Mistress Katherine hasn't heard from her since and suspects Bess is telling the judge our secrets."

"He's so twisted."

She raised her hands, signaling she was tired and would discuss the topic no further. "Do what you're supposed to do and you won't have to worry about those boys."

Cuckoo, cuckoo. Behind her from the kitchen wall, a little carved bird popped out of the only clock in the house, a gift from my godmother. Her eyes brightened. She pointed a finger in the air for emphasis. "You received the box of clairvoyant tea leaves, right?"

"Yes." My lips didn't tingle because it wasn't exactly a lie. I did receive them in the morning when the deliveryman returned.

"They really are the most accurate of leaves. Why don't you let me read yours?" Without waiting for my response, she walked over to the cupboard where she kept her heirloom porcelain teacup. The rim of the holly berry red cup was decorated with ornate gold apple leaves.

"Is the box in the pantry?"

"Yes." She was excellent at tea leaf reading, but the lack of sleep from last night and energy put into gardening flattened my enthusiasm. "I'm good, thanks." I hugged her. "I'll be in my room if you need me."

I washed up and pressed my clean, wet face against the terry plush towel, inhaling the scent of sweet mimosa fluffs from the herbal fabric softener Aunt Janie created. In the mirror, small red capillaries squiggled along the whites of my wide eyes like tiny rivers of stress surrounding the pools of dark blue. I rubbed my hands over my arms and stared at my empty neckline. A searing ripple of pain ached in my heart as I wished I could crawl into my mother's embrace and bask in her warmth. I gripped the sink, waiting for the pain and emptiness to subside.

The next evening, I pressed my hand against my empty neckline, empty not from a lack of effort on my part. I sighed as the full, white moon rose over my backyard, casting its beautiful silver light over the landscape while a warm breeze, scented with apple blossoms, spun around me, lifting my mood a bit. The garden flourished and crackled with life, except for the willful pansy seed in my palm. I glanced down at the spot in the garden where tears of herbalist frustration dropped days ago and miniature white moonflowers blossomed in their place. My bare toes traced a line in the cool earth, as if I could create a boundary between me and the twenty-nine fragile blooms remaining, blooms that marked the days left until the Seeking. I exhaled a stressful breath because I had yet to get the teeny-tiny pansy seed to sprout with the growth powder like Aunt Janie showed me, and her hummingbird trick eluded me. I returned the seed to the seed chest.

I brushed the dirt from my bare feet and slipped into the gray, patent leather, low-heeled Mary Janes—which I barely possessed the grace to walk in—and waited for Aunt Janie to finish getting ready for the monthly meeting. Wearing a stiff gray skirt and long-sleeved white shirt, I wobbled and clacked along the curving stone path in the garden, pausing once to reach up and touch the scarlet wisteria clusters gracefully suspended from the antique arbor in the east terrace. The petals looked like droplets of rich red blood against the snow white of my sleeve.

I followed the winding stone path, which began and ended at the same place; the ten-pointed sun, outlined with tangerine rocks from England. Four dividing lines radiated from the sun within the circle, sectioning the garden's terraces, each blooming with plants and flowers representing the elements: air, earth, fire, and water.

From my shirt pocket I extracted a small envelope of chamomile gum, soft from my body heat. I popped three sticks in my mouth, attempting a Zen-like calm before the meeting, but the memory of him returned, warming my blood. I inhaled the layers of flowery fragrance, trying to push the thoughts of him away, but the garden's scents couldn't compete with the memory of his alluring cologne. Flutters overtook my stomach as I twisted and tried hard to ignore them. I reminded myself he was an ordinary, and worse, a Mather. The Council forbade our mingling for both reasons. And beyond those impossible obstacles, I didn't even know his first name. I chomped the large wad of floral-infused gum over and over, trying to clear my brain.

"Sophie," Aunt Janie called from inside the house.

I headed in, pausing once to touch the delicate black-eyed daisies waving back and forth in their flowerbed. A secret part of me wanted to pluck the petals and play the "He loves me, he loves me not" game, but I pressed a hand to my forehead, instead thinking how ridiculous and juvenile that was. Of course, he didn't love me, and I told myself that was the end of it.

In the kitchen, she stood in her uniform white shirt, gray skirt, and strand of black pearls which wrapped tight around her neck. "Time to go, but first, you'll need something much stronger than chamomile." In her open palm rested a shiny chocolate candy wrapped in a piece of parchment paper. "Go on. Eat the calming confection."

I tossed the gum in the trash while she waited. I plucked the confection from her hand and took a bite, feeling the firm chocolate shell give way to the buttery warmth of her special salty caramel filling. The calming candy temporarily acted like Xanax on my tongue, keeping my impetuous comments and accidental spells from bursting forth for about an hour, but taking it long term would permanently paralyze my spellcasting abilities—which as wildly messed up as my spells were—didn't seem like such a terrible thing.

Aunt Janie and I headed to Cross Manor, which had been inherited by Eldress Mayapple and was one of the oldest homes in Wethersfield. The large Federal-style house served as a covert place for meetings and, more importantly, housed the talented up-and-coming witches who required training under the eldress's supervision after the Seeking, a great incentive for me to acquire some herbalist skills—and fast.

We crossed several streets at the corners and every time, Aunt Janie looked over her shoulder. I grabbed her hand and gently shook it. "We'll be fine. Stop worrying." She nodded. The Leos were aware of our meeting schedule since we met under the persuasion of every full moon, but recently a few of us had been stopped and questioned by the Leos inquiring about what went on at our alleged political meetings. Since word spread about their tactics, Aunt Janie and I made sure to take a roundabout way to the manor and eat one of her calming candies beforehand.

"Those wretched spies. Our meetings are an important way for our coven to stay connected. Most of us have no intention of imperiling the peace and tranquility of the neighborhood like the judge wants the town to believe," she griped.

"I don't like how those corrupt twigs twist the law to suit their needs, saying our magic is con artistry and fraud."

Her lips arched downward. "You don't think the eldress with her Council doesn't tread into the gray areas of our laws?"

"I never thought of her like that. I mean, I guess she does, but…"

"I'm no friend to the judge, but there's no point in denying the truth about our own leader." She toyed nervously with her strand of black pearls. The older witches, including the Council members, all wore the signature necklace. Its lustrous gray-colored pearls symbolized the unity between those who chose white magic and those who chose black.

"Eldress Mayapple's powers are growing darker and it has me worried."

"What is it?"

She hesitated and looked around. "I've seen her heart's desire in her cards. The judge's hatred is becoming her hatred and she wants us all to embrace black magic to fight him. It is an impossible choice to return from."

"You saw this in her cards?"

She nodded. "With her heart growing darker by the day, it seems unlikely she will stray from her chosen path."

Not wanting to see the fear in Aunt Janie's eyes, I stared at the cracks in the sidewalk, listening to the rhythm of our steps and the fabric of our skirts brushing against our legs.

"The conversion of more and more witches to black magic will change the balance within our coven and the eldress's hunger for power is growing deeper. After tonight's meeting, I fear the choices the Council makes will put us all on a path of no return." She paused, looking into the distance. "Do you hear that?"

I listened above the street traffic and heard cheering coming from the next block over. "What is it?"

"The noise coming from First Church...." Judge Mather's voice boomed from the speakers.

"Come on," I said. I pulled on her arm and led us toward the crowd gathered on the lawn around the front steps of the grand old church, which glowed under spotlights.

From the top of the stairs, Judge Mather—a tall, slender man in his fifties with sharply angled features like those of a Puritan minister minus the powdered wig—waxed poetically, hypnotizing the crowd of ordinaries. His short, dark hair was highlighted with tufts of silver near his temples and his cheeks sunken beneath the bone. His eyes, Aunt Janie described as once hopeful in his youth, now held a fiery vengeance. "Now is the time to reelect the best leaders. Leaders, like Mayor Varlet, who will uphold the traditional family values we cherish." He patted his cousin and fellow weasel on his shoulders. "The witches' magic of days gone by, the root of all our town's ills, lingers in the shadows. It is up to us to shed light upon those shadows by ridding ourselves of or rehabilitating these descendants of con artists and fortune tellers who undermine a way of life we cherish. It is why an addition to Kingshill is essential. Mayor Varlet understands and supports this and he deserves to be reelected." The men and women shook their political signs up and down, chanting the mayor's name.

I swallowed hard and rubbed the goose pimples on my arms. If the judge pointed his finger at Aunt Janie and me and told the inspired crowd we were descendants from the witches of Wethersfield, I feared they would tie us up and throw a match at our feet. My fists curled tightly at my sides. With a quick glance at my watch, I took her hand. "We should go or we're going to be late."

Cross Manor sat on two acres and, like all of our homes, was surrounded by trees and tall hedges, providing privacy to its visitors and preventing any ordinary walking by from seeing the otherworldly activities happening beyond the conservative-looking threshold. Aunt Janie tapped the antique crescent moon-shaped silver knocker on the formidable black door. It creaked open under Mistress Leta's magic. She towered over us at six feet in height, extraordinarily tall for a witch. However, she was a hybrid like me. Exceptions for both our mothers had been made with the promise that their ordinary husbands be blinded to our ways.

We greeted her, but I couldn't help to do a double take. Mistress Leta possessed beautiful blue eyes, but they were definitely more Windex blue than the last time I saw her. Aunt Janie nudged me forward.

We followed one of Mistress Phoebe's eight-inch long wood sprites. Her wings were lightly covered in dew and her moss dress clung to her little body like softly fallen snow. She led us past three huge, gold framed oil paintings depicting seventeenth century scenes of witch garden rituals.

The good old days before the Mathers drove us away or into hiding, I thought to myself.

Smoke, clove and perfumed water seeped through the black parlor doors along with the Council's tense banter. With a sprinkle of the sprite's sparkling pollen, the doors opened. "Mistress Jane and Mistress Sophie, the Council welcomes you. You may enter."

The Council was always a talented group. Our secret coven was filled with herbalists, levitators, and charm makers, but those talents weren't enough to snag a seat on the Council. The highly regarded positions were reserved for clairvoyants, spellcasters, shape-shifters, and conjurers who could summon helpful or terrifying spirits to serve as powerful guardians, if ever needed.

The octagonal-shaped parlor, a windowless room in the center of the house, ensuring even more privacy, held a head table for the eldress and her council of five. All witches thirteen and older were present at what was known around town as the monthly meeting for the Daughters of the Wethersfield Toleration Act. Our less powerful male counterparts led by the eldress' husband had their own meeting down the street with an agenda she outlined for them, ensuring their warlock efforts supported hers.

Witches in the coven uniform filled the room. Laney met my glance with a fake half-smile, her signature sourpuss. She must have hated straying from her all black emo wardrobe with the required white shirt, but she still managed to accessorize to the max with her red forked-tongue manicure.

A hush fell over the room as Mistress Deedee—the talent discerner descended from the talented black witch, Katherine Harrison—walked in holding a loaded silver tea tray. Mistress Leta, with a whirl of her finger, shifted two empty chairs in front of Aunt Janie and me.

"Please, take a seat."

I couldn't get over how much younger she looked from the last meeting. The dark magic chased away the shadows of age like the tangerine glow of the rising sun. Her lips flaunted a deep red color rather than their usual pink, and her eyes glistened with streak-free vitality. Although I hardly believed it, Aunt Janie assured me the eldress benefited from the physical enhancement of the black magic, too, but because she began with less beauty than the others, the superficial changes were difficult to appreciate.

"Stop staring," Aunt Janie whispered, elbowing me in my side. "She converted to black magic two weeks ago at the eldress' urging, and if you think opening doors and moving chairs are big tricks, you should see what she can do now."

"What?" I sat down and straightened the stiff pencil skirt, which I couldn't wait to change out of.

"A whole house. She can lift a whole house." Her eyes bugged out.

My face tensed. "What!"

"She won't show off, though. Black magic requires greater energy where white magic requires greater skill. She'll pass out if she tries to do anything grand."

"How do you know she converted?"

"Besides her obvious red lips you're rudely staring at?"

I quickly turned my attention to the head table as Aunt Janie continued to quietly fill me in. "Mistress Phoebe has kept me informed. Her wood sprites are very good listeners."

It was hard to ignore the effects of black magic. It gifted them with the Vogue Photoshop-look of glossy hair, lush eyelashes, luminescent complexions, bright eyes, and lips as blood red as my crimson wisteria.

A commotion from behind us caught my attention. I spied Misty Badeaux's warlock brother, Montel, in his way-too-skinny jeans arguing with Mistress Isobel. It was unusual for a warlock to intrude on our meetings, but he flashed a black envelope back and forth with urgency. He scooted past her and I choked on a laugh as I remembered the nickname his Glitterati sister gave him based on his talent. Smelly Montelly, the boy who could conjure the worst smells, and they usually clung to him for days. He rushed toward his sister, who was already an expert with gas and smoke herself, as she whipped up a small orange gas cloud above her head of bright auburn hair. Misty's bestie, Mackenzie, flapped her hands under her nose as Montelly shoved past her. He handed his sister the envelope, his somber eyes relaying bad news.

Ashleigh, another member of the Glitterati, oblivious to Montel's frenzied delivery, showed off her shape-shifting skills, morphing into Misty—minus the toxic smoke. The mean girls' talents had become flawless over the last few months, unlike mine. Misty elbowed her hard in the ribs until she morphed back, then she read the note. Her face bloomed red with rage. She pushed to the front of the crowded room toward the eldress and showed her the letter. The eldress wasn't upset, more contemplative than anything, as if she were figuring out where to plant the seed of information in her black garden.

Eldress Mayapple interrupted the chattering group and took her place at the head table. "Enough small talk. Time to begin."

I returned to my seat next to Aunt Janie.

"Sisters, from our beginnings in this colony, where our kind was forced into hiding because our powers instilled fear in the likes of

Reverend Mather who tried to extinguish our light, we have fought to survive." She shook the letter in the air. "Today, after the arrest of young Mistress Mina, the Badeaux sibling who is being held at Kingshill Detention Center, along with dozens of other witches, I say survival is no longer enough. We are growing stronger and it is our time to thrive." A roar of applause exploded from the group.

"Soon, the rare selenelion eclipse will be upon us, coinciding with the Seeking, where your emerging talents will be revealed to our discerner. Your placement and training will follow. We must be united for our cause—we must grow stronger. Their days of harassing us, closing our shops on false charges, attempting to disrupt our meetings, and condemning our kind to Kingshill for conversion therapy are coming to an end, and the oppressors will pay for their cruelty. From this day forward, I encourage each and every one of you to bring an end to his injustice, if that means embracing the darkness, I am all for it. We will do whatever it takes and be devoted to our cause to stop the discrimination, to stop the interference from the Law Enforcement Organization, and to prevent the judge from eliminating us."

The coven broke into a mixed reaction of applause and whispers. Mistress Deedee, nearly one hundred-and-fifty and hunched over with age, shuffled with a silver tray in her hands. She set it on the head table and spooned Aunt Janie's special Fujian Lahong Tao leaves into six porcelain symbol cups. No strainer was needed for what was about to happen.

Mistress Belladonna, a member of the Council, tucked her long, raven black hair behind her ear as her sparkling violet eyes imparted impatience. "How does your garden grow, Mistress Jane?" The candles on the wall behind her flickered.

"And what poisonous potions have you crafted lately, Mistress Jane?" Mistress Isobel purred, touching her black claw-like fingernail to her pursed lips. They both made the forever choice by embracing black magic and wanted to see if Aunt Janie was finally considering the same path.

Before she could summon an elusive response, the eldress turned her eyes on my aunt, mouthing what appeared to be a silent spell before continuing out loud. "Mistress Jane, I call upon you for your continued allegiance and help. You've explained before that time and tragedy have dulled your skills, but any foresight you can provide to us before the highly anticipated Seeking will be useful. I want to know who among our talented pool of young witches will be sorted into the spellcaster and clairvoyant levels."

There was nothing she wanted more than a new clairvoyant to replace Aunt Janie, and her request reeked of desperation. Or perhaps it was hope for her younger daughter, Laney, who would serve her well in loyalty, but whose talents were limited to conjurations of slithery reptiles and cigarettes, which would not serve her well against Judge Mather's forces.

A cold sensation snaked through me. I glanced around and saw Mistress Deedee with her lopsided bun of silver hair, focusing her energy on me. Her eyes roamed over my body like a blind person's fingers reading Braille, trying to sense my emerging abilities. Aunt Janie, already on edge, noticed my body stiffen and managed to intervene, desperate to keep them from seeing. She must have been summoning all her mental strength to get through the meeting without a fail and I worried she was going to need something stronger than valerian tea.

"Please, Mistress Deedee, pour the hot water and serve the Council their cups," Aunt Janie requested, shifting nervously in her seat. As Mistress Deedee turned her attention to the tray, the icy sensation immediately subsided. Her shaky hands tilted the sterling vessel, releasing steamy water into the jewel-toned cups. Tea leaves swirled to the center before settling to the bottoms and sides. Each Council member took a sip from her cup, and then Deedee drained the brown liquid into a waiting urn, leaving the dark straggly leaves behind. She set the nearly empty cups on the head table and summoned Aunt Janie. I squeezed her hand before she got up to do the reading.

Aunt Janie twirled each one in her hand, coolly interpreting the messages coming at her. After she finished with each cup, she tapped the leaves into the corresponding saucer and read further. Whatever she saw, her face remained emotionless, a behavior she relied on during tense times with the Council and one she urged me to learn, but my impetuous nature prevented it. She set the last saucer down and grimaced. "Mistress Belladonna, in your future I see an impending visit from your sister. Mistress Isobel, I see a rich harvest from your conjuring garden, but beware the aphids, which threaten your magenta witcheswort." The harmless forecasts continued until she clasped her hands together and finally glanced over at Eldress Mayapple. The cold connection between them was evident as the eldress crossed her arms against her chest. "For you, I see happiness. The success of a family member bringing you great pride in your very near future."

She addressed what sounded like the improvement of Laney's conjuring abilities. I looked over my shoulder and caught the beaming smile on Laney's face as she sat amongst her well-groomed friends. Her mother's shoulders relaxed as she looked to be savoring the possibility Laney might be placed into a spot worthy of her evil spawn.

"But I also see dark days ahead for us as a whole," Aunt Janie continued.

"Tell me of the dark days."

Aunt Janie's face was gripped with anxiety as she shook her head. "There is a fog preventing me from seeing more."

Eldress Mayapple pursed her thin lips. "You know I cast a truth spell on you before the reading?"

"You must be pleased your spell worked, however it does not change the fact I cannot see beyond the fog and I cannot see who will fall into the talents you seek." With both hands Aunt Janie gripped the edge of the head table, the strain wearing her down. "I can say I sense a great need on the Council's part to be prudent in the path they choose for us. Embracing the darkness will dim the light on the righteous path, the path our foremothers chose—to heal with white magic and foresee danger for the ordinaries." Although the white witches in Wethersfield no longer aided the ordinaries, those who practiced white magic tried to be helpful in other ways, like Aunt Janie with her holistic products.

Eldress Mayapple's thin eyebrows arched inward in a displeased manner. "Our foremothers believed in healing the ordinaries and warning them of future tragedies, and look what happened to them. An oppressive English king and a fearful Puritan reverend nearly destroyed us all. Desperate times require desperate measures and our foremothers did not suffer in Kingshill as we have," she said, revealing she had no intention of choosing righteousness over treating Judge Mather and his Leos to a taste of her vengeance. As soon as she sat back in her oversized silver-gilt chair, Deedee moved the cups and saucers to the tray and busied herself, moving at a slow, crippled pace.

I wasn't sure if the eldress appreciated Aunt Janie's sentiment, but she intended to remind her of the platinum rule. "Together we are united and strong. Divided, we fall."

"United and strong," Aunt Janie replied, repeating the practiced response, before returning to her seat, looking exhausted only to me.

Hearing laughs and whispers from the girls behind me, I swung around, prepared to see the Glitterati making fun. Instead, ginger-haired Josie, the witch who put the glitter in Glitterati, was crafting her sparkly charms for the others. The dazzling effect became the rage in school last spring. None of the ordinary girls could figure out how to recreate the sparkle, and the Glitterati loved being the center of a big, fat, fancy secret.

However, the chatter wasn't coming from them. Riada and her mirror-image twin Adair, sitting near Mistress Aster, their mother, levitated one of their own teacups, both of them giddy with their success as they each held one hand out to force the cup's suspension in midair. As they laughed, their shiny chocolate curls bounced.

I approached them as the Council took an informal break to discuss the revelations. "Nice work," I said, in awe of their mastery. They were a year younger than me. Why couldn't I figure out how to control and fine tune my spells as well? Maybe Aunt Janie was right about my ordinary half interfering.

"Thanks," the twins replied in unison. "Lana over there is hoping we drop it. She wants to make fun. We can feel her negativity like a spider spinning a web, using silk made of envy." Eldress Mayapple's other daughter, Lana, stood at six feet without the excuse of a tall ordinary father like Mistress Leta. Her abnormally large frame was much larger than her petite younger sister's, whose icy beauty and poise far exceeded Lana's oafish appearance and, sadly for her, she did not possess any magical ability, leaving her to chill in the huge shadow of her mother's disappointment.

"Are you sure you're not reading her mind?"

They kept their eyes focused on the cup while shrugging their shoulders. "Huh, we never thought of it." I wished I hadn't suggested it. Eldress Mayapple would kill to have mind readers under her roof. And a spellcaster, too. I shivered from the thought of living at Cross Manor with her and her awful daughters.

"How is your summer job?" Riada asked.

"Huh?"

"Your job?"

"Oh. I like working at my aunt's shop."

"We heard the Mather boys moved into their father's house next door to you and one of them has a criminal record. What's it like having all three of them for neighbors? Are the boys as horrible as their father?" Adair plucked the cup from the air and looked at me.

The lightest tickling of a feather inside my head triggered my surprise. "Oh, that's interesting," she said.

"Did you…"

Her hazel eyes grew wide. "I read your expression. Really, Sophie. You give us too much credit. Even this levitation trick. All we're doing is manipulating the air around the object, not the object itself."

I raised my eyebrows, not sure I believed them. "You should stop by one day. I'll show you around our garden, and maybe, if they're wandering around outside, you can meet the Mather boys and decide for yourself what to think of them."

"Sure," they said in unison, melodically.

Chatter picked up among the group. I rubbed my throat, struggling to breathe. My stomach churned with stress. I glanced at Aunt Janie, wanting desperately to read her face the way she read my cards. She forced an accepting smile, but beneath the agreeable surface, stress was taking her down. I followed her lead, wanting an end to the meeting as soon as possible.

The eldress raised her hand in the air to signal for silence. The thin smile on her chalky face told me she was reveling in her control of the coven. "Before we adjourn for the evening, I want to update you on a change in location for the Seeking. With such a prestigious event concurring with the rare selenelion eclipse, the Council and I have decided the old fairgrounds will be the most suitable venue and the vast outdoor location will provide the best effect from the eclipse. That's all for tonight's meeting. United and strong," she said. The coven replied in turn and the Council stood and dispersed into the crowd.

I reached for Aunt Janie's arm and tugged on her elbow. "You okay?" I whispered.

"I need to go home." As Mistress Leta shut the front door behind us, I sighed deeply.

She walked silently until we entered our house. She collapsed in the plush velvet chair in the Flower Library, her face pale and sweaty.

"What can I do?" I asked.

"Nothing. I need to sit for a few minutes and collect myself."

I kneeled in front of her, resting my hands on her knees. "What did you really see coming in their tea cups?"

She swallowed hard and closed her eyes. "I did see the Seeking taking place at the closed down fairgrounds. Beyond that…I can't see what will happen at the Seeking or who will be placed where. Those events really are encased in a fog, which means events are changing, and that has me more worried than if everything was set in place." Her lips trembled as she clasped both hands together.

"What else?"

Her face drained white as she stared at the wall. "The Leos will target two more talented young witches before the eclipse. The eldress will use this action to incite the coven further. Black-heartedness will beget more black-heartedness."

"Two more?"

"At least."

My heart rate picked up its pace. "You lied to the eldress about her tea leaves."

"I refrained, actually, and it had nothing to do with that ridiculous impotent truth spell she tried to place on me. She puts on a good show for the Council, though." She touched a nervous knuckle to her lips.

"Shh. You need to relax. Let me get you some tea."

"The family member she will be proud of is her Mexican hairless for winning a prize in an upcoming cat show. Of course, the judge who tallies the votes will be Lana, her elder daughter." Her clever restraint at the meeting impressed me, but she was feeling drained from her efforts. Her right hand held the left one steady so she could check her watch. Tiny beads of sweat dampened her brow. "No tea. I'm going to bed. You should, too."

I followed behind and walked into my room, flipping the lights on. My attention was drawn to the enchanted book. As soon as I brushed my fingers against the leather, the chill traveled through my hand as if the girl's spirit was trapped in the pages, reaching out to me. I opened it only to see the blank ivory pages. Why did she need to hide her writing from the world? What was she afraid of? I pointed my finger. "*Revela*." Instantly, the next entry appeared, the words filling in neatly, one line on top of another. I took a deep breath, pushing the lightheadedness away.

June 1662—Choices. My elder sister, Eldress Rebecca, is persuading the coven to take the dark path. Her choice, born out of fear for our well-being, has transformed into something else entirely. She is the first in our family to make that forever choice, but I shall not follow, nor shall my younger sister, Evie. If only the reverend would find tolerance in his heart. All would be mended.

I shook my head. Did I mess up the spell? I reread the entry quickly before it disappeared, making sure I wasn't inserting my own thoughts into the book. An eeriness crept up my spine as the words settled in. "Wait. Elizabeth—you're Rebecca's sister, Elizabeth? The bride who died in my house nearly four hundred years ago?" Aunt Janie told me the tale when I was a child, but I never really thought about it as anything more than a ghost story. The pages flipped to the back.

Yes.

"How old are you? Er…were you?"

I was seventeen when I wrote these entries.

She looked about seventeen when I saw the vision of her in the shop. "Why are you reaching out to me? I mean, of all the witches?"

The iron girl is an ominous warning of what happened, and of what is yet to happen if history repeats itself. Your life depends on it not repeating.

My mouth dropped open. A warning?

"Am I going to die?" I hoped to coax the answer from her, but nothing more appeared. *Just leave me hanging,* I thought. With the state I was in now, I wouldn't be able to sleep. My fingers touched the empty spot around my neck and the pang of loss hit me. I needed to search for my pendant and there was no better time than the present. I changed into my T-shirt and shorts as I played out the possibilities of getting caught. I would never do anything to add to Aunt Janie's fragile state, but by now she would be hard asleep. I had to go. Not wanting to mess with the *illuminare* spell, I grabbed the mini-flashlight from my night table drawer, being careful not to touch the iron figure that rested next to it.

The half-open window stuck from the humidity. I pointed my index finger. "*Recludam.*" Sparks flickered off the metal latch, creating a mini fireworks show, along with a headache. I patted both my hands against the latch, extinguishing the sparks so the rickety wood frame wouldn't catch fire. My enthusiasm withered. This had to get better. I shoved hard while I stifled my grunt from the strain. With a creaky *thunk* the window finally gave, and the most luxurious scent from the garden wafted into my room. I crawled out onto the balcony and unrolled the rope ladder, knowing it would save me time. I climbed down, hoping to retrace my steps from the other night to retrieve the necklace. What if it was lost forever? No. I couldn't believe that. It would turn up and if it didn't, I would put together a sachet with powdered Russian comfrey root to help me find what was lost.

The crisp moon shined brightly, its rays illuminating the garden. The manicured landscape acted like witch hazel on my restlessness, and the feel of cool, dewy grass against the bottoms of my feet energized me. The softly illuminated garden always made me feel safe, but with the judge's house in the near distance and his boys moved in, I sensed their presence encroaching on the secure feeling like long, dark shadows from a setting sun. The flashlight sputtered on and I waved it back and forth, keeping an eye out for the lost pendant.

I retraced my steps, pausing once to gaze down at the sparkling diamond-like stars, reflecting in the calm water of the fish-shaped pond. I walked past the butterfly garden and brushed my hand over the variety of newly born blossoms. I stuffed the flashlight back in my pocket and plucked tiny flowers from the lemon verbena and valerian and a red velvety petal from a dwarf rose. I rubbed them together in my palms and brought my hands to my nose, unable to resist inhaling the sweet citrus scent. The smell summoned memories of summers long gone, but I struggled to recall what the combination meant. Was it protection and luck or purification? No. I shook my head and took another sniff. Hmm. *Amantibus* something. *Ugh*, I thought. The meaning hit me like a falling tree. I gasped. The combo was "lovers uniting." The flowers were the main ingredients in Aunt Janie's Forbidden Passion Potion. I wiped my damp hands against my shorts. That was not what I needed, standing alone in the garden. *Bleh*.

The creak of a nearby hinge shattered the stillness. My breathing stopped. A door opened in the distance.

"Crud." I glanced around, spying a huge holly bush. I dashed toward it. My heart raced. "Please don't see me, please don't see me," I whispered, hoping I wasn't saying it too loudly. I finally mashed my lips together, forcing myself to shut up. Worst case scenario—I'd summon the *deleto* spell to make whoever it was forget they ever saw me. I focused my eyes apprehensively toward the Mather house.

A tall figure appeared in the doorway of the white two-story structure on the other side of the thick hedges that divided their property from ours. His face under the porch light appeared luminescent and sculpted.

He was the arrogant boy who rescued me. The no-name Mather. I bit my lip as I fought with whether to stay or run. I shouldn't have to run. This was my property. But no good would come if I stayed. I considered my escape plan. He might see me if I neared the gap in the back stone wall, which left me with one option—racing back up the terraced plots toward the rope ladder. I surveyed the backyard. I didn't stand a chance of not being heard, but I had to try. I peeked back at the boy to see if he was staring in my direction.

His gaze fixed on the shimmery object in his hand. He knelt down, dumping a small silver box of its contents onto the grass by his feet. I waited, undecided in my course of action. He extracted something from his back pocket. My leg muscles twitched, ready for an escape, but my eyes locked onto his hands.

A minuscule burst of heat and light blazed between his palms, illuminating his face. His eyes locked on it, mesmerized. He lowered the match and ignited the tiny pile of loose debris.

I froze. My muscles tensed and ached. I glanced at my balcony, knowing I should get as far away from him as possible, but anger seared through my body, scorching my throat and crackling in my fingertips. Didn't he know how stupid setting fires was? I watched as the arsonist reveled in the tiny bonfire. The shadows danced and flickered on his captivated face.

Heat raged under my skin. My thoughts blurred. I needed a simple extinguishing spell that might work, but I couldn't think. I leapt out from the holly and shoved myself through the prickly hedge, racing toward him. "Stomp it out! Right now!" My fierce and demanding tone drew his attention.

The stubbled shadow around his jaw was dark and thick and his eyes, full of secrets, burned through me. He stood tall and stamped out the small, hungry beast. With a few pats, he extinguished its life. He closed the distance with a confident gait that already set him apart from other boys his age. He stopped with only a foot of airspace separating us. Feeling vulnerable, I glanced around, already knowing we were alone.

He furrowed his eyebrows inward. "What is this? A late night visitor?" He glanced at his bold silver-faced watch, displaying no remorse or anxiety about getting caught. "You should know by now that danger thrives in the dark," he said, reminding me of the thief's attack.

"Are you dangerous?" I asked with steel in my voice.

His eyes were wary. "You already know the answer."

An impetuous ferocity took hold of me. "How dare you try to set a fire?"

His arrogance reared up in full force. "I dare because I can, and I wasn't trying. I did set fire to a few centimeters of grass. On my property," he said in his smooth British accent.

My fingernails dug into my tender palms as my fists tightened. My toes dug into the soft grass, anchoring my position. "You mean your father's property, you arrogant, metric-using twit. All it would take is one hot ember floating over here and the fire would consume the most beautiful garden in Wethersfield. Gone because of the Mathers!"

His velvety gray eyes glimmered with amusement, enjoying my irritation. "You've made your feelings crystal clear regarding my family, but calling me names like twit? What kind of thanks is that for saving your life the other night?"

I gnashed my teeth. My body trembled with anger. "Don't. Change. The subject."

His gaze broke from mine. He shook his head as if he realized he was doing something wrong and he stepped back with purpose, increasing the distance between us. Was he afraid to stand too close? "Tell me, why are you out here?"

The moisture in my mouth evaporated. An uncomfortable lump formed in my throat. "Tell me, what's your deal with fire?" I asked, using the same tone.

He ignored the question, his eyes fixed on the patch of grass he singed black. "There must be a reason you're out here so late. I hope it's not because of me." His voice held a warning.

"Trust me, Arrogant. It has absolutely nothing to do with you."

"Good. Then no need for me to worry."

My anger simmered until his head lifted and his gaze drifted over me. A jolt of electricity breached the gap between us, nearly knocking me out. I nervously played with my hair, draping the wild tresses over one shoulder. My heart thumped as I tried to clear my head, but the smell of his intoxicating cologne mixed with the thinning smoke, which encircled us and made it impossible to think. "No need at all." I gulped a breath, wanting to match his smugness, but fearing I sounded nervous instead. I whipped around, ready to leave, afraid my emotions were spinning out of control.

"The name isn't Arrogant. It's Alexavier. And yours?"

I felt his question loop around me like a rope, pulling me back. I turned around. Was he trying to be funny? He took another step back, this time into a patch of moonlight streaming through the tall chestnut trees. I studied his face, every feature regrettably pleasing to me. "Sophie Goodchild," I sputtered, ignoring the flips my stomach was doing.

"I have something that belongs to you, Sophie Goodchild." His voice lingered on my name, making it sound foreign, yet beautiful. From his front pocket he extracted my silvery chain with the red crystal pendant.

My eyes widened. I grabbed for it as I leapt closer, forgetting all about my rage. "Thank you. Thank you. Thank you. Where did you..." As our hands met, the stone surged with intense heat. He jumped, releasing the pendant to the ground. Our eyes locked on each other.

He stared at his hands. "Did that stone heat up?"

I knelt down and cautiously touched it. The stone, now slightly cooler, hummed with a subtle vibration. I wasn't sure what it meant. "Maybe you had it near your matches."

"The matches are in my back pocket. And not emitting heat, unlike that thing."

I shrugged my shoulders, unsure of what to say, but knowing it meant something. I slipped the necklace over my head and tucked the stone away. His brows knitted together with a puzzled look. It was the same expression the ordinary girls wore when I did something they thought was weird.

His expression turned cautious as if he was warning himself to keep back. "Time to go home, Sophie."

His condescending tone set my teeth on edge and my jaw ached from clenching it so tight. Who was he to tell me to go? "Look, I appreciate you finding my necklace, but I don't like you starting fires near my house, and don't worry, I definitely didn't come here because of you." As the words tumbled out on a powerful tidal wave of anger, I wasn't sure it was true. He was dangerous and awful, but I found him to be the most mysterious and intriguing person I had encountered in Wethersfield. "I'm out of here." With everything in me, I forced myself to walk away. And as I did, all kinds of emotions mixed and bubbled inside of me.

"Wait! Don't go. I…" His voice wrapped around me, urging me back.

I whipped my head around and stared with expectation. His cautious expression softened into a desperate one; a tiny and temporary display of wanting that left me wide-eyed with surprise. "I wouldn't mind if I saw you out here again."

Surprise quickly faded into shock and disbelief. My jaw dropped. *Unbelievable.* I crossed my arms over my pink T-shirt and faced him. "Keep lighting fires and you'll get your wish."

His eyes burned with pleasure as if we were playing chess and he hadn't anticipated that response from me. "I don't think I'll have to."

Was he purposely trying to provoke me? I smacked my hand to my forehead, realizing the fire I was playing with was just as dangerous. I raced up to the back of my house, climbed the rope ladder, and slipped into bed. For the next hour I couldn't stop thinking about him, couldn't stop replaying every word that rolled off his egomaniac perfect lips.

Creak.

The image of his face disappeared abruptly as I listened. The handle of the back door wriggled. I shot up in bed, opening my eyes wide. I pressed my hands into the sheets, the tendons straining as I waited and listened. It wriggled again.

My heart stopped. If I stayed in bed, maybe the trespasser would go away. If I went downstairs, I might scare him off, but I doubted it. With my petite frame, I wasn't exactly an imposing figure.

Another idea flashed in my head. I dashed downstairs as quickly and quietly as I could, not wanting to wake Aunt Janie. I slid my body along the hallway wall leading to the family room. Standing against the wall, I held my hand out into the room and pointed to the backyard, hearing Alexavier's warning in my head about danger thriving in the dark.

"*Illuminare*," I cast, hoping for a flash of brilliant illumination to scare off the intruder. I pressed against the wall and listened as the lightheadedness faded.

With fingers crossed, I peered around the wall and out the glass door. I saw tiny blinking lights—hundreds of them—flashing off and on. Light sprites? I stared harder, looking for the sparkling heart-shaped wings that distinguished the tiny creatures. Then I pressed my hand to my forehead as I realized the source—simple fireflies, illuminating under my mix-up of a spell. The winged bugs flitted about outside the door, flashing their little bottoms off and on. At least nothing was on fire. I snuck closer to the glass door and examined the backyard. No one was there. I exhaled my temporary relief. Could it have been Alexavier, playing a game of tag with me? An attempted break-in was more scary than irritating, which didn't seem like him at all, but I couldn't be sure of anything, especially when it came to a Mather.

"Good morning, Sophie," Aunt Janie said, carrying a steaming cup of pennyroyal mint tea and a plate with a chocolate doughnut into my pink bedroom.

I yawned and sat up, ignoring the sunlight drenching every corner of my room. After my midnight misadventure in the garden, followed by guard duty in the family room, and my mind racing with questions all night, I did not feel awake at all until I remembered Alexavier's little fire. My heart quickened. I sniffed my hair for any hint of lingering smoke. Aunt Janie had a bloodhound's nose and would know I snuck out last night. I sniffed twice and couldn't detect it over the scent of lavender from my pillow. I released a sigh, pressing my hand to my chest to relieve the panic.

"Good gracious. You look like you ran a marathon minus the sweat. You'll need this." She set the porcelain cup and plate down on my night table.

I arched my eyebrows, thinking her choice was overkill. "You didn't have to do this. You should be resting."

She stuck a hand on her hip and cocked an eyebrow. "Don't give me that look. I figured while I was at the market, I could pick up a treat to get you going this morning. From the color of those half moons under your eyes, I was right."

I shook my head. She ignored me and patted her dainty fingertips along the skin under my eyes. "I'll get you my Phyto-Glo powder to erase those under eye circles. Maybe I should set up an appointment for you to see your godmother?"

I swept her hand away and splayed my long, dark hair around my face, feeling self-conscious. "No glowing plant powder. No godmother."

I loved Mistress Phoebe. She was an eccentric family friend who styled herself like a great lady from the proper English Edwardian period, but I didn't need her poking around and asking questions. They would both flip if they knew I was interacting with someone worse than an ordinary—an ordinary Mather.

"Was Callum at the market this morning?" I inquired as I took a bite of the doughnut. The cold vanilla custard gushed onto my warm tongue.

She nodded. "Yes, but he was quite busy so don't go bothering him."

I wiped my chocolaty fingers on the paper napkin. "I'll bug him after work."

I showered and dressed, picking out a pair of dark blue striped shorts and a white cotton shirt. I dried my hair, jammed my feet into my worn out sneakers, and bounced down the stairs. Aunt Janie, barefoot and smiling, had already immersed herself in the garden and smelled like the exotic scent of her fragrant blue roses as she extracted their oil to make perfume. I flashed a goodbye with my hand and raced to the shop.

The welcoming scent of citrus, honey, and coriander filled my nose and a techno version of Vivaldi, one of Aunt Janie's classical mash-ups, played in the background.

The store smelled of our flower garden and its cream-colored walls and light green display shelves showed off hundreds of glass bottles and apothecary jars containing the most wonderful home and bath products. The antique crystal chandelier hung above my head, already illuminated by Mrs. Dayo, who opened the store an hour ago. I grabbed my spring green apron and tossed it over my white T-shirt and shorts, tying a bow in the back.

Ding-a-ding-ding.

Before I could turn around, the door's silver bell jingled again as a group of tourists entered.

I cleared my throat. "Hello, ladies. Can I help you find anything special, today?"

An older lady wearing various shades of purple stepped forward. "We just heard the most marvelous ghost story. Do you know the girl who lives in the Greensmith house?"

My lips pressed together, unsure what she was sniffing around for. "Yes?" It sounded more like a question.

"It's you?"

I nodded.

"During our tour of Wethersfield we were told about the bride and groom buried under that mulberry tree in your front yard."

The historic foundation started their colonial sidewalk tours early in the mornings and the last stop—the Village Cemetery—was right around the corner. In need of a good ghost story, they must have added our house to the tour. It was a good story. It had been more than three hundred and fifty years, but the tragic love tale still drew interest.

"The mulberry, which we call the True Love Tree, played a fateful spectator's part in their short lives," I said, trying to imitate Aunt Janie's dramatic tone when she told a story. "Beneath the tree is where the young lovers first met, exchanged promises, and remain together in death to this day. You see, Francis, the Mather heir, buried his bride under the shade of the tree's outstretched branches. Then, the grief-stricken young man swallowed a goblet of wolfsbane potion and dropped dead beside his betrothed's grave where he was soon after buried; ill-fated lovers resting for eternity." I paused, glancing around at their freaked-out expressions. This would have been the perfect time to push a mulberry-scented glitter soap, but Aunt Janie nixed the suggestion, saying we didn't need to sell reminders of the past.

"Any other questions?" The tourists shook their heads.

"Please feel free to browse the products and enjoy free samples of Vanilla Bean Mine tea light candles on the shelf next to the front counter." As they began to spread out and shop, Macey popped up behind me, already in her apron, startling me.

"If your aunt ever fires you from Scents and Scentsabilities, you could start giving local tours for the historic foundation," she said.

"What the…? Were you in the back?"

"No. I came in right behind the tourists. Didn't you see me?"

"Uh. No." I glanced at my wrist, surprised to see she was right on time. "I could have sworn you were…"

"Nope. You must have been early today."

Mrs. Dayo exited the back room carrying her goose feather duster and a box of white tea leaves. "Good morning, girls." Her espresso eyes smiled and her mahogany skin was luminescent from using Aunt Janie's organic Phyto-Glo powder. "Big shipment came in yesterday. Gonna need both of you to unpack today." Her graceful hands floated back and forth, adjusting boxes on the store shelves.

The bell jingled again. I whipped around expecting to see another group of tourists. My mouth dropped open. My pulse sped with panic.

"Good morning, Judge Mather. What brings you to our humble shop?" Mrs. Dayo asked, oblivious to my horror. Aunt Janie had created a line of men's face and body soaps containing chestnut extract, but I doubted that was the reason for his visit.

His dark brown and silver hair thinned on top of his head and age spots mottled the skin on his hands, which were free of a wedding band. His long, narrow face grew stern. He stood tall in his dark suit and tie, commanding our attention without words like a minister before a congregation.

I grimaced, knowing she was going to make me wait on him so she could finish organizing the shipment. I had no intention of helping *him* in any way. She nudged her head, urging me to take over. I stood next to her and under my breath I eked out, "Macey needs the practice."

She turned her attention back to stacking. "I'd prefer you do it. You know more about the products," she whispered.

He scanned the shelves of aromatherapy products, but he wasn't shopping, not for the sake of shopping anyway. "Fine." I rolled my eyes and conceded halfheartedly.

He faced me with a blank expression. His eyebrows arched.

"Can I help you find..."

"I'm looking for the aconite cream," he snapped.

I silently gasped and not from his snap. Aconite was the proper name for wolfsbane. If someone consumed the raw plant like the Mather ancestor had, it could kill them, but Aunt Janie processed it so the toxins were reduced to a medicinal level before adding it to her Tizzle Toes cream. "Aconite?" I asked, playing dumb. My lips tingled as the lies prepared to roll out. There wasn't anything I wouldn't do to protect her.

"Yes. Perhaps you call it...wolfsbane? I've heard it's good for achy feet, increases circulation, numbs pain." The words slipped off his tongue as if he had read the description off the internet.

"I think what you're looking for is over here. Follow me." My mind raced. "It really is a wonderful product. A lot of Wethersfield's elderly have benefited from it." I didn't want to tell him we delivered boxes of the stuff, free-of-charge, to the assisted living center in town.

His upper lip arched into a superior snarl. "I haven't heard that."

Crash.

The shop door flew open from the momentum of two guys pounding each other, locked in a fight of flesh slamming against flesh. I jumped out of the way before they hit the hardwood floor with a thunderous thud.

The judge spun on his heel. His face flushed red with anger and he jutted out his chin. "Zeke, Alexavier. Enough!" he said in a commanding tone. He turned to Mrs. Dayo. "My apologies. My sons have been away from home for too long and seem to have forgotten their manners."

The atmosphere in the store felt charged from their presence like it did before a lightning storm. My skin tingled from the energy like I could touch my finger to the air and make a spark. I exchanged a glance with Mrs. Dayo before taking in the details of the Mather boys' faces. Alexavier looked even more handsome in the daylight. Their crimson complexions and bulging eyes matched the intensity of their twisted mouths. The tawny-haired one gripped Alexavier by the collar with one hand and with his other, landed a punch square to his jaw. I winced from the violence.

"You need to get control of yourselves!" their father raged.

Acting like he didn't feel the brutality from his brother's fist, Alexavier stared coolly at him, as if daring him to try harder. What was he thinking? I wanted to yell, "no, don't do it," but I doubted he would listen. He paused for half a heartbeat before head butting his brother, who landed on his backside, the fury wheezing out of him like helium leaking from a punctured balloon.

Mrs. Dayo froze in place, listening to the rattling of glass jars and bottles on the shelves. She looked overhead and saw the crystal pendants from the antique chandelier start to shiver. "It's all going to crash down on us!" She grabbed the feather duster from her apron pocket and began shooing them away with it. "Get out of here! Take your fight outside."

Alexavier ran a hand through his wavy, carbon black hair and acknowledged her, catching his breath before he spoke. The fresh bruise on his cheek filled with bluish blood from where his brother scored the hit. He noticed my gaze and rubbed the offended spot. "Very sorry, ma'am. Will not happen again." He turned to his brother. "Right, Zeke?"

Zeke wiped a trickle of crimson from his lip and begrudgingly shook his head. The two stumbled to their feet. They towered over me and Mrs. Dayo, who told me before not much scared her because of the African tribal blood running through her veins. It must have been a warrior tribe because she was tough and so was her son, Callum.

Zeke glanced at me with stone-faced indifference. He was not as tall as his brother and his dull blue eyes were nothing like the dark, brooding gray of Alexavier's, but they did share the same chiseled facial features. Alexavier stared in my direction and grinned an- I-want-to-know-your-secret grin. I smiled back at him, returning the sentiment. His brother elbowed him in the side, annoyed with his distracted glance. Both exuded a mysterious air and I couldn't understand why no one knew anything more about them other than they were educated in England and one of them earned a criminal record while he was there. Where was their mother? And what was the big secret about their return to Wethersfield? I didn't know, but everything in me wanted to.

I stood there dumbfounded as Zeke looked beyond me, catching sight of a historic plaque marking the age of the shop building. He folded his arms against his chest and turned his frustration on me.

"Those were the good ole days, eh?" he snickered, looking very much like a younger version of his father.

The judge stepped behind them and rested his arms over the boys' shoulders. "People today don't appreciate the traditional values this town was founded on." A lifetime of bitterness filled his voice. He pursed his lips and eyed us as if he were standing in a pulpit elevated way above. I noticed Alexavier shrug off his paternal embrace and shift to the background. His father narrowed his squinty eyes at me. "Miss Goodchild, whenever you're ready."

I shuddered at the sound of my name rolling off his lips. Even in a small town where I tried to blend in and pretend I was nothing more than an ordinary, it always surprised me when someone knew my name, him most of all. I unclenched my jaw.

"Yes. The foot cream. Of course."

His eyes narrowed. "I'm sure it will prove...useful." He applied a thick layer of sarcasm, probably assuming I didn't have a clue about his requests to search our garden for toxic plants.

His arrogance engaged my temper. My eyes burned. My fists clenched. "I'm sure for someone your age, it will." A fistful of chamomile gum wouldn't be enough to calm me. I thought of poor Aunt Janie and the words came effortlessly to me. I reached for a jar of Tizzle Toes and aimed my index finger at it.

"*Corrumpebant*," I whispered, hoping to neutralize the wolfsbane. Not that I needed to because what was in the cream wasn't harmful, but he was searching for the smallest bit of incriminating evidence to get Aunt Janie. As the grains of magic left my finger with a tickle and dispersed into the small glass jar, my shoulders slumped with relief that the spell felt like it worked. When he had the cream tested, nothing remotely interesting would show. Before turning around, I steadied myself as the lightheadedness settled in. Something inside me told me not to show him any weakness, so I tried hard not to.

I gripped the jar by the lid and placed it in his palm without touching him. His phone beeped and as he examined it, his lips formed a thin rigid line across his face. "My son will pay for this. I have other matters to attend to."

Probably shutting down a threatening candle shop, I thought. A whirl of energy heated within me. My pendant trembled against my chest. My fingertips tingled from the force, yearning for release. I closed my eyes.

Count to ten. Count to ten.

One. Two.

"Have a good day, Judge Mather," Mrs. Dayo offered.

Three. Four.

I fiddled anxiously with my red crystal pendant, trying to calm down, but the action seemed to catch the judge's eye before he turned to leave. He stared intently, but only for a brief moment before heading out.

"I can't remember the last time a day was good. Profitable, yes. Good, no."

I protectively tucked the stone away and forced my hands to my sides, feeling self-conscious and uncomfortable.

Mrs. Dayo lowered her voice. "Will there be anything else for you boys?"

"From a soap shop? Not likely," Zeke said.

I wondered what would happen if I rubbed him all over with ground up white willow bark ointment, a hemorrhoid reliever. I started to snicker, but I held it in, however the funny thought seemed to soothe my anger. "I would suggest the Waning White Willow—"

Zeke's icy stare locked on me. He interrupted, sounding gruff and agitated, even with the British accent neatly rounding out his pronunciations. "We're finished," he said. He pursed his smug lips and mumbled, "Just like this store will be in a few weeks."

I felt a fire in my chest as I glared at him. "What do you mean by that?" My angry glare turned on Alexavier, who stood in the back, shaking his head and rolling his eyes.

"Nothing."

I pressed my hand to my forehead as a raging headache pulsed to life. "Macey will ring this up." Macey dropped the price sticker gun and shifted to the register as I stood against the back room door. Zeke snatched the bag from Macey's fingers and turned to leave.

"Hope you have a better day than your dad expects to." I mashed my lips together, mad at myself for letting them get to me.

He whirled around and shot daggers at me from his narrowed eyes. "You have no idea what our lives are like." He gnashed his teeth together, restraining himself from saying more, but I sensed there was more.

I wanted to keep jabbing at him and see what else fell out, but Mrs. Dayo grabbed me by the elbow and yanked me back. She held firmly. Her fingers dug in to warn me that there were better ways to provoke them, but I preferred the direct route. I was tired of taking the roundabout way to avoid a Mather. They disappeared from the shop window and the only thing remaining of them was the echo of the bell and the alluring scent of Alexavier's cologne.

She shot me a warning look. "Wait a second and follow them. Without being seen," she stressed. "Take the dirt path behind the store. It runs parallel to the street. I'm curious where they go with the cream."

Although Mrs. Dayo was an ordinary, she was a good friend to Aunt Janie and me. "You know where they're going."

"Just follow."

I removed the store apron and sneaked out the back door. Halfway down the path, I heard Zeke's voice. I followed the sound and leaned out from the edge of a doctor's office, spying them at the corner as they waited for the light to change.

Curiosity stuck my feet to the ground like superglue. I bit my lower lip nervously as my fingertips pressed against the rough wall. I leaned out further, my heart beating faster than a hummingbird's wings.

Zeke spoke vehemently. "That girl needs to be taken down a notch."

"You can't fault her for dishing it back to you. She's quite cheeky." Zeke's body went rigid and shook like a quake rumbled beneath him. "You look like you're going to kill someone. Calm down. Would it make you feel better if I said she's not worth the trouble?"

I gulped as I fizzled under his harsh summation. Damn Mrs. Dayo's concern and my curiosity. I closed my eyes, not being able to stop listening, even as my heart pulsed louder in my ears.

"She isn't, so make sure you remember that," Zeke replied.

"Not worth the trouble?" I repeated to myself. I should have kept my mouth shut. My head ached even worse. I wrapped my arms around my chest, mad and hyperventilating.

"Sophie," a deep voice hollered, heading straight for me from the other side of the path.

I jumped. "Aaah!"

"Whatchya doin'?" he yelled in his booming voice.

My body stiffened. "Shh!" My mouth hung open as I flashed my eyes to the Mathers, waiting for their realization.

"Hey, what's wrong with you? You're as red as a steamed lobster."

I hushed him again, tugging on his arm to shut him up, but it was too late. I pinched the bridge of my nose, waiting for the explosion as Zeke rushed toward us, his nostrils flaring.

"Are you following us?" he demanded, glaring at me.

I held my fists tight against my body so nothing could shoot out of my fingers.

Callum's large paw clamped onto my shoulder, keeping me steady. "You Mathers don't own the streets, so shut up. My mom sent Sophie to meet up with me," Callum spoke coolly. His voice resonated with steely determination.

Zeke fixed his cold metallic stare on me until his beady eyes narrowed to tight slits. "I doubt that's true."

The hair on my neck stood at attention, sending a shivery chill through me, but I refused to back away.

"Do I look like I care?" Callum challenged. He locked his gaze on Zeke's and his jaw clenched. His stance threatened a fight without words. The muscles in his arms flexed beneath the short sleeves of his navy blue polo. I could barely breathe from the testosterone in the air. Callum was taller than Zeke, and although he was tough, Zeke possessed an indifference that made me think he could eliminate a problem without consideration of any rules.

"My brother's right. She isn't worth the trouble," Zeke snarled as he turned to catch up with Alexavier who watched from the corner.

A little piece of me crumpled up on the inside, but another piece of me wanted to set his hair on fire like I had accidentally done to Misty's which, thanks to my *deleto* spell, she didn't remember or she would have doused me in a green gas cloud. However, there were too many spectators and being so upset, who knew what kind of mishap I would cause?

Callum eyed me. "You okay? If you're not and you want me to say something, I will," he said, full of confidence.

I kept my fists balled up, not wanting to release any magic. "I'm fine, really. I'm tired. That's all."

Five. Six. Seven.

He studied my face. "You should keep walking—not near them. The sun will do you good. You always perk up in the sun."

I looked at him curiously. "How do you know that?"

He grinned. "I'm observant when I want to be."

"I'll be fine. I need to get back to the shop." I already knew where they were taking the foot cream and following them would make no difference in the outcome I had already fixed.

"Here." He grabbed my hand and placed a silver key ring with a house key in my palm, the ridged metal cold against my skin. "My mom forgot this. Can you give it to her so I can get back to work?"

I nodded and promised to catch up with him after my shift ended. I approached the back door of the shop and paused, letting the summer sun warm my tense muscles. *Not worth the trouble.* I bounced my head against the door, wanting to curl into a ball and disappear.

I worked hard at appearing less than special for the ordinaries, so why shouldn't the effort be noticed by them? My whole body sighed with confusion and frustration. I sniffled, letting the thick, quiet tears stream from my eyes.

The crunching of gravel underfoot caught me off guard. I stood straight and wiped the wetness from my cheeks. Then I turned. Alexavier stood next to me, his height forcing me to look up.

"I want to apologize for Zeke's rudeness. Well, he had no right," he offered in his smooth British accent.

The remorseful tone, meant to soothe my irritation, only rankled it further. He was the one who needed to own up to what he said, not his brother, but why should he apologize if that's how he really felt? "Trust me, I get it. What I don't get is why you care?"

His brow crinkled with what looked like surprise. "He was rude and..."

"Yes, behavior expected from a Mather. What's surprising is that he was honest, you know, to my face instead of saying things behind my back." My lips pressed thin.

He crossed his arms against his strong chest. A puzzled expression spread across his face. "How do you know so much about my family?"

"Duh. Small town. Hard to believe you don't know." I inhaled a breath, unable to shut up and leave it at that. Then I pointed my finger at him, as if he embodied the worst of them. "Since it was your family who persecuted mine."

His eyebrows arched with bewilderment. "Persecuted? Like back in the dark ages?"

My lips pressed together. "Puritan times were not the dark ages if you were lucky enough to be a Mather."

"From what I do know about my family, the word 'lucky' doesn't really apply." I watched him search his memories for meaning. His brow smoothed. "So you're related to the witches the old reverend hanged?"

I stomped my foot. "See? You do know."

"Okay, but the hangings were a long time ago and I had nothing to do with it," he said, putting his hands in the air and sounding so innocent.

My blood heated. "Are you serious? Your father supports the same kind of intolerance today as your ancestor did back then. I suppose you don't know about Kingshill, either, right?"

With his eyes locked solemnly on mine, he closed the gap between us. His tone dropped to a more serious level. I watched his chest expand as he took a deep breath.

"I am not my father."

"You are a Mather."

His eyes delighted in the sparring. His lips pursed. "And are you a witch?" The tone of the question was more matter-of-fact than trouble-making.

I gritted my teeth and inhaled through my nose. "What do you want with me?" The edge in my calm tone advised caution.

He looked at me, his straight-faced expression turning suddenly somber. Then, he set his eyes upon the path, detaching from the moment. He stepped back, a favorite move of his. "Regrettably...nothing." He paused, apparently wanting to say something else, but I wouldn't let him.

My body shook with another wave of anger. I glared, hurling invisible daggers, not being able to help myself. I was impetuous. It would be my undoing one day, but at the moment, I didn't care if I knocked Wethersfield's oldest oak trees down for the whole world to see.

"Nothing? Because I'm not worth the trouble, right, Mather?" A spell bubbled on my tongue. The winds whipped up within me, licking at my insides. All of my tensed fingers flashed straight out by my side. "*Ictus*!" I called to the wind in a whisper.

"What did you say?" he asked, interrupting my concentration.

I tried to ignore him as I waited for the gale force winds. Or a curtain of rain to fall between us. Or a chestnut tree to start pelting him with nuts. I finally looked up and all around.

I smacked my hand to my head as I watched a ballet of delicate pink and white flower petals drifting from the sky, swirling toward us on the warm summer air current like little dancers. They floated gracefully down, landing in our hair and all around our feet. I swatted the little traitors away and brushed them off my shirt. I went over the spell in my head. Where were the hundred miles per hour gusts to match my temper? The falling oaks? My shoulders slumped. Another fail, this worse than all the others, including Misty's hair.

As disappointment battled with the lightheadedness, the stark realization of what I had done hit me like a whip. I flashed my eyes wide and waited for the shocked expression, for the fear of what I did followed by an immediate call to his father, reporting me for tampering with the weather or some other pathetic reason to throw me in Kingshill. The *deleto* spell fumbled around in my head unable to get to my tongue fast enough. I pointed my finger at him. "*Del-Del...*"

I wobbled to steady myself, but he didn't notice, watching the dancing petals circle around us. He put his palm out to catch one like a child waiting for a snowflake. His lips curled into a half-grin. "It's raining flowers and only on us." A thoroughly satisfying laugh choked out of him. "How fun."

My hand retracted. My face crinkled in confusion and my head swam in dizziness. Fun? "Uh!" My eyes narrowed. My lips mashed together. I spun around, imagining puffs of steam billowing from my ears as I stomped back into the shop, and out of his detestable sight.

Disenchanted

A glance at the dwindling moonflowers in my garden set off the countdown in my head again, reminding me I really needed to nail down an herbalist trick before the Seeking. I spent every day of the next week shoving thoughts of Alexavier out of my head and practicing with Aunt Janie, which left me no time to explore the secret journal. Where the herbalism tricks failed no matter how many times we tried, my spells were slowly improving since the flower shower catastrophe that rained all over Alexavier. My magic seemed to fall apart whenever I was near him, and that thought led to another. I couldn't get the problem of him out of my mind, no matter how hard I tried.

I headed downtown, looking for help. The summer sun bathed Goody's Market's red and white striped awning in hot rays of golden sunlight. The awning protected two tourists from the heat as they licked the chocolate jimmies from their melting ice cream cones.

Inside, the air conditioning vent whirred above me, blasting frigid air onto my sun-warmed skin. I noticed the disheveled floral department and glanced around, making sure no one was watching. "*In ordinem.*" I whispered with half-confidence, pointing my finger at the tilted flower bouquets in their galvanized buckets, asking them to align. Giddiness bubbled inside me as I watched the power of the spell bounce off every other bucket, straightening the ones it hit. Not perfect, but pretty good, so maybe I didn't totally suck. I took a deep breath, waiting for the dizziness to subside before heading to the back, completely oblivious to Mr. Geoffrey, the manager, until I bumped into him in aisle three, canned goods.

I staggered backward, knocking six cans of Le Sueur peas to the floor. I bent down, unsteady from the unexpected thump, and picked the tall cans up, two at a time, waiting for Mr. Geoffrey to help. He didn't, though. He stood there staring at my chest, the same way he did a week and a half ago, although not looking as surprised this time. Not that there was anything surprising about my small chest, but the staring definitely creeped me out. "You okay, Mr. G?"

Weirdness rippled off the market manager. He stood there, average in height and build, with a cleft in his chin and tufts of mousy brown hair tilted in varying directions. His muddy brown eyes squinted, giving him the look of eyestrain. "Sophie." He finally snapped out of his creepster delirium.

He should have been used to seeing me by now. I was here after school nearly every day hanging with Callum and eating damaged packages of Milano cookies. "How are you?" His mouth smiled. His eyes didn't.

"Fine, thanks. Is Callum here?"

"In the back, unpacking." He chewed on the ragged fingernails of his right hand, seeming preoccupied with his thoughts.

"Okay…" I paused for an awkward second, staring at my faded gray T-shirt hem, waiting for him to say something else, but he didn't. "Thanks." A warm, cinnamon-scented wave of air drifting from the bakery swept over me, reminding me of Mistress Phoebe and her cinnamon-pomegranate tea biscuits, an unnecessary bribe she brought over occasionally to persuade Aunt Janie to read her cards.

In the back, Callum popped up from behind a stack of cardboard boxes. He wore the navy blue store apron over his fitted navy polo. His bronze skin glowed and when he smiled his straight white teeth peeked out from his infectious grin.

"Hey Short Stack! What are you doing here?" He approached closer, holding a box cutter in his right hand. He was tall with sculpted cheekbones and amber eyes, which laughed with amusement even when he wasn't talking.

I pouted and placed my hands on my hips. "You need to come up with better nicknames." Five-foot-one wasn't tall and the rest of me was pretty small, too, but I didn't want to encourage the shorty nickname.

He grinned, not taking me seriously. "Well, you are way shorter than me. It's like you have pixie in your genes. How 'bout Pixie Stick?"

Definitely not Pixie. "Since last summer *everyone* is shorter than you. You've got to be over six feet tall."

"Yup. So what's up, Pixie Stick?" He shrugged and went back to slicing the seams on the cardboard boxes.

"I need help."

He stopped and turned his full attention on me. "Since when?"

The way he said it made me feel like I'd never asked for help before. I grimaced. Maybe I hadn't.

I explained my distaste for the Mathers, mentioning the fire Alexavier set in his yard, how his dad and the Leos wanted to inspect our garden, and Zeke's rudeness, which he witnessed himself. Without bringing up the Seeking, which, as an ordinary, he knew nothing about and would never understand, I told him my whole world, in general, was unraveling.

"Unraveling? You got me, babe. What more do you need?" he smiled and grabbed my chin, trying to shake a smile out of me.

I brushed his hand away. "I'm serious."

"Lighten up. The Leos have been trying to check on my mom's garden, too, but nothing has come of it and, if Zeke or his brother is messing with you, I can handle them." He flexed his sizable bicep for me.

If I could figure out how to keep my cool around them, I could handle them, too. "I don't think you starting a fight is the answer." I plopped into the desk chair, slouching over like a limp tulip. There had to be a better solution.

"Mr. Geoffrey will hire you in a microsecond if they keep coming around your aunt's shop to give you a hard time." He laughed out loud. "I think this store would stop making a profit on its chocolate cookies, though."

I jumped out of the chair and shoved his shoulder. He shoved mine back, enjoying the horsing around. My momentary grin straightened. I pursed my lips into a thoughtful twist, pondering. "They just get under my skin and make me so angry."

The father buying the Tizzle Toes cream, Zeke saying the shop would be finished in a few weeks, and Alexavier dismissing me as not worth the trouble amounted to one big pain in my butt. Maybe I needed the white willow bark ointment.

"You hardly know these guys."

I paced back and forth in the small cluttered space. "They are Mathers. I don't need to get to know them."

He shrugged and stepped back toward the boxes. "You sound a little judgmental today. That's not like you."

My defensiveness bubbled up. "I'm not judgmental." My lips tingled, as I feared they would. He was right, but it wasn't what I wanted to hear. I needed an idea. A suggestion. Something to make them leave us alone or go away.

He set the box cutter down. "My mom taught me a saying. 'Hate darkens life, love lights it up.' I think it's from Martin Luther King, Jr. It means being a hater just makes more haters."

"Ha! I am so not a hater." My lips tingled from the lie I didn't think was a lie and I didn't like it. I didn't want to be a hater, but I couldn't sit back and watch them light fires near my house, threaten to close our shop, lock my sister witches up at Kingshill, and do nothing.

"You don't sound so sure about that."

He was supposed to be on my side. My face heated. "What are you saying? If I learn to love them it will brighten my life?"

He threw his hands in the air. "That's not what I'm saying at all. Why are you being so difficult?"

"Why do you like them so much?"

"I've only seen them twice and, trust me, I don't like them, but I'm not a hater and neither are you."

"Wanting that family to back off doesn't make me a hater. It makes me a realist." My lips tingled again, which I ignored, and then an idea popped in my head like a bubble bursting. The job would require Macey's special connection. My eyebrows furrowed as what he said sunk in. "Wait a minute. You've seen them twice? You mean facing off in the path wasn't the first time?"

"They came in here last week. Placed a rush order of the weirdest food from England. Stuff normal, red-blooded working guys from Connecticut don't eat."

"Like what?" I expected the list to include crazy things like tripe and kidney pies. I could picture Zeke tearing into an undercooked haggis.

"Outside of the frozen shepherd's pies, they ordered a bunch of girlie food. Get this—candied ginger, almond cakes, and these weird fried mistletoe things. Cost a fortune for the food and another fortune for the shipping, but your Alexavier threw down cash like it was nothing."

I flashed my hands out in front of me in a stop motion. "He's not *my* Alexavier," I corrected. "Fried mistletoe...you mean burned?"

"Yeah. Do you know what it's for?"

"Yeah," I said, shaking my head, the mistletoe order surprising me.

He stared at me with his big amber eyes, waiting. "Girlie food, right?"

If I remembered Aunt Janie's lessons correctly, the burned mistletoe wasn't for eating. "Where in the world did they order this stuff from?"

He slapped the top of a box and shook his head smugly. "Girlie food. I knew it. A shop called Black & Spencer in London."

I glanced at the clock. Ten after six. "I'm meeting Macey. She's going to help me with a special project." Even if she didn't know it yet.

I walked next door to Gracie's Good Eats, the Mayapple's sandwich shop on Main Street. Macey was hooked on their Witch Wraps, no doubt in part to the addictive Parisian basil I had tasted in their mayonnaise. They were secretly adding it to their sandwiches and wraps to keep customers coming back. It was black witches like them making us all suspect in the judge's eyes, but they got away with it because the shop appeared so...ordinary. And harmless.

Kitschy tin signs featuring Coca-Cola, club sandwiches, and a variety of ice cream treats decorated the aqua blue walls. The smell of greasy french fries and onions saturated the air. Macey, already waiting in line to order, waved me over, the ruffles of her black mini skirt swishing from the motion.

"Sophie, I want you to meet Jenna. She's a Boston girl. She'll be going to our school in the fall." Jenna stood behind the counter in a pink uniform shirt. She had stick straight sandy blond hair and big brown eyes that smiled as she blew a shimmery pink bubble.

"Jenna, this is my bestie, Sophie."

"Hey Sophie," Jenna said cheerily, chomping on the big wad of pink gum.

"Hi," I said, watching Laney behind the counter. I had never actually seen her work.

Jenna noticed me staring at her. She leaned toward me and whispered, "Laney Mayapple is the owner's daughter. Huge harmaceutical. And what's with all the black outfits?" She pressed a finger to her lips. "Shh." In a louder voice she added, "What can I get for you two?"

I chuckled to myself. Laney needed to work on conjuring a better personality because the ordinary girl already had her pegged. As soon as Macey and I paid for our orders, Laney slinked into the back. I was thankful she chose to ignore me.

"I guess with a mother like Laney's you can't expect her to turn out much different. She acts so privileged. Sort of like your 'aristobrits'."

We picked up our food and sat at the table by the window. "They are not *my* aristobrits. They're not even Brits, by the way. They were born in Wethersfield like the rest of the Mathers."

"I know, but they talk like Brits and they dress like Brits. And"— she said, shaking a fry at me—"the younger one can't seem to take his eyes off you."

Blood rushed to my cheeks. I patted my hands over the warmth and looked away to stare at the pattern of white speckled floor tiles. "No doubt spying for his dad."

"I don't get the narc vibe from him, and why do you suddenly look so embarrassed?" she asked.

I rolled my eyes. He was arrogant, condescending, and he liked to play with fire. "Nothing to be embarrassed about."

"Uh huh," she said, not believing me.

"Anyway, Jenna seems real sweet."

"She's great." She eyed me suspiciously. "What's up with you today?"

I wore my emotions on my face and, apparently, Callum and Macey had no problem reading the messages I posted.

"I need your help."

She dropped her wrap on the tray. "What did you do?"

My mouth dropped open. "Nothing. Why would you assume I did something? Never mind. What I'm saying is, the Mather family has to go and we are just the girls to make that happen."

"The boys are way too Hottie-McTottie to go. And what if the younger one likes you? We could double date for the junior prom this year," she said like the eternal romantic optimist she was.

I gave her *that* look. "Firstly, the prom is almost a year away. Secondly, I heard him say something about me that wasn't very nice, so let it go."

She wiped her hands on a napkin and sat back in her chair, resolved to set me up with a wretched Mather.

"I don't believe it."

"He said I wasn't worth the trouble. I'm not making it up. I swear." Macey liked to play matchmaker, even when the matches were blatantly off. She wanted me to find a guy, any guy. I understood her self-interest, but I wasn't going to settle for just anyone so the four of us could hang at the mall together.

"Fine. What's your plan?"

I did, however, love that she was always on my side. She leaned forward and dipped a handful of fries in my ketchup, then stuffed them all in her mouth at once.

"I was hoping you might come up with the plan. You know, because of where your mom works..."

Her face lit up. She gulped most of the chewed up fries down. "You mean the fact she happens to work for a locksmith?"

I slammed my drink down with emphasis. "How are you failing history, but you can read my mind?"

She laughed and soggy bits of fry flew out of her mouth. "I'm not a mind reader. I just know how curious you are."

"I'm sure his dad keeps records of everything regarding himself and the boys, and what better place to look than his home office?"

She chomped into her wrap, smearing the mayonnaise on her lip.

"You really should cut back on those."

"I like them too much. The spread tastes like sparkles on my tongue, like I'm eating magic. Now, let me think." She took a long sip of her Coke and bobbed her head back and forth. "Okay, this is how it's gonna work. I'm going to snag her set of lock picking tools and we're going to figure out a time when they won't be home. Got it?"

I sat there with an open mouth, in awe of the way she thought. When she graduated college, she would have no problem securing a job with the FBI. "Got it."

She squinted, thinking. "B—T—W, if you find info, what are you going to do with it?"

"I have no idea. I'm hoping there's something there to prove the father isn't the community pillar he pretends to be and when he's confronted, the truth will be enough to drive him and the boys out of town.

Her face squished up. "Politicians are never squeaky clean. You might get lucky, but I doubt something as sweet-sounding as the truth is going to drive a man like that out of town."

I only had to think about what he did to Bess and all the other girls at Kingshill. Plus, Zeke's harsh attitude paired with Alexavier's desire to set fires didn't make him father of the year.

"Let's hope we get lucky." She wiped the green mayo from her mouth and balled the napkin up. We left the restaurant and waved goodbye. I kept glancing at the billowy thunderheads stacked like a tall heap of freshly picked cotton as I walked home.

A tingle of nervousness snaked the length of my spine as I hurried past a narrow opening next to Carson's Guitars. I glanced over my shoulder, almost expecting to see one of the Mathers stalking me. I scanned the shadows of the deserted space, and then wiped the sweat from my forehead and continued on my way, brushing my fingers along the rough bark of trees that shaded the town storefronts. Uneasiness gnawed at me. I cocked my head slightly to take another look around. Locals and tourists out on the town crowded the street behind me, all dressed in light, casual summer clothes. All except one. He sat on a black motorcycle parked beside the curb, head down, wearing a black hoodie and revving the engine.

The hairs on my arms stood at attention. I planned to cross at the next corner and, if he followed, I would know for sure.

The distinct gurgling sound of the engine grew louder behind me. Nervousness shivered down my back again, jump-starting my hyperventilating. My rising temperature mixed with the heat of the Connecticut summer. The motorcycle engine growled louder.

At the next corner, I managed to break into a run. I cut through a path out of his sight, but the biker drew closer, speeding up to cover the distance between us. I couldn't breathe. I couldn't think clearly enough to cast.

With a flash, lightning seared across the tall illuminated summer clouds, crackling through the hot air. My heart skipped a beat. A boom of thunder exploded. Rain gushed down, drenching the streets. The violent screech of metal hitting pavement resonated through the rain. He was down. I stared straight ahead as my numb legs kept moving in a motion that resembled running.

Footsteps smacked furiously in quick succession behind me. I sped up, gasping and coughing for air. His arms wrapped around my shoulders. He wrestled me down to the ground.

"Give me the necklace or I'll kill you."

I recognized his menacing voice from the last attack. It dripped with danger and desperation. I had to get out of here or I was going to die because giving him the necklace was not an option.

I was alone, my heart raced, my body ached to be free. I twisted and kicked, landing a hard blow to his shin with the back of my heel. He groaned. Thunder roared above. Adrenaline raced through me. Sensing his weakness, I stomped on his foot. He moaned and loosened his hold. I broke free and ran like a tiny gazelle on fire.

With one terror-filled leap, I hurdled a cluster of trash cans and dashed down a city street to my house. I shoved the front door open and slammed it shut behind me, latching the lock in one swift motion. I leaned my back against it, dripping wet and shaking. A serious freak-out commenced.

I slumped to the floor and tried to think straight. The attacker's tattoo flashed back like a searing blaze of lightning. Wasn't it bad enough that my mother had been taken from me, now I had to hand over her necklace, too? I thought about calling the police, but the judge recruited most of the force. No. I desperately had to pretend the attack didn't happen, just like before. I needed to protect Janie from the stress and try to figure out why those Leo bastards were chasing after worthless jewelry.

I scanned the empty house, relieved Aunt Janie wasn't here to see me. I pulled myself up, walked to the kitchen, and wiped my face dry with a tea towel. I dragged myself to my room and plopped on the bed, wet clothes and all. Within minutes, sleep enveloped me.

Plucky harpsichord music floated up from the main floor. The perfumed scent of blue roses filled the air. I swept down the stairs, hearing a ghostly girl humming the haunting melody while it played. I took a deep breath, my ribcage constricted by a tight dress bodice, which flared into a full skirt that extended all the way to the floor. The low neckline was ruffled in heavy blue silk and the lace sleeves draped loosely to my wrists. I gasped, realizing it looked like the dress painted onto the iron girl figurine. I glanced around, searching for the mysterious harpsichord and the humming girl, but instead, a man in a pre-colonial coat and breeches entered the sitting room. His face remained in the shadows. I stepped closer, curious. His hand glided to my waist and we began to dance in a formal, old-fashioned way I had only seen in movies. A shiver of excitement rippled through me and my heart rate accelerated. Darkness dispersed as the flicker of candlelight began to illuminate the room. The details of his face emerged. The girl's voice with the hint of a Puritan accent, whispered to me, "Do not fear him." He searched my face with his stormy gray eyes, not quite letting me in, but wanting to.

I shot up in bed, ripped from sleep by the realization of who he was.

After the strange dream, I spent two hours attempting to conjure helpful sprites in the garden, drawing on the power of the stones from Essex and their connection to the otherworld, but whatever I was doing wasn't working. I watched the burned offering fizzle into a thick line of smoke as the summoning gift of golden dwarf apple and dandelion root, set upon the British stones, smoldered to sweet-smelling ashes. I watched for sprite wings and listened for the patter of little pixie feet, but heard nothing except the beating wings of brightly colored finches chirping at the feeder in the east terrace.

Clearly, I wasn't an herbalist or a sprite conjurer, but I was tenacious and desperate. My quirky godmother was quite good at summoning wood sprites for herself and pollen pixies for Aunt Janie and I figured it couldn't hurt to summon a pinkie pixie or two. They were helpful and would give me a heads up when they sensed danger, and with the danger that had been coming at me, I needed something.

I exhaled a breath, blowing a wisp of wavy hair from my eyes as I struggled to connect to the otherworld. And it wasn't just the lack of pinkies. I hadn't asked Elizabeth to reveal her writing in days and I found myself needing our connection. We seemed to have a lot in common even for having more than three hundred years between us. My lips puckered into a pout and as I was about to gather more dwarf apples for another offering, I heard the faintest *ding dong* come from inside the house. I spun around and raced inside.

"Coming."

I glanced at my watch and grabbed for the door, not expecting anyone. I twisted the knob and pulled, feeling the warm air from the front yard whoosh past me into the house. Two shiny, smiling faces wearing their frilliest summer dresses and pretty leather sandals greeted me. "Riada. Adair." I looked around to make sure they were by themselves. My brow crinkled. "What are you doing here?" I asked, studying their faces before they could respond.

"Hi Sophie, may we come in?" they said in unison, their voices pleasant and melodic.

I pointed to the garden through the back door. The twins shared quick, knowing glances with each other as we walked outside. They sat in a synchronized manner on the bench under the red wisteria-covered arbor. They straightened their short flowery dresses and turned their attention on me.

"Just like your aunt, always walking about the garden in bare feet. Really, Sophie."

"I don't like wearing shoes. They're so binding, it's like I can't breathe."

"Obviously, the earth is your element and it energizes you. It's not surprising considering your family background. The air is our element, what with our levitation tricks and all, but tell us. What is it we don't know about you?"

I felt a tickling in my head like the movement of a feather. "Stop that."

"I knew it. You can do something amazing and it has nothing to do with dirt or plants. Ooh and a *deleto* spell, too. Cool," Riada said excitedly. "Show us."

I shook my head. "No one is supposed to know that and I can't."

"You're not supposed to know about our mind tricks, yet you do. We trust you not to tell anyone on the Council about it. You need to trust us."

Sharing my secret with someone other than Aunt Janie was dangerous, but the camaraderie made me feel light like a dandelion's downy blowball. "I'm not that good. I practice, but my spells are erratic." My gaze drifted down. "And I'm feeling a bit lost."

"Our mom knew your mom. She said she was pretty good with casting spells, especially in the garden. And your dad was talented, too."

"I figured since my mom got an exception to marry him, he must have been an extraordinary ordinary, but Aunt Janie's never said anything about him."

"He could make things happen with his mind. Our mom said he was a special ordinary. What do you call that?"

"An oxymoron?" Riada said in a snarky tone.

"No. Telekinetic," Adair said, correcting her sister. "But not moving stuff like Mistress Leta. More like he could will things or objects to do what he wanted, like make a seed grow or ignite a fire."

Riada jumped in. "What if you have both their abilities? Casting spells and telekinesis. That would be amazing. Do you have a seed?"

I threw my hands up in disbelief. "I'm descended from a Greensmith. Of course I have a seed. Follow me." We walked over to the seed chest. I plucked out a teeny-tiny Padparadja pansy seed. I stared at Aunt Janie's growth powder in its small cubby next to the seeds. I wanted to try this my way with no powder, only spellcasting.

"What do you want it to do?" Riada asked.

The answer was obvious. "*Flos.*" Flickers of magic sparked on my tongue like Poprocks as I asked it to bloom. Excited, I focused harder on the tiny speck in my palm. "*Flos,*" I repeated, picturing velvety, dark orange petals. The tiny black speck vibrated with magic, but refused to sprout for me. "*Flos?*" Again it trembled and rolled around my palm. My head started to ache.

"You're expecting too much from yourself. Baby steps," Adair said.

I took a breath and spoke the spell again. This time I added more intensity. "*Flos*!" The tiny plant trembled. Then it spun around in my hand like a tiny dust devil as if the gift of my mother's spellcasting was really mixed with my father's telekinesis. Was that even possible?

"Quick. Stick it in the dirt!" the twins shouted excitedly.

I stepped into the dirt, dipped my thumb in the soft patch of damp soil, and plopped the seedling in. I heaped a tiny mound of dirt around the short white roots and waited. I repeated the spell.

"Demand it. Will it to grow, Sophie. Show us your hybrid awesomeness," Riada shouted.

My lips scrunched up. "Hybrid and awesomeness don't belong in the same sentence."

"Says who?" the twins said in unison.

"Whatever."

I took a deep breath, feeling the earth invigorate me. My confidence surged. The pendant trembled against my chest. "*Flos*!" I said louder, my voice vibrating, my thoughts directed on the tiny plant. "*Flos*!" I commanded, this time with more energy. The dirt began to shake loose from the mound. Tiny green leaves grew larger, soaking up oxygen and reaching for sunlight. Buds formed and expanded. They sprung open with a pop and then a burst of brilliant orange as if the sun itself had painted them. Within seconds, dozens of rich, dark orange petals unfolded before us like a fan dancer. I had to catch my breath from the dizzy feeling consuming my head.

The girls applauded. "Sweet!" they cried together. "Again. Something bigger."

Shock paused me momentarily. I regrouped and turned my attention to the scarlet wisteria on the arbor beside them. "*Montem*." Intensity shook my voice as I asked it to climb. "*Montem*!" The vines crackled and stretched their way to the top of the wood structure, creeping along the arbor as new leaves and crimson blooms emerged. It slowly draped through the slats until it touched their heads. I held my finger in the air. "*Desine*." The magic whooshed out like a sandstorm. The vines stopped. Silence fell upon the three of us.

"That was amazing, Sophie. How do you feel?" Adair asked.

My cheeks tugged on my lips, stretching my mouth into an easy smile. "Lightheaded like I've been on a merry-go-round for hours, but thrilled. I guess I needed a little pushing."

"It would have happened without our help. Eventually. What are you going to do at the Seeking?" they said and tilted their heads in opposite directions, but at the same time.

I glanced over my shoulder at the remaining moonflower buds, which would reopen when the moon rose and flash their delicate white petals at me to remind me of the days left until the Seeking.

"I hoped to make the seed sprout like an herbalist. If I try it this way, the Council will know immediately that I can cast. I won't be able to hide it and they'll take me away from Aunt Janie for sure. She's too fragile."

Riada grimaced, understanding. "It's our secret. We won't say anything, but you'll have to come up with something believable because the eclipse will heighten your natural magic. You're right that you won't be able to fool them into thinking you're an herbalist when your ability to cast spells will be at its peak."

I tilted my head to the side. "What do you mean, 'peak'?"

"The eclipse will enhance your talent. If they find out you lied, well…it won't be good," Riada said.

"What about you two with the mind altering and reading?"

"We are equally gifted with that and levitation. We will be able to choose which talent to display for them. You won't," Adair offered.

"What do you mean, 'It won't be good?'"

Riada grimaced. "Our mom read from our histories that hundreds of years ago, when we used to help the ordinaries, a very talented young witch tried to hide her gifts from the Council. When her sister, the former eldress, Rebecca, read her diary and found out about her secret gift and about her forbidden affair with an ordinary, she went ballistic, used her black magic to punish her. She paid with her life. Her own sister." The twins looked at each other with shock in their expressions.

A creepy chill shivered through me down to my bare toes. They were talking about Elizabeth. "I know that story, but I don't remember reading it in our histories."

"The current Council removed it," Riada said.

I swallowed hard. "Why?"

"Eldress Mayapple doesn't want the former eldress's punishment to reflect on what she's doing, which is trying to create a strong unit with unfailing loyalty to her," she continued.

My mouth dropped open. "Unit? We're not soldiers. We're witches, meant to help the ordinaries, not hurt them or wage war against them. What's happened to us?"

They shrugged their shoulders. "She wants us to believe it's war," Adair said.

"It's wrong. She's wrong. She's letting her position and power go to her head."

"You need to worry about you and your Aunt Janie. Be careful, Sophie," they said together.

"Thanks," I managed to eke out. I walked the girls to the door and said goodbye before tearing upstairs to the enchanted journal. I had to know what was going on within my coven and as parallel as Elizabeth's life was to mine, I wondered if her entries would provide me with insight. I pointed to the book. "*Revela.*"

July 5th—Secrets. They are mounting. I cannot bear the weight of them. I have been hiding the gift of my clairvoyance from my sister and the Council. They will employ me against their enemy, the reverend, and I do not desire to be a weapon of revenge for them or anyone. From what I have seen, there will be no victors. The choices they have made from their blackened hearts will destroy most of us. I must follow the dictates of my heart and save myself and my loved one in a way they can never touch. If Providence permits, my gift and Evie's gift shall touch the future. Their gifts shall not.

July 12th—Tragedy. Eldress Rebecca has discovered my love for the ordinary boy. I do not care about her law and what she threatens. I do not care about the Seeking. I will not choose the path of darkness. I have already seen what becomes of it and their future does not compare to mine. My heart has chosen him. Regardless of the present consequences. The power of it overwhelms not only my body, but my determination to save us from their black magic.

I sat at the kitchen table, my head slumped in one hand and the fingers of my other hand drumming madly against the tabletop. Aunt Janie, back from her visit with Mistress Aster, brushed into the room, wrapped up in her chaotic thoughts.

"Sophie." Panic drenched her voice. Her brunette bob swished. In her hands, she held her deck of gold-rimmed Lenormand cards. She gestured to the stack.

"Shuffle."

She meant to read them for me, no doubt looking for answers and clairvoyants could never read their own cards. I sat up. "What's going on?"

"Mistress Phoebe is leaving for England tonight."

My lips parted with a gasp. She must have been headed to Essex to seek out the Grand Coven's Council. "Why? What's going to happen?"

She closed her eyes and took a deep breath. "I sent her on a difficult errand for me. However, if events have changed, which I will be able to see in your cards, what she seeks will no longer be necessary. In the meantime, you should know Mistress Aster's daughters are being watched."

"Riada and Adair?" A prickle traveled down my spine.

She nodded. "The girls are free-spirited and Aster is very afraid the Leos will see their talents and take them both. Conditions at Kingshill Detention Center are harsh. The conversion therapy alone deteriorates and permanently damages a weak body and mind. I cannot even imagine what happened to Bess when she went there." She paused and cast her eyes down. "I haven't told you the worst. This morning, I found a headless hummingbird on our doorstep. It's a terrible omen, Sophie."

"Are you sure it wasn't a hungry gnome who discarded the bird there?" Her grave expression imparted her stress. My fingers trembled nervously above the cards. I pulled back. I didn't want her to see in the cards what happened to me with the Leos' attacker. She would freak for sure. "Wouldn't a reading for Mistress Leta be more revealing?"

"You are here right now and I need to know. Go on. Shuffle." This time it was a command.

I bit my lip and took hold of the large, gold-rimmed oracle cards. By touching my fingers to the sides and sorting through the thirty-six card deck, Aunt Janie would be able to see what significant events had and would take place in my life and in the lives of those closest to me.

"Choose three cards and set them here," she directed, tapping the left side of the table. "Then three more in the center, and three more on the right. All face up."

She was looking for a revelation and I worried it had everything to do with me. I set the deck down and extracted the cards from various layers in the deck and followed her instructions.

"Now, choose carefully the last card and set your heart's question upon it. Place that card face down."

I knew exactly what I wanted to ask that card. As a witch, it was the only question to ask.

The long fingers of her hands glided above the cards, feeling vibrations emanating from the symbols. She shook her head grimly to herself, absorbed in what she was seeing. She passed the first set of three cards, which showed a snake, an inverted house, and a book. "Betrayal, a change in house leadership. The conspirator betrayed one of her own kind, took the leadership role, and hid the secret of how she did it."

Sounded like what Rebecca did to Elizabeth. I wiped my forehead, relieved the reading had nothing to do with the thief's attacks or Alexavier. Her hands floated above the second set. A ship, an inverted anchor, and clouds.

"A departure because of uncertainty and impending trouble. This is the present state. Mistress Phoebe's journey to England, although she won't need a ship or a plane for the trip, and an impending change. But who will it hurt and who will it benefit? Let us take a look at what is to come..." She closed her eyes and listened to the three cards: a whip, a scythe, and a bear. She seemed to strain herself over the last card and finally took a deep breath. "Anger and danger, strength and death. The bear brings strength, but he also lies under the scythe." She leaned her head into her hands, looking frustrated and more helpless than I had seen her in a long time.

"You need to lie down and rest," I suggested.

"I'm too involved. I'm involved. And you're involved. That's why I can't see more clearly. And there's danger and death."

"Stop worrying. Your readings are not concrete. Events can change. We'll be fine. What of the last card? My heart's question," I said to distract her from the anxiety she was drowning in.

She flipped the card over and to my surprise, her lips curled at one side of her mouth. She drew back in her chair. "What was the question?"

I evaded for no obvious reason. "What's the answer?"

She eyed me with a puzzled expression. "The moon signifies dreams of romance." She hesitated. "Your dream shall be realized." She nodded toward the deck. "Pull another card."

I backed away from the kitchen table, not wanting to know more. "I know what you're looking for."

"Tell me who he is."

"No one. The card is wrong. It's not a possibility. Dreams of romance? That's not what I asked." How could I tell her? I could barely imagine it myself. The cards were wrong. I wanted to know when he was leaving town. The stress was clearly affecting her talent.

As if she could read my mind, too, she smiled. "The cards are never wrong. And neither am I. Draw another."

I shook my head vehemently. "No. We're done here."

I arrived late to Scents and Scentsabilities. Fortunately, Mrs. Dayo walked in right behind me. She said nothing about the time. Macey was already there, apron on and ready to go. I didn't know how someone who liked to sleep in as much as she did was never late. I threw my apron on and twisted my wild hair up into a messy knot, securing it with a skinny perfume pencil in a dreamy honeysuckle scent.

A group of early morning shoppers scuttled into the store, sampling the None of Your Beeswax Ouch Ointment. I glanced at my watch and straightened my apron. I took a deep breath, trying to focus on the shoppers and not think about the card reading. As I guided the group of local book club ladies around the store, I noticed Alexavier standing outside the front window, watching me. My jaw clenched. My face muscles trembled from the pressure. I peeked around and saw Macey texting on her phone. I excused myself and tapped her on the shoulder. "Help these ladies, if they need it. I have to take care of something."

Her eyes bulged. "Mrs. D will kill you if she sees you're gone, so make it quick."

"And Mrs. D will kill you for texting on the shop floor instead of working." She shut up and waved me on. I rushed out to Alexavier, lowering my voice to a furious hush, wanting to unleash on him for everything his family had done recently and in the past, whether he had anything to do with it or not. "What are you doing here?" I barked.

His masculine eyebrows arched inward with genuine astonishment. "Can't leave me alone, can you?" he uttered, completely ignoring my rage.

I glared at him, my lips taut. I wanted him gone. All gone. "Are you crazy? You're standing outside where I work! And leaving you alone is definitely not my problem." The egomaniac probably perceived my reaction as interest, but I didn't care.

His brow crinkled. "What is your problem then?" Without hesitation, he stepped closer to me, our bodies mere inches apart. Flutters filled my stomach. His eyes locked onto mine.

I gulped, not meaning for it to be loud. "I'm wondering why you and your brother came back to Wethersfield." I wanted him to say it. To admit he wanted to work with his father. I wanted my hate to come easy.

"I can't speak for my brother, but I will tell you this much. I am here to get away from a past I don't want to see repeated."

Against all efforts and weak from the flutters I couldn't even begin to understand, I fell into his mesmerizing eyes. "What past?"

"I don't know if I can avoid it, though. The rebel in me wants to jump off that cliff and see what happens."

He eyed me with a devilish gaze that made my heart flip. I swear if he touched my hand and told me to follow him off the edge, I wasn't sure I would be able to resist. The surprising conflict between my heart and head tore at me. I needed to get away before I made a bad decision.

"I...I have to go."

"When do you get off work?"

He grasped my hand to impart the seriousness of his question. Where he touched, an explosion of sparks tingled. My lips parted. My hearing went fuzzy. What did he say?

"When you're through here, meet me at your house. Under the mulberry tree. I'll be waiting."

I flashed my eyes at him and stood breathless under his dark gaze.

"That's the...the..." The words stuck in my throat. I couldn't disconnect from him. My hand burned from his touch. I felt dizzy, hypnotized, absorbed by the intensity which ignited between us, making me forget who I was, and what I was angry about.

He tugged me closer. His stubbled cheek lightly bristled against the smoothness of mine. I worried he would hear my heart racing as it pounded against my chest. He slid closer and whispered in my ear, "The True Love Tree."

I gasped, the last of my breath expelled from my lungs. I managed to yank my hand away. The sparks lingered like crackling embers, snapping and popping. He grinned and turned away. As my senses came back, so did my ability to breathe evenly. I raced back into the store.

From my back pocket, the journal I was carrying around sent its chill to my fingertips. I touched my hand to it and a cool minty sensation prickled the hairs on my arm. She wanted to tell me something. I walked to the back room. I rested the journal in my open hands. The pages flipped open and the ink flowed.

Be warned. Her curse lives on.

"Curse? What curse?"

The true love curse. Only the one who wears my ring can break through her darkness, but the cost will be great.

"Are you talking about Eldress Rebecca?"

She cursed me to death, but it was an easier death than suffering as the Mathers have.

"Why would she do that?"

Before they hanged her, she cast the curse on them. Her hatred for them lives on as strong as the curse does.

Fear trembled in her writing as if after all these years the mention of Rebecca's name and her black magic continued to instill fear. From what I learned of the black witch, fear was a palpable weapon. I thought of Rebecca and her hatred for the Mathers. I understood it, but knowing she chose black magic and the kind of witch she was sent a chill sweeping over me. I didn't want to be like her. I didn't want to carry on her hate. Her words settled uncomfortably in the pit of my stomach. "Elizabeth, did you tell me in my dream to not be afraid of him? Was that you?"

The book slapped shut. She was gone. Why was Elizabeth worried this curse would affect me? I shoved my hands out in front of me in a stop motion. I would think about that later. At the moment, I had more serious problems. However, the mention of the Mather name left me glancing at the time. He had to be kidding about meeting under that specific tree.

Soon enough, the shop's grandfather clock chimed five times. Before Mrs. Dayo started to do her evening round of straightening the products on the shelves, I rushed to the door and back to my house. Alexavier stood there with his hands in his pockets, staring at the ground beneath the tree's branches, seeming distant. He heard my approach and greeted me with a welcoming smile.

"Tell me, Sophie. You have spent your life in Wethersfield. What do you like most about it?"

"Questions about my life? Why would you care?"

He grinned his seductive grin, letting me glimpse his dangerous streak. Most likely a family trait and I had to make sure I didn't forget it was there. He did seem different from them, not as affected from the poison running through their veins.

"I'm curious about you."

My heart pleaded with my head to ignore the doubts and questions, to be in the moment and believe it was possible. "I love my garden, but this is what I like the most about Wethersfield. Right here. Where the star-crossed lovers are buried. Their story...well, it's an interesting one."

His lips pursed. He drew back, dejected. "Their story? Their story is a tragedy. One of many in the Mather family history."

"The end is tragic, but it's still a love story and this tree..." I raised my hand, admiring its lushness. "It's a symbol of their forbidden love. Centuries with no berries and now look at it." The mulberry swayed with the breeze as if it were dancing. The branches flaunted multitudes of pale, red berry clusters that had begun to ripen for the first time. I liked to think the tree was finally done mourning, but I had no idea why it picked this year of all its three hundred plus years.

"You sound like you believe in happy endings."

"I want to. Don't you?" He was kind of young to be tainted, I thought. My mind drifted to the possibility he had been jilted by a beautiful duchess during his time in London.

"Like I said, I come from a long line of tragedy in my family."

I bit my lip for a second. He was right about that. For as long as we knew his family, they had been dropping dead, and usually in the prime of their lives, except for the really mean ones like the reverend, and his father and Zeke.

"You know you have to fight for your own happy ending. You have to will it to happen."

His eyes held mine, leaving me breathless again. I struggled to think straight.

"I'd bet you're good at willing things to happen."

A tendril of sable hair tickled my cheek. I brushed it away. "I'm good at making mistakes. Lots of mistakes."

His eyebrows furrowed with disbelief. "You make it rain flower petals, yet you wallow in self-pity?"

He was aware I created the storm of blossoms. Crud. Of course, he was. There was no good explanation for it. My stomach sank. "I...uh...uh."

He grinned, not fazed at all by what I could do. "How would you feel about having me as a friend, Sophie?"

My heart fluttered when he said my name, but I glanced at him curiously, not understanding what he was offering. "I choose my friends carefully." I thought back to my dream last night. I wasn't afraid of him, but how could I trust him?

He grimaced from my pause. His threw his hands out in front of him. "Look, I know you hate my family. And we haven't exactly gotten along swimmingly, but I was thinking, it might be easier for both of us if we could find some middle ground."

Incredulity colored my tone. "You want to be friends?"

"Why not?" he replied.

I shook my head. "Surprisingly weird."

"Me?"

"Your suggestion."

"It's not weird at all." He extended his hand to me as if he were serious. "Shake on it."

My heart yearned for his touch, but it wrestled against the logic from my head.

"I can't."

I glanced around, knowing that since the Wethersfield Witch Trials, minus the rare exceptions, witches were forbidden to enter into any kind of a relationship with ordinaries, especially the Mathers.

"This is crazy. Our families are enemies and...and I hate you." My lips tingled from the devil's bit, confirming what I already felt. It was a lie. I didn't hate him at all. In fact, I feared it was the opposite.

"Tell me what you really want from me." I subtly pointed my finger in his direction. "*Verum,*" I whispered in a hushed voice, attempting to cast a truth spell on him. The magic trickled out. I watched for a change in his focus, but as I watched him, a heart shape carved into the bark of the mulberry's tree trunk behind him. My eyes popped. I closed my mouth, still staring at the engraving. "Wha?" I uttered in disbelief. Mishaps were guaranteed when I was near him.

"What do I want from you?" he repeated back to me, unaware of my fail.

I averted my eyes, feeling ridiculous.

"I want you to be you. You've got everyone thinking you're thoroughly ordinary when you're the farthest thing from it."

I peered up at his beautiful face from beneath my lashes. Did he see through me? Did he really know what I was? "What would your father think about you wanting to be my friend?"

"It's no one's business but ours."

"Ours? Like you and me together?" My brow crinkled. "A secret friendship?" I tried to ignore my quickening pulse. Everything in me wanted to believe him. My head railed against the idea. I would be breaking rules and there would be consequences.

He stepped closer. "I think we're both good at keeping secrets. Why not one more?"

I swallowed hard. "You seem to have everything, including a terror for a brother who's got your back. Why do you need a friend?"

"Everyone needs a friend."

He held his hand out, wanting me to shake it while his eyes held me tight. In that moment, dizziness crept in and an overwhelming feeling of falling from a cliff followed. The intensity of it scared me. I put my hand up in a stop motion and pressed my other hand to my stomach, hoping the plummeting sensation would pass. I backed away. My head and heart tore away at each other. "I can't do this."

His face bore a forlorn expression. "You're right. I'm playing with fire, a bad habit of mine. This was stupid of me. I'm sorry."

Curiosity creased in my brow. "What do you mean 'playing with fire'?"

His eyes, holding tight to his secret, burned through me. "I mean you. I'm pretending I can control something that's out of my control. I can't be around you without getting burned, yet I'm completely drawn to you." He parted his soft lips. "Like a moth to the flame."

He disconnected from me and left before I could argue about the irony of me being the flame. Instead, I watched as he disappeared beyond the house. I didn't know what to make of him. I smacked my hand to my forehead. First, he says I'm not worth the trouble and now I'm the flame to his moth? He was certifiable. I felt for Elizabeth's journal in my back pocket and realized I had taken it out and hidden it in my store apron. I raced back to the shop to grab it, hoping it had gone undiscovered. Macey was on her phone in the back room as I reached for my apron hanging on its hook.

She stuffed her phone in her pocket. "Thought your shift was over?"

"I forgot something."

"I was about to call you." She grinned smugly at me. "That was my mom. It's all arranged." Her voice dropped to a whisper like what she was about to say was vital, top secret information.

"Tomorrow afternoon. I told her I wanted to meet at the locksmith shop so we can go to lunch"

Her confidence was inspiring. "Thank you." I checked the time on the wall clock. "I gotta get back to make dinner for Aunt Janie."

The fragrance of simmering purple puzzle tomatoes and pink Parisian garlic wafted up to my nose as I dipped my clean finger into the pot and cast a puree spell on the sauce, zapping the savory lumps into liquid. So much easier than using the blender. I guessed I was beginning to appreciate the small successes. And the simple spells weren't causing as much lightheadedness as before. I dabbed my finger to my lips and tasted.

Mmm. Perfect.

The jingle of a keychain against the front door alerted me. "Aunt Janie?"

"Who else?" she said, walking into the kitchen.

I stopped myself from rolling my eyes. "Where were you?"

"Went down to the small business association to file a complaint against the judge. He has been acquiring my products, secretly testing them, and sending false toxicology reports around town that state my products are dangerous. You'd think I was adding poisonous frog skins to my creams and lotions the way sales have dropped. I'm going to have Mrs. Dayo post a list of ingredients on each shelf next to each product to ease our customers' concerns."

She looked me over. "Have you noticed a decrease in sales?"

"Seems as busy as ever." With everything going on I hadn't really been paying attention.

"That's not what the books say. So frustrating." She began pacing back and forth.

"You need to relax. Dinner's almost ready."

She smiled and stared at the sauce pot. "What are you making?"

I took a deep breath. "Mom's recipe for purple spaghetti sauce."

"Oh, yes. I can smell the Parisian garlic. Yum."

"Aunt Janie, I have a question about Mom." I dropped a tablespoon of fresh, chopped Sicilian herbs into the pot and stirred.

She tucked her hair behind her ear. Apprehension gripped her face. She was Mom's sister and had known her better than anyone, but she didn't like to talk about her or anyone else in the family. It was like she wanted to keep her memories in the same mysterious box where I found my mom's necklace, locked up tight in her closet. She reminded me of Alexavier with his conflict.

"What is it?" She picked up a wooden spoon and dipped it in the dark tomato sauce for a taste.

"Look." I grasped the long silvery chain attached to the pendant and held the stone out to her. The mounting questions were wearing me down and I was tired of looking over my shoulder every time I walked somewhere, wondering if the thief was hiding behind the next bush. "I know this was my mother's and I'm sorry I took it without asking." I didn't try to explain my wrongdoing. There were more important matters pressing on me. "Did she tell you anything about this necklace or its history?"

She paid too much attention to the sauce, keeping her eyes averted. "You should have left that where you found it." A foreboding tone I had never heard in her voice sent chills through me.

My lips trembled. I squared my stance in her direction. "Why? What's wrong with it?"

"I don't know anything about it except that it belonged to your mother and she should have taken it with her to the grave."

"Don't say that!" I gripped the rectangular red crystal between my thumb and index finger. The cuckoo bird clucked from the wall clock. I thought about Aunt Janie's talents and an idea came to me. "Will you at least read its memory?"

She glanced up at me. "That stone holds no answers for you so don't go looking for any."

"I'm asking for your help. Will you read it?"

Her eyes creased at the corners. "The instant you put the necklace on, it became yours, its memory became yours." The finality in her tone suggested she was glad I had put it on, erasing its readable past, and she was done talking about it. She mumbled something that sounded like, "Don't want you ending up like Elizabeth."

"Did you say, Elizabeth? As in the unlucky bride?"

Her lips formed a thin smile. She tucked a strand of hair behind her ear and put the spoon to her lips. "No, I didn't. Sauce tastes delicious. You've outdone yourself. Maybe you should use this as your herbalist trick for the Seeking," she said as if I had never brought the subject of the pendant up. Her eyes focused on nothing as she headed to her blank place.

"Umm. Can you finish up dinner?" I glanced at the rolling boil of water and the noodles submersed within it. "Pasta is almost done."

She snapped out of it and glanced at me with curiosity. "Where are you going?"

"Gotta run an errand." There was one place to go for answers. Somewhere out of her sight where I wouldn't stress her. I grabbed a small, plastic box of orange Tic-Tacs from the drawer in the foyer table, listening to the familiar baby rattle sound when I shook it. I stuffed the candy in my pocket and ran out the door in the direction of the library.

Inside the refurbished brick building, the smell of parchment paper, old leather, and copier ink from the machine whooshing in the background greeted me. Three open sections branched off the center atrium and when I gazed around I could see dozens of tall, dark bookcases standing row by row, pristine and orderly. Mistress Katherine, Bess' mom, peeked over the rim of her reading glasses and greeted me. She wore a thin, white sweater to keep the air conditioning chill off her short, lean arms. I couldn't help to notice the small cluster of flowers pinned to her sweater. The corsage was a combination of holly, lily-of-the-valley, and passionflower—a special mix from our garden Aunt Janie must have crafted to keep her hopeful for her daughter's return.

"Sophie! How are you?"

There were a few patrons milling about so I needed to watch how I addressed her in public. "Good evening, Ms. Johnson." In public we always addressed each other with the ordinaries' titles. "It's been awhile since I've seen you."

"What can I help you with?"

I played with the chain of my necklace. "Personal research. Can I use a computer?"

"Absolutely. Follow me." She nudged her glasses up the thin bridge of her nose and directed me to a quiet reading room. She pointed to a desk with a computer in the center of the empty room.

"Would it be okay if I had a desk against the wall? Like over there?" I pointed to a dark corner.

"Whichever you prefer. There's only a few people here with summer break in full swing so you won't be disturbed." She walked me over and switched the computer on. "You can access the internet and the library's intranet from here."

I waited for her to leave, pretending to straighten the already neat pile of scrap paper and tiny pencils on the desk. I didn't want her telling Aunt Janie what I was researching. As soon as I was alone, I logged into the main search engine and typed like a maniac. I fiddled with my pendant, waiting for the results. The red stone seemed to grab the fluorescent light and hold it without returning a sparkle. I keyed in a description of the stone. As I waited, I reached in my pocket for the box of Tic-Tacs and poured a few orange-flavored pellets into my mouth, tasting the orange baby aspirin flavor. The results popped up.

Jewelry book titles glowed on the screen, but none of their synopses offered an exact description of rough red-looking stones like mine. I typed in "rough, uncut, gem" and clicked on the images. Thousands of photos of colored stones similar to mine in shape appeared. I tried again, this time changing the word "gem" to "red crystal." Suddenly, the word "ruby," not "red crystal," appeared in every search result.

I double-checked what I typed, shaking my head. There had to be a mistake. I held my hands away from the keyboard, afraid to search further. My necklace wasn't a ruby. My family couldn't afford a ruby of this size. I didn't even have a college fund. The idea of it didn't make any sense.

The screen continued to glow, the word "ruby" blaring from each result. I read on, scrolling down to an image of a stone that was close in size to mine. The value was estimated to be in the tens of thousands of dollars. I had to push my chin up with the back of one hand to close my mouth. Completely impossible. How would a normal person even get their hands on a ruby like that? I glanced at my stone again; it looked different from the ginormous ruby. Maybe it was the intensity of the color or the lack of sparkle. I tucked the stone under my collar, not believing it could be anything except enchanted crimson-colored glass, but nonetheless, feeling a little more self-conscious and protective of it. The thief believed it was valuable. I glanced cautiously around the room, paranoid. I cleared my search history and switched off the computer.

I tossed about in bed all night and dragged myself up in the morning, showered, and rushed to Scents and Scentsabilities, arriving perfectly on time. I found Macey struggling in the back room with her apron

"Here, let me help," I said, watching her wrestle with a knot.

Macey turned back around to me with a laugh. "Call in the National Guard. Your hair is a disaster! Did you even brush it this morning?"

I automatically touched the tangled strands. My hair was the least of my worries. "I washed it, but the only thing that got brushed was my teeth."

"Yeah, that's only important to your dentist, not guys. Well, not at first." She grabbed my shoulders and twisted my back to her. Her hands twirled and pinned my long wild waves into a disheveled knot, securing it with bobby pins she pulled from her pocket. Macey may have poked fun at me every now and then for obvious reasons, but her intentions were gold.

"I don't know why we can't leave our hair down."

"We can, but Mrs. Dayo and Aunt Janie think it looks more professional when it's pulled up."

I twirled around and patted my head. "How do I look?"

"Gorgeous," she said with a terrible fake British accent, which made me laugh. "Oh, and I acquired the necessary tools we need for you know what." She raised her eyebrows up and down to remind me of our covert operation.

My confidence in her was solid, but as I weighed the consequences, my level of angst rose. My fingers trembled nervously, fiddling with my pendant. Whether she wanted to say it out loud or not, breaking and entering was illegal. Was I willing to risk being thrown in juvie for information on the mysterious Mather family?

"Got it. I'll figure out when they'll be gone."

Mrs. Dayo heard from her gossip connection the city was hosting a big political black tie fundraiser. Judge Mather would be attending, along with his boys, whom she said he wanted to introduce to political life. I rolled my eyes, thinking another Mather in Wethersfield politics was the last thing the town needed. A quick internet search of the hotel revealed the event's start time, tonight, seven o'clock.

Macey and I, dressed in black from head to toe, hurried to the Mather home for the special op we dubbed Clean Sweep. The white two-story home seemed suddenly black and impenetrable. We kneeled down by the back door and eyed the simple brass knob. She turned to me. "You're sure they're not home?"

"There isn't a single light on inside. No one is home."

I glanced all around, making sure no one was watching, though. Crickets chirped and gnats flitted about my face.

She pulled the roll of lock picks out from an expensive leather tote bag that also held the flashlights. On the outside of the tote, a diamond shape with painted interwoven tree branches was engraved. I did a double-take, surprised to see the French sorceress' symbol for time on an ordinary's bag. I had only seen the image before at Cross Manor in an antique book of symbols.

"Stop humming. You're making me nervous. I already have to pee."

A laugh burst through my lips. "Focus. You can do this. You could kickbox your way out of any trouble, and you didn't think twice about us breaking in."

Without skipping a beat, she chimed in. "You're strong, too. You just don't see it."

I didn't feel strong at the moment as the heat built up beneath the black shirt and pants and my throat swelled up. She nudged me twice in the leg with her elbow when I started to hum again. "Chill," she eked out under her breath.

I shifted my weight from one foot to the other and tugged at my collar. "I'm trying."

She set the roll on the ground, picked an L-shaped pick and inserted it, twisting it around. Her head tilted and she paused. "Oh my gosh." She pulled the pick out and set it back in the roll with the others.

"What's wrong?"

With a twist, the door pushed open. Macey sat back on her feet and laughed out loud. "World's dumbest crooks."

I helped her up and the two of us entered the house. From the bag, she handed me a flashlight.

"Where's the judge's office?"

"There's only so many rooms on the main floor. It's got to be one of them." Within two minutes, we located his office, the walls lined with heavy dark oak and the built-in bookshelves filled with thick law texts.

"Let's search his computer files." Macey went to flip the switch on the desktop, but I grabbed her hand.

"He wouldn't keep anything private on there. He's too smart for that. Whatever we're looking for, it's probably going to be in a locked file drawer."

"Right." She flashed the light onto a tall file cabinet near his desk and immediately set about testing each drawer. The metal drawers squeaked, but they all opened. "Now, what?"

I tapped a finger against my lips, thinking. "This is going to sound crazy, but Aunt Janie keeps her legal papers, like the deed to the house and stuff, in the freezer in case of a fire."

With that idea, Macey darted out the door to the kitchen.

"Wait," I said, trailing behind her and keeping my voice low. "He wouldn't put them in the kitchen freezer. The garage. Come on." She followed me through the connecting door into their garage where the father's silver Jaguar was housed. We shined our flashlights toward a humming sound coming from along the far wall and made our way toward it.

I pulled the handle of the tall freezer, but it wouldn't open. Macey flashed her light on the side and the light glinted off a small metallic object. "Someone installed a lock on this freezer. That's not weird." She set the tote down and pulled out a straight pick.

"Don't damage it. We don't' want them to know we were here," I whispered.

"I got this." With a few wiggles of the pick, the lock released. She slipped it off.

"You really need to consider a career in espionage. I'm in awe." I opened the door, the light turned on and cold air rushed out. I searched through layers of frozen fish filets sealed in plastic bags, my heart sinking as I worked through the pile.

"Do you see anything?"

"I guess the judge likes fish."

"What?" She stood next to me. "What's that?"

Underneath the twentieth bag of fish, there was something different. A plastic bag filled with papers and copies of checks. "Bingo!" We pulled the bag out and rested it on the hood of the Jag. I gave half the stack to Macey to search through.

It was difficult to understand the legal lingo on some of the documents, but there were several copies of police records regarding Alexavier and his time in London. He had been arrested seven times for arson and destruction of property. Seven times. From what I read, it appeared he finished his probation in London.

"Here's some stuff on Kingshill. Take a look at this. I think it's what you were after."

I had already seen enough. I slid the papers over and held them under the beam of light.

"How are we going to copy this stuff?" she asked.

Without taking my eyes off the papers, I explained. "I saw a printer in his office. That will do, but we have to be quick. We've already been here too long."

A scurrying sound outside the garage door startled me. The papers went flying. "Crud!" I froze, trying to listen.

Macey grabbed my hand. "Stay calm. They're not home."

My breathing raced out of control. My stomach tightened. I glanced back and forth at the scattered papers, the white seeming fluorescent in the darkness. I wiped the perspiration from my brow, and took a deep breath.

We both gathered the papers and set them back on the hood. I flashed the light on my watch, but I didn't care anymore. Curiosity urged me on. I needed to know how the judge was so connected to Kingshill. I saw a bunch of documents with the address for the old psych ward, and some property and tax forms. I skipped through the pages and picked up copies of written checks made out to Judge Mather for tens of thousands of dollars from a prison management company. My head pounded, but I couldn't tear my eyes away as I tallied the sum.

A total of two million dollars written out to him. Kickbacks for filling up the privately owned detention center? He was making money and getting rid of the witches at the same time? It would explain why Wethersfield had a conviction rate ten times higher than the surrounding towns. I searched through the remaining pages until I found what I was looking for, the actual owner of the dilapidated building. Mayor Varlet, his cousin.

I dropped the papers, shocked by the privileged information I wasn't supposed to be privileged to, especially Alexavier Mather's criminal record. All the dirt was right in front of me, although surprisingly, nothing on Zeke. However, there was enough to force the judge to leave town and never run for reelection again. "I'm going to copy these. Be ready to re-lock the freezer.

In the office, I copied every page I had in my hands. The judge, proud of his tough on crime reputation, would not want to be disgraced, nor have their true colors revealed. I snatched the evidence and folded it up, then stuffed them into the waist of my pants. I bit my lip and fiddled with my pendant. I should have felt satisfied after years of watching the judge condemn girls like me to Kingshill for losing control of their harmless white magic, but a stomach-upsetting mix of guilt and remorse settled in instead.

The door leading to the garage creaked open. "Hurry! I think they're home. I heard a car pull up."

I stopped breathing and raced toward her voice. Adrenaline flooded my muscles. I dashed back into the garage, stuffed the papers into the plastic bag and shoved it under the piles of fish. Macey threw the lock on and grabbed her tote.

The sound of the electric garage door opening and the hum of an idling car sent a rush of panic that swept up from my feet. Macey panted. We tossed the lit flashlights into the bag and from memory, retraced our steps out of the garage, back through the dark house and out the back door.

Once outside, we hurried into my yard. On the other side, I bent over and leaned on my knees, hyperventilating. My hair draped all around my head. What was I doing? My curiosity over the Mather family had prompted me to do things I would never think of doing. Illegal things. Gray area things. Slippery slope things.

I looked up at Macey who stood there with her hands on her hips. "I can read your face, even in the dark. You're such a goody-two-shoes."

"Are you kidding me? That was a serious violation of privacy. A crime."

She shrugged her shoulders like it didn't matter. "We didn't get caught and you got what you wanted, right?"

I nodded, staring straight ahead, still in shock. The papers burned against my skin like a glowing ember.

"Mission accomplished then, right?"

"I guess."

"Sooo?" she asked with her hands out, fingers wiggling, waiting for the info.

"He was busted seven times for arson. It's all true. He's a rich, delinquent aristobrat…"

"Aristo*brit*," she corrected, preferring the Brit part even though I had told her a thousand times he wasn't a Brit. "You know what they say. If he talks like a Brit and he looks a Brit, he's a Brit."

"He's not a Brit! He's a Yank and a Mather." Although he didn't talk like a Mather or look like a Mather.

"And an arsonist. What about that stuff on Kingshill?"

"It was bad. The judge is morally and ethically bankrupt, but I'm not sure I can call him that since I broke into his house to get the information."

"That doesn't make you worse than him and it doesn't change what he did." She waited, like she expected my enthusiasm to kick in at any moment. "So, now you can send them packing, right?"

I looked at her, angst creased in my brow. Everything I needed pressed against my waist. I could make more copies and show the judge, convince him his career was over, and if he didn't comply, I could threaten to send it all to the papers. Why not add blackmail to my list of growing crimes?

"You said Alexavier was mean to you, right?"

I nodded.

"So why do you look so freaked out?"

"He was mean, but he doesn't deserve to have everyone know what I know. It's his business." He was obviously a bad boy. I saw the streak of danger in his eyes and I watched him revel in the fire he set in his backyard, which he didn't try to hide from me. And, it was a gut feeling, but I doubted he knew anything about his father's Kingshill activities. There was something else bothering him. Something that had everything to do with his family and with me being the metaphorical flame he needed to avoid. The papers I copied had nothing to do with that.

Macey grabbed my arm. "What's wrong?"

"It's not that simple."

"Seems simple enough to me."

Callum's words came back to me about not being a hater. I didn't want to be. And I definitely didn't want to be like Rebecca or the judge. "I can't do anything with this. They'll know I broke in and I'll get in trouble."

She twisted her mouth to the side. "That's an excuse and you know it. You could snail mail the papers anonymously to the newspaper. The truth is the truth no matter who finds it."

"What if discrediting them doesn't change anything? What if…"

She shook her head, her curls fell into her eyes, but it didn't stop her from seeing my truth. We both knew the paper would print it. The judge would be disgraced and they would all be forced to leave town from the shame of it. His public relations team would work overtime to try to erase the tarnish of greed and corruption but it would never be wiped away completely.

"Listen. You know I'm on your side. If you want to go public with the info to get rid of the family, you should, but I think it would be easier on your conscience if you admit you like Alexavier. What's so wrong with liking him?"

The answer to that question was everything, but I said nothing. She couldn't possibly understand the hostile history between the witches of Wethersfield and the Mathers. Liking him was not an option, in fact, it was forbidden, but I couldn't punish him for mistakes he made in his past. His father could do it to us easily enough, but I didn't have it in me to do it to one of them.

She bounced her head side to side, full of energy as she jabbed the air practicing her kickboxing moves. "The adrenaline rush made me hungry. Let's go to Gracie's. I'm craving a Witch Wrap."

My stomach churned with stress. "Maybe you should lay off their wraps."

"Maybe you should try one," she snapped.

"I don't like their food. Look, I don't want you to think I don't appreciate your help tonight. I do, but I'm not hungry. I'm gonna head inside. See you tomorrow and take my advice. Switch to the Cove BLT, no mayo."

"Okay, but cheer up."

I walked inside, my head hanging low. I tossed the evidence in the trash and trudged upstairs. In the bathroom, I glanced at my reflection in the mirror. At first, all I saw were loose tendrils of wavy hair clinging to the moist skin along my cheeks. Then I looked deeper and saw someone else staring back at me, a girl I hardly recognized and I didn't like the reflection. My ribcage tightened. I couldn't breathe. I started to hyperventilate. I dashed downstairs and into the garden again, succumbing to the fresh warm air. My breathing relaxed until it all rushed back. Did I make a mistake throwing the proof away?

"I prefer your hair down," he said, his warm, familiar voice came from behind me, sending flutters right to my stomach.

My pulse quickened. I closed my eyes, feeling guilty. "I don't care what you prefer." Macey was right. I liked him. As much I didn't want to, as much as I knew it would bring me nothing but trouble, I couldn't pretend any longer. All I could do was try to avoid him.

"I think you do."

I swirled around to face him. "Said the reckless boy wanting to run from his problem."

A "v" formed over his nose. "I'm here and I'm not going anywhere." His voice resonated with steely resolve.

Had something changed his mind? I narrowed my eyes. What did that mean? "You are nothing but trouble."

He studied my expression and my tensed frame, both of which exuded anger. Anger with myself for not walking away from him as soon as his pleasant voice sounded in my ears and his alluring scent wrapped around me. "You're right, but so are you. That's why we should stay away from each other, but since we can't seem to manage that and you don't want to be friends, I have an idea."

My hand pressed to my forehead, feeling the force of falling off the cliff again.

He squared his stance and stared into me with his piercing eyes. He pursed his inviting lips. "Have dinner with me."His arrogance remained firmly intact, irritating me enough to argue with him.

"Why? Because I can't leave you alone? Oh wait, that's your problem," I said, applying a thick layer of sarcasm.

He grimaced from my tone. "I don't mean to sound obnoxious. I only thought it would be good to get to know each other better."

I stared at the ground, not wanting to be mesmerized. What if I told him I knew about the arson charges? What if I confronted him with the truth of what I had done? He would be so mad I snooped into his private business he would want nothing to do with me. He would finally leave me alone and I wouldn't have to worry about it anymore.A lump formed in my throat as the truth accumulated there in a tight little ball.

"I...I saw your criminal record," I blurted out, knowing there was no turning back.

Strangely, his expression remained unfazed. "How did you see that?"

I waited for anger or rage or some ugly emotion to surface, but it didn't. He remained calm and steady, unbothered with my prying. He stepped closer to me, his scent as pleasant and intoxicating as ever. I felt myself unraveling, my inhibitions slipping away. My head grew cloudy. "That's, uh, a secret." I peered up at him, unable to resist gauging his mood. Did he hate me?

His eyes brightened under the long black eyelashes and a smile crossed his face. I watched as his strong hand rubbed his square, shadowed jaw. Then he threw his head back and laughed.

Part of me sighed with relief while the other part wondered why he was so messed up.

"What's so funny?"

"You are as curious as you are interesting. What time should I pick you up?" He seemed thoroughly smug and satisfied with his assumptions, which was the perfect antidote to the daze in my head. I gnashed my teeth and exhaled loudly.

"You...you...are so arrogant!"

"Seven o'clock? Tomorrow night?"

I shut my eyes and shuddered. "I have other plans." I stomped back into the house without another glance.

"Callum!" I shouted into the back office of Goody's Market, scanning the room. I froze in my shoes as an unexpected sound came from behind me.

"God, Sophie, take it down a dozen decibels. Your voice is like a fork scraping on glass." I spun around to see Laney approaching me. She jumped on the desk and sat there like a cat watching its prey.

My forehead crinkled in surprise. "What are you doing here?"

She shifted, crossing her legs in front of her, looking comfortable like she hung out in the back office on a regular basis. "Nice greeting. Callum invited me, of course." Her eyes narrowed.

Callum shook his head and rolled his eyes at me. "Laney, you invited yourself to hang out. All I said was that I didn't care." He hung his store apron on its hook and winked at me.

She arched her head back and twirled a strand of blond hair around her index finger. "So Callum and I were talking about you before you got here," she said, pausing intentionally before batting her eyelids in Callum's direction.

I flashed a look at Callum. He shook his head. "No. Laney was asking questions about you. I simply answered them to kill time."

As a witch, she knew more about me and my family than Callum ever would, so what was she up to? She tossed her head up, letting the straight strands of white blonde hair fly over her shoulders. Her attempt at sexiness came across uber-weird. "He said you're into…gardening. Is that true?"

She already knew it was. The Mayapples had always frowned upon my family's interest in herbalism, but they were nothing more than average conjurers. I furrowed my brow. I had watched her and the other Glitterati play this game in front of the ordinaries before. "Well, Laney, I work at my aunt's aromatherapy shop, so it's kind of a prerequisite to like gardening since that's where her products come from."

"Scents and something, right? And how are you getting along with the Mather boys who moved in to the house next to yours?"

Callum choked out a laugh, probably thinking of Zeke. "I think that's enough questions, don't you?" My anger rose up like mercury on a hot day.

She scowled and I swear I thought I heard her hiss at me. It was about all I could take.

"You know what our *family* thinks of the Mathers?" she said, referring to the forbidden law. "Anyway, I'm interested in conjuring a great future for myself, not being stuck in some retail boutique with dirt under my nails."

I smirked. She was full of herself today, hoping the upcoming Seeking would make her a star in her mother's eyes. "Conjuring a great future? It's gonna take more than a magic trick for you to conjure anything great. But that's a craptacular goal." I tried to downplay her references so Callum wouldn't figure out what she was rambling on about.

She leaned forward with ice in her eyes. "I'm not into gardening, but if I were, I would be better at it than you," she challenged.

My fists curled at my sides as my anger simmered past hot. "No, you wouldn't. You and your horr-ronic mother have less talent than any other…any other…"

Her lip arched into a severe snarl and her gaze grew icier than usual. "At least I have a mother, you orphaned mutt."

"Laney!" Callum yelled.

My eyes widened. The veins in my neck strained from the pressure building in me. I stared at the framed print hanging on the wall behind her. My finger snapped in its direction. "*Prolapsio,*" I eked out under my breath through clenched teeth. The magic rushed out of my hand like a sandstorm. The picture crashed with force onto the desk. Glass shattered and sprayed into jagged bits all around her. I stepped backward, suddenly sick to my stomach and very lightheaded. I flashed my eyes to Callum's. Crud. Showing off in front of an ordinary was Laney's territory. Not mine. She screamed and scrambled to her feet. Her icy eyes blazed as she jumped in my face.

Callum threw himself between us, creating a physical barrier. "Laney, you need to apologize."

"Didn't you see what the half-breed did?" she said, referring to my father being an ordinary. She pointed a narrow finger at me. As my temper cooled and my sensibilities returned, the only thing flashing in my head was the *deleto* spell. I readied my tongue, but before I could say a word Cal interjected.

"That's it, Laney. Stop with the name calling. Bigger people like me might take offense since I'm actually a mutt." He flashed his large bronze-colored hands in front of her for effect. "You shouldn't throw those kinds of words around so loosely. If you have a problem with people of mixed races, then you need to leave," Callum yelled, interrupting my thoughts. I couldn't think straight to cast the spell. Crud. I could hear the clock ticking on the wall.

Breathe.

Laney stood there with a shocked expression, surprised that an ordinary could be so threatening to her. She had no idea when she said, "mutt" and "half-breed" she would be insulting Callum.

"Now!" he yelled.

Her lips mashed together as she threw the door open. Cal turned to me, changing the topic to clear the hurt he could see in my expression. "Epic comeback about her mother, Sophie, although I have no idea what you were talking about."

I flashed a hand at him to wait a second as I stepped toward the closing door. A sliver of fluorescent store light leaked through, the time constraint jarring my memory. My pulse raced. "*Deleto,*" I cast, pointing in her direction. The door shut. I gasped for breath, unsure if I got the spell out in time. Proximity never factored into my spells before so I had no idea how close she had to be for it to work. What if it didn't work? What if she told her mother what I could do? I snatched the doorknob, ready to race after her.

"Wait," Callum said.

I shook my head. "What?"

"What you said to Laney. Very feisty."

"Back at ya."

He suddenly creased his eyebrows together. "Why did she call you a mutt?"

My lips tingled. "No idea."

Callum smacked his hands together, the clap shaking me out of my head. "That's what I figured. Let's clean this up and we can go."

"Hold on." I whipped the door open a smidge and scanned the store for her blonde head of perfect hair. My heart sank as I spotted her. She stood next to her mother, pointing her finger in my direction and talking quietly to her. The look on Eldress Mayapple's face quickly phased to displeasure. I shut the door, pressing my small frame against it. My head ached. Did the spell work? What did she tell her?

"Grab the dust pan over there."

"Huh?"

"We gotta clean this glass up before we go." He picked up the nail that held the picture on the wall. "Crazy this fell down right when you two were fighting."

"Yup. Crazy." I rubbed my neck, knowing there was nothing more I could do at the moment. "Where are we going?"

"I told you. Daniel and his bro, Drew, invited us to join them on their sailboat tonight. Should be fun."

"Oh. Right. Fun."

Locals crowded the Cove Yacht Club, filling the eateries that advertised half-priced pitchers of beer and lobster rolls. Seagulls squawked above us, circling a group of small children throwing animal crackers in the air.

I chatted with Macey and Jenna as we followed behind Daniel, Drew, and Callum to the boat. Along the edge of the dock, ducks swam in clusters, quacking periodically as they waited for sandwich crumbs and ice cream cones to drop.

"What do you think of the boat?" Drew asked proudly. His mop of brown hair almost covered his eyes and his attempt to grow facial hair created a patchy look.

"It's beautiful. The prettiest one I've ever seen." The long, sleek sail boat with antique wood trim and a glossy wood deck boasted a strange name. On the stern, Ghost from the Past, was printed in bold black letters. Something about it didn't sit right with me.

"What's up with the name?"

He shrugged his shoulders. "My dad had a boat just like this and wrecked it in the Caribbean five years ago. This is the replacement. The ghost."

"Replacement? No. It's too beautiful to be called a ghost. It should have a pretty name."

"Like Sophie?"

Like Elizabeth, I thought. "How big is it?" I asked, not comfortable with the compliment from him.

His voice thrilled as he explained. "It's a thirty-one-foot Beneteau Oceanis."

"A Benna what?" I said, still distracted.

He smiled. "It's the maker. Let me help you." He offered his hand to me and Jenna as we lightly leapt on board, his grip lingering longer than necessary. Callum followed.

We descended into the galley with its shiny, golden brown wood walls. The seats were cushioned in taupe and stacks of soft blankets sat on the table.

Above, we heard cursing and the intermittent sputtering of the engine as Drew and Daniel attempted to start it. The smell of gasoline fumes drifted down to us. Callum and I glanced at each other. He shrugged his shoulders and grabbed a bag of grapes from the small refrigerator. "Snack time?" I asked, staring at the cellophane bag of magenta pearl grapes.

"Hungry boy needs food," he said, patting his stomach and making me laugh before we climbed up to the deck.

"What's wrong, Drew?"

"Battery cables are torn. We can't get the engine to turn over, so what do you want to do?" he asked, disappointment shrouding his mood.

I considered attempting a fix-it spell, but I knew nothing about engines and with ordinary witnesses standing around, it would be stupid to risk it. Macey, already blissful with Daniel next to her, smiled. "So what? We are all together on a beautiful boat in a great town. Let's hang out here for a while. It'll be fun."

The warm air smelled of summer and sea life and the sloshing of water against the hull buffered the town's noises in the background. Daniel took Macey by the hand, maneuvering toward the front of the boat while Callum and I drifted to the back, sitting on the edge so our arms rested on the rails and our feet dangled over the side. Drew, realizing he was not invited to sit with us, reluctantly joined Jenna in the galley where they were probably content playing with the satellite radio and sharing her pocket stash of warm gummy bears.

"What's that thoughtful gaze for?" Callum asked. His short dark brown hair shimmered, glistening in the fading sunlight.

"Nothing. Just feeling contemplative right now. Is that okay?"

"Yeah. You've been kind of out of it lately." He glanced at me like his comment was an invitation to explain. I resisted. "What's going on with you?"

My shoulders rose then fell heavily.

"Gonna make me work for it?" he persisted in his humorous way.

"Callum..."

"I like it when you call me Cal," he said in a low, throaty voice.

I closed my eyes and shook my head. "You're such a flirt."

"Nah! I'm playing. What is it?" He popped a grape in his mouth, waiting for my question.

I slipped the pendant out and held it in my palm for him to see. The crystal looked like red glass in my hand. "Do you think this could be a ruby?"

"I never really thought anything of it." He stared at me for an uncomfortable second. "It's hard to get past those blue eyes of yours."

I grimaced. "I'm being serious. What do you think?"

His gaze broke from mine and his voice softened. "I have no idea. Why don't you ask Sam, the jeweler next door to the market?"

"I'd feel stupid. What if it turns out to be a piece of seaglass? Besides, I don't have money to pay for an appraisal."

"Then you have to live with not knowing because I sure as heck don't know." He leaned closer, his broad shoulder brushing against mine. "If you're really worried about it, we can meet after work one night and go over. I'll introduce you. Maybe he'll give you a discount for knowing me." He smiled big, reassuring me everything would be fine.

I wanted to laugh. "You don't lack confidence, that's for sure."

"Why should I?" he said, still wearing the grin.

"You shouldn't and that would be great." I loved the camaraderie we shared. It was innocent and fun, like it was when we were children playing together, but times were changing. The Seeking was quickly approaching and one way or another it was going to change my life. Aunt Janie worried for the twins she continued to foresee locked up at Kingshill. And the judge was threatening to close Mistress Phoebe's nut shop, her only source of income, for a rodent infestation she believed one of his henchman caused.

I looked out at the cove, watching the countless sailboats glide back and forth across the dark sparkling water. On the land around the cove, tall, lush trees watched over a handful of illuminated businesses and historic barns. He tossed a grape to a passing flock of ducks scooting past.

"Not to change the subject, but why don't you tell me why you've been hanging out with Alexavier Mather," he said, sitting straight again. "I didn't think you liked him."

I arched my eyebrows at the mention of his name.

"I know your aunt doesn't. She was asking my mom questions about them."

I stared harder at my distorted silhouette in the brackish water below, my hair succumbing to gravity as it draped in long sable waves around my face. "So my aunt asked questions. It doesn't mean I'm hanging out with Alexavier."

"My mom said she saw you two on the path behind the shop talking. She likes to keep an eye on her favorite employees." When I peeked at him, he was staring out at the horizon that was changing from red to painted streaks of purple. He looked as if he weren't overly interested in my response, but his unpleasant interactions with the Mathers and my knowing Callum told me otherwise.

"The only things said were pleasantries."

"Pleasantries behind the shop? You know, I get the impression the older one is very protective. Doubt he wants his little brother hanging out with locals."

"The way you say, 'locals' doesn't make me want to hang out with them either." I tried to stifle a snorty laugh, but failed.

"I mean it."

I sat back, twisting my lips to the side. "Did Zeke tell you that himself? He said those exact words?"

"He didn't have to. I can tell." The muscles around his jaw tensed like he was angry.

"Uh-huh. Well, they happen to come from a long line of locals."

"You know what I mean."

"Yeah. I know. The wrong kind of locals. So what happened when they came into the market to place their order of weird specialty food?"

"You mean, girlie food? I wasn't impressed with either of them or their cash roll, although Mr. Geoffrey loved making that sale. He was kissing up to them like nobody's business, trying to meet his quarterly sales quota so he gets his bonus. Made me sick. Anyway, Zeke complained about the quality of the market's food and told his brother the locals were about the same in quality and to remember to not get involved with any of them."

My lips pressed tightly together. Dreadful Zeke. But I had to not care what he said or thought, just like Laney. "There's nothing going on between Alexavier and me, but I'll tell you this," I paused and peered around to make sure the others were not in listening range. I wagged my finger at him for extra emphasis. "I swear, if you tell anyone I'll kill you. Do you understand?"

"You're too tiny to be the threatening type, but what is it?"

"And don't laugh either."

His lips pursed as he possibly considered a negotiation, but he resisted, eager to hear what I was going to tell him. "I promise."

"I had a dream about Alexavier."

He drew back, disgusted. "What the heck kind of secret is that?"

I waved my hands for him to calm down. "You don't understand. You told me I wasn't a hater and this dream was like a nudge, a good nudge to make me rethink my feelings toward the Mathers."

"Exactly what kind of dream was this?" He raised his eyebrows and tilted his head.

"Not a dirty one so get that look off your face." I figured the joke would make him laugh, but it didn't. "Alexavier was in it and a ghost told me to not be afraid of him. End of dream."

He frowned. "That's weird. Are you sure the ghost wasn't your subconscious?"

"Very sure," I said defensively. Too defensively.

He knitted his brows together with concern as he studied my expression. "No, you're not a hater, but you sound like you like him, really like him."

I remained silent, not arguing against the idea. His face instantly wrinkled in disgust.

"What are you thinking?"

Crimson surely colored my cheeks as the warmth radiated from my face. I grimaced and twisted my fingers together. "Why do you care so much?" I asked, feeling despair seep in as I contemplated that Alexavier was a Mather with a shady background and a hidden secret.

"You've been my friend forever. Is it okay if I care about you?" He shrugged.

My small hands wrapped around the cool metal bar of the rail in front of me. I leaned back and gazed up at the twilight sky

"Cal, I swear there's nothing going on with him and me."

"Good. You're better off that way." He swallowed hard. "So do you ever dream about me?" he asked, his big toothy grin appearing as he beamed his attention on me.

The boat rocked gently back and forth. Small waves splashed against the hull, sounding like a thirsty dog lapping water from its bowl.

"You're such a goof," I complained. I bumped his shoulder with mine teasingly as I set my eyes on the water again, feeling uneasy. Seagulls squawked above us, searching for one last evening snack. Cal tossed a grape to them, causing a flurry of white and gray wings as they descended to scavenge.

"So he hasn't made a move to ask you out?"

"He did ask me to dinner. Tonight. I think he was kidding, though," I added, but I didn't believe that. "I told him I had other plans."

Callum shook his head. "Don't say I didn't warn you."

"I don't want to talk about it."

"Me either."

"Good."

He popped two grapes in his mouth and mashed them with his perfectly straight white teeth. Macey suddenly appeared and leaned down to whisper quietly in my ear.

"Uh, Alexavier Mather is standing on the dock, staring at this boat. I think he's waiting for you."

I didn't want to alert Callum after his warning.

"Girl stuff," I said, excusing myself. I walked with Macey to the front of the boat. She waved at him and pointed to me. I tugged on her frilly tank top. "No," I pleaded with her.

"Look. He's just standing there, staring, behind the crowd. Weird, but kind of romantic."

"Weir-mantic?"

She grinned. "You should go and talk to him." She was playing matchmaker again. "I'll tell Cal I sent you for tampons. He won't ask one question after that."

I bit my lip and nodded. This was the last thing I needed. If I didn't go, he was capable of standing there all night, leaving me unable to concentrate on anything else. I leapt off the boat onto the dock and approached him. He wore dark blue jeans, a white T-shirt, and a chambray blue button down over it with the sleeves rolled up. It was the most casual I had seen him. He ran one hand over his black as midnight facial scruff and his eyes set on me with a smile.

"Are you following me?" I asked.

"No."

"Then why are you out here?" My hand gestured to the yacht club.

He stared out at the water. "The grocery manager mentioned you and your friends were heading to the cove."

Mr. Geoffrey, the brown-noser, was handing out my location for a sale? "You were at the market earlier?"

"Yes."

It was too much of a coincidence—him being near the yacht club and the boat engine not working. "Did you tear the cables on the boat's battery so we couldn't leave?"

No remorse showed in his eyes, only determination to overcome any obstacle in his path. "I promise to repair the damage in the morning."

I pressed my hand to my forehead. My heart beat loudly in my ears. His bad boy streak was a huge red flag. How could I like someone like him? I grimaced, already knowing the answer.

"Do you know how crazy that is?"

"No." He said seriously, not even considering the possibility I might be onto something.

"You're earning yourself a bad reputation." He probably didn't care since he already had one.

"Are you hungry, because if you are, I'm still available for dinner. I found a nice place."

My mouth dropped open, always surprised by the enormity of his ego. "Clearly, I'm in the middle of my other plans for the night." I hesitated. "And I think it would be better for both of us if we didn't."

"You're probably right, but here I am. Moth to the flame."

The muscles in my body tensed. I tapped my foot against the ground as I crossed my arms over my chest.

His expression softened. "Look, I'll take you home as soon as you want to leave."

The dose of humility softened my stubbornness like he probably knew it would. Then his eyes did that brooding thing I found utterly appealing.

I looked up at him, trying to sense what he was thinking. If only I could read minds. "What about your father and brother?"

"What I do is none of their business."

"You sure about that?"

"What about your friends?" he asked, being very clever.

"Better if they don't know." Cal would freak and Macey would never stop talking about it. My head reeled from the deception as my heart insisted I consider it. After all, he did promise to fix the boat engine. "You think you can resist the flame, Mr. Moth?"

"My life depends on it." He said it jokingly, but it didn't seem like a joke.

"Let me tell them I'm leaving. Where should I meet you?"

I stepped back onto Ghost from the Past. My lips tingled from the nectar, but there was no other way to handle the situation. "Hey guys, I'm tired and feeling a little seasick. I'm gonna head home."

Drew, about to jump onto the dock to help me off, was held back by Cal. Cal stepped forward and examined my face, looking at me with suspicion. "Let me walk you home," he offered.

"No." I pulled a few ones from my pocket. "I can grab a cab ride if I need to, but thanks." I stuffed the money back in my pocket and said goodbye. I headed to the corner where Alexavier told me he would park, glancing behind me in case Cal decided to follow. He didn't.

The shiny white Audi waited. Alexavier jumped out and dashed around the front of the car to open the door for me before I reached the handle. I sat down and clicked the seat belt. Hearing the click, I realized there was no turning back.

What was I doing? My friends assumed I was on my way home because I lied to them and, now, I was alone with Alexavier Mather, a sworn enemy of my family and the witches of Wethersfield. But it didn't seem so black and white anymore. The witches in my coven weren't exactly innocent, either. Conflict bounced around inside me. I draped my hair over one shoulder and played with my pendant, feeling its magical hum.

His car roared to life with the press of a switch, sending powerful vibrations through the seats. After a short drive, he parked on a street on the edge of town and led me through the woods with a flashlight he brought with him, along with a large handled basket he had hidden in the trunk. The smell of sweet grass and wildflowers swirled around us as we entered a field in the middle of nowhere. The sun had set and the stars blanketed the sky with their twinkling beauty. I smiled.

"Where are we?"

"It's an abandoned field. The land abuts the Stonefield's farm." In the distance, the soft whinnies of horses echoed on the cool evening breeze. He set the basket down on the grass and pulled a wool blanket from the top. "I didn't know if you would come with me or not, so I packed just in case." His steely determination to get what he wanted impressed me.

I spun in a slow circle, taking in all the details. A damp evening breeze brushed over my warm skin and a shiver shook through me.

"I'll fix that in a minute," he said, noticing. He spread the blanket across a small patch of field and extracted matches from his back pocket.

"Do you ever not carry those?"

"No," he said without regret or apology. He scratched the match to life and set the flame to a small stack of wood near the blanket. Within seconds, the kindling crackled and a fire glowed, giving off enough heat to ward off my chill. The light from the fire illuminated his face and cast dancing shadows on the grass behind us.

"You had this all set up. I must be so transparent."

He shook his head, his eyes expressing only a tender argument. "No. Not at all. I'm just optimistic. For the first time in my life. And it feels good to feel this way." His hand touched his stubbled chin, drawing my attention to his masculine features. "I thought if there was even the smallest chance you might be persuaded to come with me tonight, I wanted everything to be perfect."

My lips parted with surprise. His honesty overwhelmed me and I felt myself getting lost in the moment. My stomach dropped as if I were staring over the edge of a steep cliff. I closed my eyes to stave off the flutters. Friends only, I reminded myself.

Alexavier took me confidently by the hand and led me to the blanket. The flutters intensified. Sparks ignited where he touched. I gasped, not meaning to, and tugged my hand back.

He released it. "You okay?"

"Mm-hmm. Great. Fine. Good," I said, trying to play cool, yet feeling everything but cool.

"Sit down, please. Would you like something to eat?" He grabbed the basket, taking containers out and setting them between us. He sat down after me and pointed to the spread. "Brie in there, loaf of French bread there, and fruit here. It's not exactly dinner, but I'm hoping it will do."

"I'm fine, really."

He furrowed his brow inward. "No, you're not. I can hear your stomach grumbling."

With Callum rushing me to the boat earlier, I had forgotten about dinner. He offered me a handful of voluptuous Bing cherries. I popped a few in my mouth. The dense flesh was sweet and delicious. He passed me a dewy slice of pear. The nectar sweetness of the summer fruit dissolved in my mouth. I plucked a blackberry, hoping it was as sweet. His eyes followed the movement of my hand. I popped it in my mouth, more slowly than I normally would, and pressed it against the roof of my mouth, squeezing its sugary juices from the plump flesh.

"Are you eating with me or is this all mine?" I asked, wondering if he would join me in the nighttime picnic.

He laughed. "Of course, but I like watching your lips move. Heart-shaped and very good at communicating exactly what you're thinking. I swear, sometimes you look at me with an expression like I'm the worst of the Mathers."

I frowned. "I'm sorry if I do that. I don't mean to." I popped another berry in my mouth while he ripped a chunk of bread from the loaf and took a bite. "So where are your dad and brother?"

He lowered his eyes and waited. "Attending a political rally downtown." He didn't look at me when he said it.

I sat up straight and crinkled my brow. "What kind of rally?"

His head dropped lower if that was even possible. "My father is desperate to get funding for a new addition to Kingshill and he is trying to generate support from the town to do it."

"What?"

"Don't worry. It's a waste of time. The town can't afford it and Kingshill is privately owned so the current owner needs to foot that bill."

Did he not realize the current owner was his father's cousin? "If your dad needs more space to lock the rest of us up for the smallest of crimes there won't be anyone left, including you." The anger dripped from my tone.

He closed his eyes and sighed. "I agree with you, but my father prefers to see me as a victim during my time in London. He's wrong. He's so blind when it comes to me and Zeke, but he has laser focus when it comes to everyone else who won't obey his laws. He's a bitter man."

"Bitter about what?"

"His lot in life."

"Can't you do something? Try to make him see? I mean, you made me see that you could be different, can't you try with him?"

"I have tried. He won't listen to me. He's beyond help." Tension creased in his brow. He was telling the truth and I could sense his frustration.

"There must be something that can be done."

"I don't want to talk about my father any more. Do you mind?" His eyes pleaded.

My lower lip stuck out. "What about Zeke?"

"He's no better. Desperate for our father's love and approval, he's willing to throw his hopes away to follow him. We all have to make choices in life. They have made theirs."

My eyes narrowed. My skin felt hot. Talking about Zeke being like his father brought the memory back. "You're very charming when you want to be and you've managed to talk me into this picnic, but there's something I need to know."

"Anything."

"Explain to me what you meant when I heard you tell Zeke I wasn't worth the trouble." A witch couldn't forget that kind of crushing statement. I had to know.

He laughed immediately, sounding amused by my curiosity. "Yes, you overheard what I said to my brother on the street corner the day we were fighting in your aunt's shop. What you don't know is there was a reason I told that lie."

I knitted my eyebrows together. "Lie?" I interrupted. "The only reason you would say that is because it's how you really feel."

He sighed, sounding exasperated with my lack of trust. "Why were you eavesdropping?"

I pouted and said nothing.

"Because you were curious. You wanted to know more about me," he answered for me, in his priggish, arrogant tone.

"It doesn't matter anyway," I cringed, curling up into a ball on the inside.

"It does matter. You have accused me of an offense and you owe me the chance to explain myself," he said in his soft British accent.

"I'm not a moron, Alexavier. Being an outcast isn't new to me. I get how things work. People say one thing behind your back and another to your face."

He concentrated his stormy gray eyes on me, commanding my attention. "Listen to me—my father doesn't want us to get involved with anyone here for reasons I cannot disclose. When Zeke caught me looking at you in the shop, he wanted to tell Father."

"And what did he see?"

He sighed with exasperation. "That I like you."

My temper began to cool. I stared at him, blinking as I considered it. "How do I know you're telling the truth?"

"You can't see it?" His eyes held mine tenderly, imparting his honesty, causing me to tremble in an unfamiliar, yet pleasant way.

I sucked in a breath, impressed and relieved that he wasn't as awful as I first thought he would be, what with being a Mather and all. A bit of guilt settled in as well, knowing how angry I had been with him for saying it and not knowing why. "Maybe we should get to know each other better."

"As friends?"

"Why don't you tell me something about yourself that I don't already know," I mumbled with my mouth full of cherry.

He sat back, looking at the starry sky. "You've already researched the sins I committed in England and my family's history...I'm not sure what's left, curious girl." Humor filled his tone.

Crickets chirped their songs and fireflies flashed their tails in search of love. A breeze whirled around us. "Have you ever been in love before?" I blurted without thinking, wondering about that beautiful royal girl I had pictured breaking his heart. As soon as I said it, I totally regretted it. It didn't matter. Friends only. My eyes darted to the trees surrounding us.

"I wasn't expecting that question," he said.

"Sorry. It was a stupid question. You don't have to answer…"

"No. It's fine. The answer is definitely not," he said very quickly and sounding very honest, but how could someone so perfectly handsome have avoided the charms of an ordinary pretty girl?

I peered up at him, nervous. His gaze caught mine. "Did you go to an all boys' school or something?"

His expression suddenly turned somber. "I don't have the luxury of falling in love. I have lived a life without it. I have a distant father, a mother I never knew, and a lunatic brother who is my complete opposite…" He stopped short. "What about you?"

"No. Never," I said innocently.

"No one? That's hard to believe."

"It's true." No one had ever really noticed me. I was betwixt two worlds—not quite fitting in with the witches and warlocks and an outcast among the ordinaries. "So why are you here…going to these lengths"—I gulped—"with me?"

"Moth to the flame." He stared at the glowing fire. The citrus-red flames danced in his eyes like demons. He seemed lost in it for a moment.

"Alexavier?"

He smiled, but I wondered about his troubled past. "What's your deal with fire?"

He continued to stare at the flickering flames. "It's an escape."

"You have money and a new start in the States. What do you need to escape from?"

He shook his head, still lost in his thoughts. "I wish you could understand."

I stared at him. "Try me."

"My family comes with baggage I didn't ask for, and I have no choice but to deal with it. I want to escape from all of it, but I can't. Ever. None of us can." His voice imparted his desperate state of mind. He paused, his expression full of conflict, his breathing deep and shallow.

"Every family comes with baggage. I live with my aunt because my parents died when I was young. You just have to go on."

He turned his attention on me, his eyes wide and his mouth parted. "I'm sorry."

"It was a long time ago."

"My parents might as well be dead to me. I don't want anything to do with my father and I never met my mother. She was a surrogate he hired. At least you were loved by your parents." He picked at the cherries, not eating much.

"Your dad's so big on traditional family values. Why a surrogate and not a marriage?"

He pressed his palm against his forehead and closed his eyes. The firelight enhanced the dark shadows on his face and the blackness of his sideburns that segued into scruff around his jaw, and lips that looked so soft. "It's not that he didn't want to marry. He wanted to. However, there wasn't a choice."

My brow crinkled, not understanding. "Even if that made sense, why can't he see that if having a traditional family wasn't a choice for him, it might not be a choice for others?"

"Nothing he does makes sense. He fathered children he doesn't want to be a father to. He's drowning in unhappiness because of the curse."

"What curse?"

A flash of pain crossed his face. He stood up, running his hand through his thick black hair. "I've said too much."

I jumped to my feet. "Tell me."

"Your knowing me…will bring you nothing but misery," he said, his voice wracked with frustration and conflict. "It was wrong of me to ask you here. I can take you home."

I grabbed his arm, feeling the electric current running between us. "Wrong because I'm not the kind of girl your family wants you to bring home?"

He shook his head. "No. Because I'm not the right kind of guy for you. I'm selfish and reckless, like you said."

I stared into his eyes and willed him to understand. "What if I want to stay?"

"Why would you want to do that? I'm a Mather. You've made it perfectly clear how you feel about us."

Desire burned deep within my soul, igniting every inch of my body. "I…I don't know, but I find myself not wanting to leave."

His shoulders relaxed as if we breached an impossible barrier. He grabbed my hand in his and tugged me gently toward him.

"Whatever this curse is you're worried about, there has to be a fix and even if there isn't, I don't care. I'm here, breaking rules and taking chances."

"I like you, Sophie, no matter the obstacles, or whether our families approve or not." He stared at my lips again, sending pleasant shivers through me.

"Our families have been enemies forever for a reason."

He looked at me with his piercing eyes. "What if that reason doesn't make sense anymore?"

"It doesn't make sense anymore." I closed my eyes as my head lost the argument to my heart, which ached with longing.

"Your hands are so soft, so very feminine," he whispered, his sweet breath catching on my cheek. "I don't know what to do around you—unfamiliar territory." He sighed as his fingers glided up my arm.

Pleasurable chills spread to every part of my body. I stared at his shoulder, trying to think other thoughts, but he could still see my eyes. He moved his hand to my chin. I bit down on my bottom lip.

"Look at me." He stared into my eyes for a moment. "I can be your friend, if that's all you can offer me, but I know how I feel about you, no matter the repercussions, or whether our families approve or not." His eyes consumed me and his expression turned serious. His words burned with more than sincerity. He was solemn and unwavering in his sentiments.

The torment in his eyes began to change. All I could see now was a delirious longing that matched my own, willing my lips to part with anticipation. He shifted closer and our bodies met. My head spun in a daze, leaving me vulnerable to his touch that sent sparks from my lips to my toes and my breathing quickened as I waited, yearning.

He held me firmly in his longing gaze and leaned down, slipping a hand along my cheek. I closed my eyes. His lips touched to mine. They tasted sweeter than I had imagined; soft, yet dense like a sun-ripened peach. His other arm slipped around my waist, pressing me closer to his warm body. His chest against mine imparted the excited thrumming of his heart. We blended into each other, passionately satisfying the urgency and heat, which had been building between us from the first day.

Whoosh! The steady bonfire beside us roared to life, responding to my emotions. He didn't notice and I didn't care.

My mouth lingered on his until he pulled back. He looked at me and inhaled. "We need to stop," he murmured softly, not convincing me that was what he wanted to do, but knowing he would not let himself go any further.

I nodded as his heated gaze held me tight, but I sensed the frustration returning.

"You deserve someone better. If we continue, something bad will happen. To both of us. I can't let that happen." Despair drenched his tone.

My breath grew rapid and shallow. Panic settled in hard. "Because of the curse you believe in?"

He closed his eyes, pain seared across his face. "You don't understand. That bride and groom buried in your front yard—we're both part of that. It's a reminder of what can happen and nothing can change it."

"History doesn't have to be repeated over and over. We can figure this out."

"There's nothing left to figure out."

I looked up at him from under my eyelashes, trying to grasp his fear.

His sultry eyes took me in as we paused in silence. "I'll take you home now."

"But you said—" I found myself desperately wishing I had applied Forever First Love Lip Balm to my lips, but no. I wanted him to want me on his own. No potions or spells.

He interrupted, upset. "I thought I could control my feelings, but I can't."

An earthquake rumbled in my head. I still didn't know what happened and I didn't have time to think about it further at the moment. Aunt Janie walked down the stairs. "Ready? Mistress Aster is waiting for us. She's desperate for a card reading. Anything to keep Riada and Adair away from trouble."

In the kitchen, we packed up sachets of powdered angelica to spread around her house for protection. Then, we walked to Mistress Aster's house two blocks away. When we arrived, we were too late. I grasped Aunt Janie's hand, bringing her to an abrupt halt. I nodded at the scene and yanked her behind a row of tall hedges before the stress overcame her.

Although the summer sun shined on us as it continued to set over the town, a cold chill shook through me. We saw Judge Mather and his henchmen leading the twins away from the house and into his long black Cadillac, which looked like a hearse. Riada glanced over in our direction and nodded her head as if to quietly acknowledge us. Adair looked stressed, no doubt feeling her mother's intense emotions. The judge's burly assistant held them each by their forearms in a vice-like grip, escorting them into the back of the car while Judge Mather slithered into the front passenger seat. The girls' mother stood there helpless with tears streaming down her face.

I wondered what went wrong. Then I saw him. Zeke was the last to leave the small row house. He must have spied on them and reported them to his father, no doubt trying to earn his admiration. My blood curdled as I clenched my jaw so tight my body shook. "We have to do something!"

Unable to control my impetuousness that rose up in a whirlwind of rage, I lifted my arm and pointed my finger in their direction.

"Stop," Aunt Janie said, clasping her hand onto my forearm and bringing it down. Her fear was palpable. "You already know using our magic at the moment will not help them or us. We are more effective if we regroup and find a sensible solution to get them out of the detention center without getting ourselves in trouble." She stared blankly at the hedges in front of us, and I knew she was trying to keep it together as she considered what had to be done. "Besides, our white magic would be ineffective against someone as black-hearted as Judge Mather. His work can only be overcome by equal force. Eldress Mayapple is correct about that. We will have to figure out another way to fight them."

I thought about the possibility of having to embrace the darkness. Would the loss of one's soul be worth saving someone you loved? I sighed, frustrated, my fists clenched again so tightly, my fingernails dug into my palms.

"They want to lock us all up and take away what makes us special, so they don't feel more ordinary than they are. If we don't stop them now, there won't be anyone left to do it later."

She narrowed her eyes, looking determined to do what she could, but holding back, afraid they would take us both.

"No. There's nothing the two of us can do by ourselves." Her lips trembled and panic resonated in her voice.

I slumped under her fear, knowing I couldn't act. "I can't stay here and watch. I'll go mad."

Her eyes filled with concern. "Go then."

"I'll take the grassy paths and head to the shop," I assured her. "Will you be okay?"

She nodded.

"Then stay, read Mistress Aster's cards. Find out what you can."

I looked over the product returns from yesterday. As distracted as I was, it was easy to see the judge's efforts to shut us down were making a dent. The basket was filled with unopened jars and bottles of Aunt Janie's organic items. I re-ticketed and re-shelved them.

Macey slipped into her apron behind me.

I peered all around. "Did you come in the back?" I glimpsed the front door, which was still locked.

"Uh huh. So are you recovered from your seasickness?" I sensed a twinge of doubt and curiosity in her tone.

The truth that I left with Alexavier wouldn't have bothered her at all. I think she already suspected it, but I wasn't ready for her questions, mostly because I didn't know how to answer them. I nodded.

She brushed her curls behind her ear, but a few dared to dangle alongside her rounded cheekbones. She glanced at her reflection in the window. "Alexavier acted so weird last night. Tell me someone that hot with that sexy accent isn't a complete loser."

A smile sprawled across my face. "He's got problems, but he's not a loser."

She raised an eyebrow. "Problems—more than what's on his juvie record?"

I shrugged my shoulders. "People have problems and I have no idea what his are." It was only a half lie and my lips barely tingled. Although I'd offer a bag of elusive black rose petals to a nosy flower nymph to score more info on that curse he was so upset about.

"I think he's got a stalker problem," she said, fishing for more.

"I think he's terribly lonely and afraid." Afraid for me. It's like he didn't care about himself, but he acted like he needed to protect me.

She looked at me sideways. "He said that?"

"It's a feeling."

She keyed in the code to unlock the register for the day. I gathered my wild waves of hair into a knot and held it tight with a pencil.

Outside, we saw Mrs. Dayo approaching the shop door. She held a small white notecard in her hands. The lock clicked and she entered, greeting us with a smile.

"You'll never guess who I ran into."

Macey and I stood there dumbfounded. "Who?" I asked.

"Alexavier Mather. Saw him just a few moments ago pacing the sidewalk outside. He wished me a good morning and politely asked me for a favor. He seems so unexpectedly different from the rest of his family." She handed me the small envelope. "Special delivery for you."

Macey held her breath, watching. "O—M—G."

I ripped the seal on the envelope and read the words. My hand dropped, barely having the energy to hold the note. Macey grabbed for it and examined it thoroughly.

I'm sorry —Alexavier.

"'I'm sorry,'" she said, reading the note. Her mouth gaped wide.

I shook my head. "I'm more confused than ever."

She rolled her eyes and stared at me in disbelief. "I knew you weren't seasick. What happened? What's he sorry for?"

"He took me on a picnic last night."

"I knew it! Woo-woo!"

"We argued, we kissed, and then he said he didn't want to hurt me. Now, he's sorry. Sorry I went with him? Sorry we argued? Sorry for the life-altering kiss? I have no idea."

"A life-altering kiss, huh?" Her lips formed a pout of pity for me.

Thoughts of him washed over me like warm ocean waves. The shop bell jingled. I whirled around and nearly lost my balance when I saw her face. Eldress Mayapple. My mouth hung open as I slipped the note in my back pocket. She walked right up to Mrs. Dayo, firm in her request for a specific cream to help with liver problems. I would have guessed it was for those scaly hives of hers, but then I felt bad for thinking that. Mrs. Dayo hurried to the back room, searching through our newly delivered stock. I slipped behind a tall display shelf, trying to regroup and hoping Mrs. D could find it. She dashed back out, empty-handed. The crimson color of impatience filled Eldress Mayapple's cheeks. As Mrs. Dayo jotted down her contact information, I overheard the eldress say my name. When I looked out from the shelf, she lowered her voice.

A warning from Riada and Adair to be careful flashed back to me. What if she was mad because my *deleto* spell didn't work on Laney and she told her mom about the crashing glass at Goody's Market?

"Sophie. Come here."

"Yes?" My lips trembled.

"Mrs. Mayapple is looking for a lotion with a special ingredient. I was wondering if you could run home and see if you have the ingredient growing in your garden and ask your aunt to process it for this special customer?"

"Of course." Inside, I sighed with relief. "What is the ingredient?"

"Milk thistle seed."

I nodded, recalling the plant thriving in our garden. "We are growing it."

Mrs. Dayo turned to the eldress. "I will call you as soon as we have it ready."

She eyed me up and down. "Please do."

I darted out the door and down the flower-filled sidewalk, dodging tourists and slow-paced locals. I needed the fresh air to clear my head anyway. I raced around the corner and dashed into my house and into the vast garden in the back.

As I strolled through the herbs and flowers I overheard a heated conversation coming from the Mather's yard. "You incompetent fool! You know what will happen. It's inevitable. Time has proven that!" A fiery fury ignited Zeke's bellow from across the way. They were outside and obviously unaware of my presence.

"I don't want to bear this cross anymore," Alexavier said unapologetically.

"You don't have a choice. Neither do I. And I won't let you mess up what's left of the life we have to live." Zeke slammed into their house. The engine of Alexavier's car revved to life and the wheels screeched.

My mind buzzed as I spied the tall milk thistle plants. A few pink flowers still bloomed on the stems, but a few withered blooms had already dropped and seedpods took their place. I plucked a few and brought them inside. I left them with a note to Janie before racing back to the shop. Mrs. Dayo was pleased with the news, but rested a concerned hand on my shoulder, garnering my full attention. "Watch your back with the Mayapple woman. She's very cunning and good at getting what she wants."

Mrs. Dayo was intuitive, and so was I.

After work, I asked Macey to join me for a gelato at Celia's Creamery on Main Street. I left the notecard in my khaki shorts pocket and shook my hair out of its messy knot, letting the wild dark waves frame my ivory face.

A small table in the window opened up as we walked into the whimsical blue creamery. I snagged it and we ordered Cokes from the waitress.

"No problem, sweethearts." She tucked a pencil behind her ear and stuffed her notepad in her apron pocket.

Five minutes later, two Cokes with lots of ice arrived, much appreciated as I tried to cool down from the saturating heat outside. I coaxed my straw from its wrapper and plunked it into the carbonated beverage. I stared out the window at tourists wearing "Wethersfield" sun visors and sweating from the oppressive heat clinging to the town.

Macey tousled her curls. "You're so quiet. Don't let that note get to you and don't give up."

"Doesn't seem like I have a choice."

"You like Alexavier, he's freaking hot with a bad boy streak, and sorry to mention the obvious again, he is freaking hot. Outside of the juvie record and the sorry note, what's the problem? Go after what you want."

I shook my head. "I can't. The sorry note is kind of a problem." I folded my hands under my chin and looked outward at nothing in particular. The waitress returned and took our order for one chocolate chip gelato, two spoons.

"Are you sure it wasn't your kissing?"

"Pretty sure. I mean, I'm not an expert, but I thought it was good."

"What about the way you dress?"

I threw my hands up. "Feeling kind of offended over here."

"Don't change for me, Argentina, but seriously, look at your clothes. Basic T-shirt and boring shorts. I don't have a problem with it, but you could stand to spice things up."

I glanced over my outfit and shrugged. "I like pockets. Besides, what if the problem is his? What if it's because his family has some weird issue?"

"I wouldn't let his creepy dad or idiot brother get in the way. You'll regret it." The waitress returned with our frozen treat. Macey took a big spoonful of creamy gelato and smiled smugly, a piece of chocolate chip stuck to her front tooth.

As I laughed, my cell rang. "Hold that thought." I glanced at the name. "Hi Aunt Janie. What's up?"

"Mistress Phoebe returned from England only to find her shop closed."

I strained to hear her over the noise in the creamery. "What? Hold on. I need to go outside." I stuffed the phone between my shoulder and ear and walked out the door, strolling past a few stores to a quieter spot.

"The judge had the health department put a lock on the door last night."

"No!"

"Yes. A little girl whose mom shopped there came down with some illness. They are blaming the illness on the shop's vermin problem, which she wouldn't have had if the Leos hadn't snuck the mice in, in the first place."

My face drained of its warmth. The cool harsh reality settled in. "Try to stay calm. How is Phoebe handling it?"

"As well as can be expected, but without the nut shop, I don't know how she's going to get by."

"We'll help her." A cold chill shivered through me and not because of the bad news or the frozen gelato. From the corner of my eye, I spied the would-be-thief in his black hoodie. Hood up. He watched me from the other side of the street, tucked into a tall shrub. Anger ripped through me and my temper flared.

"Drink your valerian tea. I gotta go. 'Bye." I clicked the cell off and walked away from the creamery and Macey. My thigh muscles strained as I lengthened my stride.

I glanced over my shoulder. The stranger followed behind on the other side of the sidewalk, keeping his distance and his head down. With each glance I stole, I tried to focus on his face to see if I recognized him. He revealed nothing. My breathing accelerated. My heart raced as sweat dripped down the side of my face. The whirlwind of emotions accelerated inside me. I clenched my hands into fists, hoping to keep my temper under control in the crowd of ordinaries. I darted into Goody's Market. He crossed the street in my direction. A spell sizzled on my tongue. My finger pointed behind me, wanting him to fall down. "*Ceciderit*," I eked out with as much force as I could summon.

The crash of clanging metal hit the sidewalk. My head whipped back. My shoulders tensed. An empty scaffold collapsed into a heap of metal bars and a cloud of dust. The thief changed direction, heading away as a crowd drew around the debris. At least the spellcasting mishap worked in my favor, this time.

I ran into Goody's, searching for my friend.

"Callum!" My breath returned to me. I steadied myself from the lightheadedness and grabbed his arm. We walked in the direction of the back office.

"Seriously, girl. What is that song you're humming? It sounds like the theme song from the last zombie movie we saw. What's wrong with you?"

I stopped the unconscious humming. I leaned against him and tried to catch my breath. "There was a man. Out there." My heart continued to hammer in my ears. "Following me. I swear." I wiped the hair clinging to my sweaty face.

He eyed me. "For real?"

I nodded, pressing my hand to my forehead, reeling from the incident.

"What did he look like?" He stood on his toes, not that he needed to, and surveyed the store and outside the windows.

If only I had a pinkie pixie to watch out for this sort of thing. I was going to have ask my godmother for one on my next birthday. "Average build, black hoodie. Hood up."

His forehead wrinkled. "Hood up? It's like eighty-five degrees outside."

I flashed my hands for emphasis. "Right?"

"Wait in the office." He left my side and raced to the front of the store. I peeked out the office door and watched. My breathing started to slow.

Callum peered outside the doors in both directions. When he walked back to me he shook his head. "I don't see anyone like that."

"I swear I wasn't imagining him. I swear!" In that moment, I remembered poor Macey. "Crud. I forgot about Macey." I called her, hoping she would pick up.

"Where are you?" she asked, sounding worried.

"Down the street. Stay put. I'll be there in two minutes." I looked up at Cal. "Can you walk me back?" With Cal by my side, the thief wouldn't dare come near us.

"Yeah, but I have to wait for Mr. Geoffrey to get back. Can you hang for a few minutes?"

I nodded. He left the office door propped open as I sat on the desk, waiting for him to return from helping a customer.

After a few minutes, a strange feeling forced me to look up. I jumped to my feet. "Judge...Judge Mather?"

"I happened to walk past and caught sight of you. Seemed like a good time to ask a question," he said with his hands clasped behind his back.

I stared hard at his beady eyes, trying to ignore the intimidating school headmaster tone he took with me. "I don't have any answers for you."

"Mrs. Phoebe Jenson. A family friend of yours, yes?"

I stared blankly at him.

"She recently went missing for a few days. Her house and shop were locked up tight. What was the reason for her disappearance?" He crossed his arms over his chest while a smug look crept onto his face like he already knew the answer. Did his Leo spies keep that close of an eye on her shop and whereabouts?

"No idea. Maybe she wanted a break from your surveillance team."

His thin lips puckered. "I am the law in Wethersfield."

"Yes. You and your corrupt cousin," I replied, hinting at their Kingshill connection.

"Don't mess with me, young lady." His head tilted up at a smug angle. "Although, lady isn't the proper term among your kind, is it? It's mistress, correct?"

My breathing grew shallow. We all strived to keep our witch heritage quiet. Even the obscure painting of Rebecca Greensmith hanging on the shop wall lacked a nameplate. Family or not, we couldn't afford for the ordinaries to link her dark deeds to us, so the idea of him even guessing freaked me out. "What do you want?"

"I want you to know your kind has caused enough trouble from this town's beginning and it's going to end with me. I'm cleaning up."

It was like bad history repeating itself. The Wethersfield Witch Trials all over again. And like last time, I wasn't sure there would be any winners. "Cleaning up, like how you fill up Kingshill with innocent girls?" It was difficult to not say anything about the kickbacks he was getting for each witch he locked up. He needed a reason, anything small, to add me to the population and I had no intention of giving it to him.

His eyes momentarily slipped to the red pendant dangling from my neck. I quickly tucked it away. "Girls? They're not girls and they're not innocent. They're riffraff and every town needs a place to hide the riffraff. The more your kind use magic, the more I will fill the detention center, proving the town's need for a new addition to it. An addition to make room for more disruptive, unruly young women like you so you can change your wicked ways and become productive members of society instead of contributors to its ills and unhappiness."

I couldn't think straight. My thoughts raced as he spewed his plan to grow the detention center and throw more of us in, no doubt lining his pockets with cash in the process.

"I do not contribute to this town's ills. If anyone does, it's you. You're greedy and corrupt."

"You look strong and healthy. I'm sure you would survive the special therapy, although, not everyone does. Do you want to know what happened fourteen years ago when we first started the program?"

An icky sensation crawled across my skin. I shook my head. "Is that when you destroyed all the public parks and gardens?"

"I figured the less plants, the less concoctions your kind could make, but that's not what I meant."

Bess had been filling him in and I had a bad feeling about what he was going to say next. "I want to leave now."

"Make yourself disappear or whatever it is that you do. Give me something." His eyes glinted, challenging me. A sadistic grin crawled across his face as he waited for me to slip up.

I grabbed for the doorknob with my hand.

"Our first patient was known around town as a passionate mischief maker, causing all sorts of trouble with her finger pointing and gardening skills. I thought maybe she could help me, but I was wrong." His tone was controlled and vicious.

I turned back to him. "Help you with what?"

"A little problem I have courtesy of a witch from long ago."

What was he talking about? "What happened to the mischief maker?"

"She wouldn't help me. None of them would or could, so they claimed. I had her arrested and thrown in Kingshill with its iron locks." He paused, staring hard at me, looking for recognition in my eyes. I recalled the witches' histories, but I didn't know which witch he was talking about. "She was the first to undergo my conversion therapy. Figured if she couldn't help me with my problem, she could help me with my mission." He shook his head in a fake display of compassion. Something he was incapable of possessing. "Poor thing. Therapy back then included electroshock combined with psycho-hallucinogenic drugs. The technique was not quite perfected. She died, unable to withstand the trauma to her troubled mind."

I drew back, disgusted, afraid, and angry. My stomach ached. Where was Cal? I glanced at my watch, unable to pull myself from his repulsive presence.

"When her husband showed up—with a gun—well, we had to defend ourselves." He made it sound as if they were all standing around watching her suffer. He bit his lip and narrowed his glare at me. "What I had to do, well I claimed it was self defense. Hell, I may have given him the gun before I pulled the other one from my holster. Who knows? Pity they were so young, so in love."

I leaned against the wall, my knees weak.

"Who...who are you talking about?"

"Your parents, Mistress Goodchild."

I staggered sideways along the wall, bumping into the desk. My throat swelled shut. I couldn't breathe. "No. No. You had nothing to do with them." My body shook.

He lowered his voice, his tone etched with wickedness.

"You watch your step with me and steer clear of my sons. Am I understood?" He paused. "Your aunt has been looking very frail lately. Wouldn't want to see anything happen to her. Would you?"

I locked eyes on my target. I lunged, pulling and ripping at his shirt, ignoring the ache in my strained hands. An ice and fire hatred filled my heart.

That's when I first felt it.

The liquid black ice seeping into my bloodstream, licking at the core of my soul. "I hate you!" I seethed.

He gripped me by my wrists and peeled my hands from his shirt. "Still no magic tricks for me today?" He pushed me back and left me in a collapsed heap of sobbing on the floor.

I paced barefoot in the garden, hoping to draw calmness from the earth. Aunt Janie had said she knew nothing about my parents' deaths. I refused to tell her what the judge said or what he threatened. Not only could I not bear to speak the words, I knew Aunt Janie wasn't strong enough to hear them.

I put my thoughts aside and focused on what I could do at the moment. I couldn't change the past. There was no magic I knew to do that, but all the anger whirling inside me needed to be focused on the one who took them from me and the danger he posed to my aunt. I sat down at the garden table where the journal rested. A wisteria scented breeze ruffled the thin pages.

"Elizabeth, help me." I needed to never feel helpless like I did listening to the shell of a man speak so callously about my family as if they were garbage he could kick aside without consequence. "*Revela.*"

> *July 19th—the future and the past, the past and the future*
>
> *I desire so wholly to be a spellcaster, tho I am not. Clairvoyance is my gift, allowing me to foresee the future. All will be lost if the one to come does not realize the magick within her. Magick more than spells. It is greater than any inherited magick. This power can heal black hearts and change lives in my present time, which will be the past and the future to her. It can set things right. How shall I bring awareness to her eyes? This question tears at my soul as the sands of time run with rapidness through the hourglass.*

"Who was the one to come and how will she change your past?" The pages flipped to the back, her elegant script rolled across the page in a bolder print than usual.

> *Though it is difficult to see, she must. She has to.*

"What does that mean?" I shook my head, frustrated. "Elizabeth, I need a spell. I need to punish the one who has hurt me." I waited anxiously for her reply. Something. Then the pages flipped back to the July twelfth entry, of which one line reappeared.

> *I do not desire to be a weapon of revenge for them or anyone.*

"I don't understand. Why are you connecting with me then if not to help me?" The doorbell chimed. With reluctance, I left the journal and raced to the foyer.

"Riada! Adair!" I yanked them both into the house and hugged them, feeling drained, but so happy to see them. "What happened to you at Kingshill? My aunt and I were hiding in the hedges across from your house when they took you. We were so afraid."

The twins stepped back, wearing their short summer dresses in contrasting colors of purple and orange.

"Barefoot again, Sophie? What are we going to do with you?" Adair asked.

I grimaced. "Never mind about me. How are you here?"

They grinned, mischief sparkled in their eyes. "Zeke Mather caught us floating straws to each other at Summerfield's Smoothies. He ratted us out. Our mother is not happy with that family, naturally," Riada said.

"Join the club. So what happened?"

They smiled the same crooked smile. "The Leos now believe we are talentless and that idiot Zeke made a mistake in what he saw."

I silently cringed at the sound of those names.

"Then we convinced them we are aligned in their beliefs and vowed to devote ourselves to a traditional way of life, which includes reporting those who practice magic and cause mischief."

"I don't understand. What?"

"That's what they think anyway," Riada assured me as Adair laughed her melodic giggle. "I read their thoughts and Adair projected her thoughts into their empty heads, convincing them they had completed the fastest conversions in the history of Kingshill Detention Center. I mean, seriously. Did you really think we were gonna spend another three weeks hanging out at that creepy psych hospital under their misguided junior therapists? Plus, the orange uniforms did nothing for our complexions." She wagged a finger. "I don't think so."

My head tilted as I absorbed what they were saying. "How does the reading and projecting your thoughts work exactly?"

"It's what our mom has shielded from them and the Council. She and your aunt believe the Council will use us as pawns if they find out what we can do. We let you in on it because we like you, but no one else knows, a side effect from her shielding charm, and it has worked. But the levitating trick is so cool, it was hard to hide from the ordinaries. When Zeke reported the floating straws, the Law Enforcement Organization jumped on it. I guess they are desperate," Adair said.

"Yeah. Desperate to make money," Riada added.

"Huh?"I shook my head. "Never mind. Go on."

"Once we convinced them we couldn't do anything magical at all, they had us repeat an oath to live a moral and non-magical lifestyle. We were more glad to make Zeke look like a liar," Adair said.

A lightheadedness came over me. It was all so much. "You look worn out. Are you okay?" Riada asked.

I pressed my hand to my cheeks, feeling a cool dampness. "What's there to be anxious about? They closed Phoebe's nut shop, Eldress Mayapple has been sniffing around me, and I haven't mastered one herbalist trick for the Seeking. Oh, there's nothing to be worried about." I couldn't even mention the huge black hole the judge ripped into my heart. I shoved the thought aside, not wanting the rush of emotion to come over me.

They looked at each other and grimaced.

"Tell," I said.

"We know why the eldress is asking questions. Laney told her mom she thought she saw you flirting with one of the Mather boys. She wants to keep an eye on you. Make sure your loyalties lie firmly with the coven. We know it's super forbidden, but we don't really care if you like an ordinary, even if he is a Mather," Adair said.

"As long as it's not Zeke," Riada added, sticking her tongue out as if she were gagging on a spoonful of pokeweed tea.

My pulse picked up. The eldress was questioning my loyalty? "I don't flirt!"

"I'm sure, but Laney has always been one to embellish," Adair said.

I exhaled my stress. It could be worse. At least she didn't tell her anything about my casting, which meant my *deleto* spell worked on her at the market and from a distance.

"Never mind Laney. We have good news. The dozens of other witches detained at the center? We can get them out," Riada said, tapping her fingers together like a scheming mastermind.

Adair smiled, teasing my curiosity. "And the iron locks won't be a problem. We plan to revisit as volunteers, you know as part of our oath to live a traditional lifestyle devoted to advancing the Law Enforcement Organization's mission."

My eyes brightened. "That would be amazing. Did you see Bess Johnson while you were there?"

They looked at each other, the hope in their expressions faded. "She came in once. With the judge. She works directly for him. It's too late for her," Adair said.

"No. There has to be hope. There has to be a way to change her back."

"It will have to come from within her. Stay optimistic. By the end of the week, we should have most of our girls back. Judge Mather won't know what to do with himself," Riada added.

A smug grin spread across my face. "I like that. Maybe you can imprint a story in his head about them breaking out and running to Canada or something?" I said, looking at Adair.

"I don't know, Sophie. Breaking through to a mind is like cracking a nutshell. Once I'm in I can imprint my thoughts, but it's the getting in that's tricky. The therapists at the center were easy, but Judge Mather is firm in his beliefs and black in his heart. It will be like breaking through a granite wall. I don't know if I'm strong enough for that," Adair said.

"You've got to try."

Adair flashed her small hands up. "I can't guarantee anything."

"I'm sorry. I know it's a ton of pressure. Right now, I'm just glad to see you here." My shoulders relaxed and I hugged them both. "We've all been so worried. I know your mother told us not to worry, but still."

A few minutes after they departed, the bell chimed again. I pulled the door open, expecting the girls to have forgotten something, but before I could look, his jarring voice raked through my aching head.

"What have you done to my brother?" he demanded, anger vibrating in every syllable.

Zeke.

I widened my eyes in disbelief. Irritation at the sight of him on my doorstep rankled my nerves. "What are you doing here?"

His eyes narrowed and his thin lips curled downward into a scowl. He tugged aggressively at the collar of his white shirt.

I curled my fists into tight little balls and focused on his frame that threatened to invade my personal space and home. A glacial sensation swept over me. "What do you want?" I seethed, wanting to push him and hoping he would push me back. I dangled from a precipice by one fingernail and only needed the slightest nudge.

"You don't get to ask me anything, you no good nightmare of a girl."

The crack in me exploded wide open. A saucy spell sizzled on my tongue. My thoughts centered on the door, imagining it slamming in his face. My lips trembled. I focused. "*Sapit!*" My voice rumbled in my throat as I directed my attention at the target. With a thunderous force, the door slammed into the jamb. His arm, which reached in to grab for me, crumpled in the crack.

"Aaah!" Three throaty obscenities followed the agonized moan.

I shook myself out of the lightheadedness and stepped back in shock, staring at the door. Waiting. With a violent roar, he struck it with his good arm and tore into the house.

"You dirty little witch!" Scarlet colored his face. His cheeks puffed with each rapid breath. "You're under arrest!"

Immediately my finger twitched, pointing in his direction. Dizziness encompassed my head. "*Deleto*," I sputtered, feeling the adrenaline interfere.

His eyes went blank for a moment, but his focus remained sharp and intent. "Did you cast some kind of spell on my brother? Is that how you do it?" He rubbed his injured forearm. His rage-filled eyes looked about to pop from his head. The agitated bull charged further into the house.

I stumbled backward, trying to maintain the divide and calm myself. My lips tingled. "I don't do magic. You need to leave. Right now." He matched my pace, deeper into the house, closing the distance between us. All these weeks, how I cringed with each spellcasting mistake and, now I wanted nothing more than one huge mishap, even if the house collapsed around me. My pulse beat faster.

His eyes grew enraged. "What have you done to my brother?"

From the kitchen, the cuckoo clock chirped. The echo of the wooden birds resonated in my head, and suddenly I thought of something. This was my chance to see if he was the hooded attacker. Zeke was smart enough to fake an American accent. With his sleeves rolled up, I searched for the lion tattoo, but I couldn't see the undersides of his wrists.

I stumbled backward into a table, knocking two wood figurines over. I gripped the edge, trying to steady myself. If I couldn't summon a distraction, I needed to create one to divert his attention. My thoughts ricocheted in my head.

"How are we going to solve my problem?" Instantly, his face drained from blood red to pale pink as he stared at me. Pressing an index finger into my shoulder. "You are going to stop seeing my brother. Immediately."

My throat tightened. My tongue swelled. I wiped beads of perspiration from my brow. Dammit. This was ridiculous. This was my house. I smacked his hand off me. My other hand pressed to my chest, my heart hammering against my ribcage. "You need to leave or I'm calling the police," I bluffed, knowing they were as corrupt as his father.

He stood back and laughed. "Go ahead. Call them."

My throat felt dry as cotton. I snatched my cell from my pocket. His sharpened blue eyes pierced me with loathing. I pressed nine. One.

"You realize of course my father and cousin hired most of them." My finger hovered over the one. He gripped his hand around my cell and ripped it from me, tossing it to the floor. "I'm going to make this simple. If you don't leave him alone, you're both going to be sorry."

"Both of us? What are you going to do to him? I've seen you fight and he won without a problem." I fully regretted not knowing where Aunt Janie kept her banishing powder, not that I could make it work, but I was ready to get him out of here.

He studied my quizzical expression. "You mean, he hasn't told you?"

"He told me you're following in your father's footsteps. He was right about that." I searched all around for the banishing powder in the purple bottle. I reached for a table drawer and tugged on the knob.

With force, he grabbed my arms and shook me, wanting my lost attention and reinforcing his danger potential. I winced from the pressure of his fingertips digging into my soft flesh. I wriggled to free myself, but it was no use.

"Let go of me!" I stomped down on his foot as hard as I could.

He gritted his teeth from the pain. "Stay away from him. You'll both end up dead. I'm warning you."

The words chilled my blood as he continued to stare me down, his icy eyes bulging. Either he was going to kill me or he wasn't. "What do you mean?" My gaze drifted to his wrists. No tattoo. Only a strange pink birthmark shaped like a broken heart showed on his white skin. He wasn't the thief, merely a dangerous rat, like one carrying around bubonic fleas.

He snorted with contempt. "You've been warned." He turned abruptly and left, slamming the front door behind him. I ran and flipped the lock. I pressed my back against the door, seething.

The next day, I walked around the garden, counting the butterflies flitting about the blueberry bushes, undisturbed by my angst as they pursued their search for love and nectar. Lucky bugs— they didn't have to worry about feuding families and complicated relationships. My fingers brushed along the hi-gloss leaves of the boxwood topiaries. As I grazed my hands over the unopened buds of the blue roses, grains of magic trickled out of my fingers without a thought. The roses began to unfold and bloom. I glanced over my shoulders, making sure no one could see, a habit I wished I didn't need to have. If I were an herbalist, I could make the flowers bloom with special concoctions and rhymes rather than spells that trickled out of my finger. But I wasn't an herbalist and as my spell casting magic grew stronger, fooling the Council became a more distant possibility. Mistress Deedee would have no problem sensing what I could do, especially if Riada and Adair were right about the eclipse's influence.

I worried what would happen to Aunt Janie. There was so much at risk. I cleared my head and focused on the annuals. Their fresh clusters beamed bright crayon colors of purple, pink, red, and yellow, enhanced by actual crayon shavings Janie worked her magic on. But as much as I tried to focus on other stuff, the horrible memories broke through the mental dam and flooded back; the relentless thief, Zeke busting in my house, and his father spewing his hatred for my family all over me.

I reached the third terrace and stopped. Zeke's voice drifted over the hedges. I shuddered from the sound of it. I rubbed my arms and swallowed hard. His overbearing tone told me he was talking to Alexavier. Uneasiness settled in like stomach acid. Part of me wanted to run away, but the other part had to know what he was saying. I knelt down and peered through the greenery.

"The meeting is at the Mayflower Hotel down the street. Six o'clock tonight. Black tie. Governor will be there this time. Don't forget."

"I made it to the last function without any reminders from you."

"It's important to Father." He flashed the underside of his wrist at him, the one with the funny birthmark. "Never forget."

My insides rumbled with nausea. What was his problem? I pressed my hand to my stomach and tiptoed along the border hedges back to my house. Paranoia forced me to glance back and make sure Zeke wasn't following, but as I faced forward a figure flashed in front of me. "Aaah!" I squeezed my fist against my heart and bent over to catch my breath. "Macey! What are you doing here?"

She blocked the doorway, standing there with her arms crossed over her chest as if she had been watching. "What are you up to?" Her foot tapped against the floor.

She wouldn't judge me. She had done worse. "Eavesdropping on the Mathers."

"Why?"

I pushed her into the house and shut the door behind us. My voice dropped to a whisper. "Zeke showed up here last night. Forced his way in, I should say, and acted like a lunatic. He demanded I leave his brother alone. He was so dramatic, like the world was going to end if I didn't do what he said, so I was helping myself to information because I can't figure out what in the world is going on with that family."

Her lips curled into an impish smile. "Time for another covert op?"

"Shh." I looked outside. "I already have an idea."

"I'm in!"

I released an exhausted smile, mentally drained, but grateful for her enthusiasm. "You don't even know what I'm going to say."

"Doesn't matter. I'm your bestie. I'm in."

"Mrs. Dayo is closing the shop tonight, so we can leave early. Let's meet back here. I want to break into their house again."

"How do you know they won't be there?"

"Zeke said they are going to another meeting at six tonight. Sounds important."

"Wow! You little scheme-aholic." She eyed me with an approving look. "Something's changed about you, you sound so determined, so risky-licious."

I nodded. "I feel kind of risky-licious." My problems were mounting and whether Aunt Janie approved or not, things had changed. I was changing. There were truths that could not be taken back and there were going to be consequences.

At five o'clock, we left Scents and Scentsabilities, taking different paths to my house. We waited upstairs, spying out the guest bedroom window. Well, I spied and Macey practiced her kickboxing jabs. I ducked down as if they could see me and I laughed at myself, realizing they couldn't. After waiting for what seemed like forever, Alexavier exited, looking fa-mazing in his tuxedo. He straightened his silver tie as he walked toward the driveway. Zeke followed a minute later, taking time to fix his cuff links before shutting the door behind him.

"Macey, it's time," I whispered. If Zeke came back early and caught us, he would kill us or have his dad throw us in Kingshill. Alexavier would no doubt hate me and what would happen to Aunt Janie if I were thrown in Kingshill? Why was I doing this again? Hyperventilating commenced. I needed chamomile. I patted my pockets. Where was my chamomile gum? Deep breath.

Macey approached closer. "You don't need to whisper. They can't hear us from here. And remember, you're risky-licious. No more stressing. Worst case scenario, police show up and we calmly explain that you live next door, you're on strong cold medicine, and got the address mixed up."

"Right, because I sound like I have a cold." I could always count on her for assurance, but it wasn't helping. I tapped my finger against my chin while I hummed. We were gonna wing it and hope for the best. A wave of nausea swelled up. I pressed my hand to my stomach to contain the sickness. "Let's go."

"You sure?" she asked, "'Cause you look pretty pale."

"Positive." We made our way along the hedges of the garden until we reached the sparsest shrub. "Fingers crossed the back door is still unlocked. When you see me open it, run for it." I took a deep breath and shoved my way through to their yard. I dashed to the back door and as the knob turned, I did a quick fist pump, thankful. I let myself in, motioning for Macey. She rushed up and slipped in beside me. My sweaty hands pressed against the inside of the door and pushed it shut.

I exhaled. No turning back, I thought. I ignored the incessant churning in my stomach and nudged her. "Upstairs this time. You find Zeke's room and search for anything incriminating."

We climbed the winding staircase and then Macey tore through Zeke's while I entered Alexavier's. A full-size bed, a large antique armoire, a dresser, and a night table accented the cool summer white of the walls. I glanced around. His jeans lay across the bed with a black T-shirt folded neatly on top of them. He wasn't here, but his pleasing scent was everywhere. I pressed the soft shirt to my face and inhaled while my eyes scoured the dresser and armoire. I dropped the shirt and went about pulling drawers open and lightly lifting clothes in search of anything to provide a clue to their family secret.

Beside his bed, I noticed the corner of a hardback book peeking out from beneath. I reached down for it. Blake: Poems. William Blake?

On his night table I spotted a handwritten note. I unfolded it, my eyes searching for the signature. His father. Why was he sending him a note when they lived in the same house? I guessed the hours his father worked didn't allow for much of a personal relationship. I greedily read the information. The old man wanted Alexavier's support to raise money to build the addition to Kingshill. My hand dropped to my side.

From the other bedroom, Macey shouted. "Surprisingly, no sacrificial animals, pitchforks, or brimstone over here."

Her voice startled me. My fingers lost their grasp of the note. The piece of stationery slipped under the bed, riding the air current.

"Bunch of political propaganda books, but nothing incriminating. I even checked in his hamper. You're welcome and, by the way, yuck."

"Thanks."

"Do you want me to start on dad's room?"

Jangle, jangle.

My heart stopped. I pressed a hand over my gaping mouth. Someone was home and at the front door. I ducked on the floor, scrambling blindly to find the note. It landed dead center under the bed, beyond my reach.

"Crud!"

Macey grabbed me by the arm, tugging fiercely.

"They're back. We gotta get out of here," she whispered in a frantic hush. "We're both gonna get locked up."

"Why are they at the front door? They always use the back door and the dad uses the garage."

"Does it matter? Someone's here."

My heart pounded in my ears. I searched for an escape. Alexavier's window faced the front of the house where there was nothing below to break our fall except the person trying to get in. "Does Zeke's room have a window?"

She nodded. I clamped onto her hand and wrenched her across the hall. I quietly eased his door almost shut. I snuck to the window and flipped the latch, but it wouldn't budge, probably painted shut. Macey raced back into the hall, looking for another window. I closed my eyes and thrust my hand to my forehead. No. I was cool, I was risky-licious.

I turned my attention back to the window, thinking of nothing else but my desire to get the heck out. "*Aperi!*" I grunted in Latin, but nothing. I listened for police sirens. I thought of Zeke finding me in his room. I focused harder on the panes. The memory of his flushed angry face and rude words urged me on. My finger swirled and I focused on the lock. "*Resera!*" I demanded the lock to unlatch. Magic sparked on my tongue. Instantly, the lock unlatched and the window flashed open with a loud crack of the paint seal, alerting

Macey. If she asked, I would blame it on adrenaline. She raced in and stood there, dumbfounded.

"How did you…?"

The lightheadedness encroached. "No time for questions. Go!" I urged, wanting her to not think, only to move fast.

She dashed toward me and wiggled through the open window, grabbing for a sturdy branch on the chestnut tree right outside. She was graceful like a flower nymph, floating from limb to limb. I dashed to the bedroom door and peered out. My jaw clenched so tightly, I thought my teeth would crack. No one was there, but approaching footsteps sounded from the staircase. My pulse jumped. I ran back to the window and squeezed through, leaping for the same branch. The roughness of the bark scraped at the tender skin on my hands. I scrambled to get down, not half as graceful as Macey.

"Sophie! I see you. Stop!" Alexavier shouted, leaning out the window in his tux.

I peeked up. Heat flooded my cheeks. My brain swam in guilt and embarrassment. I didn't know whether to stop or run, but I couldn't look at him again and I didn't have the nerve to erase his memory. I jumped from the last branch and hit the ground with a thud. I wobbled to my feet and raced after Macey, trying to catch up. I watched her scramble onto a bench and throw herself over the six-foot-tall stone wall at the bottom of their property. I didn't stand a chance of doing the same, but if I could make it to the hedges…

"Hurry, Sophie! Hurry!" Macey yelled from the other side.

I ran, but adrenaline worked against me. My heart raced out of control. My knees buckled. I stumbled. "Get out of here!" I yelled back to her. No need for her to go down, too. It was my idea. My fault. Alexavier raced out the back door, heading straight for me.

I laid there, face down, keeping my gaze locked on the ground. My lips trembled. He would hate me forever. "I'm so sorry. I feel terrible and guilty. If you want to call the police…"

"Do you really think I have any right to call the police?" he asked in his British accent. A brief bout of laughter greeted my wholehearted embarrassment. I slowly glanced up at him. He shook his head. "Let me remind you again, I am not my father." He extended his hand and helped me to my feet. Seeing him up close in his black tuxedo left me dazzled. He was unbearably handsome like a youthful 007 and I was a ridiculous half-witch with tangled hair and dirty knees.

"And you are not sorry. Your curiosity leads you and you would do it again if you could. You can't help yourself." His eyes sparkled with amusement. "I find that desire in you quite endearing." Lightness filled his voice and his accent sounded softer than usual.

I glanced up at him, bewildered. "You're not disappointed?" His gray eyes gazed down on me, smoldering and full of acceptance, stirring butterflies in my stomach. His cologne smelled sweet and masculine. I moved closer to inhale it.

"Hardly. Look at your hands and legs. You're a mess."

"Huh?" I brushed the grass off my limbs and rubbed my hands gently together.

He eyed me curiously. "How did you get out of that window? It's been stuck since we moved back."

"I…I'm stronger than I look, I guess."

"Are you telling me you think you are physically stronger than Zeke and me?"

There was no point sticking to the rules. I broke into his house and cast my way out. I couldn't deny it, rules or no rules, because an honest explanation was the least I owed him, even if he didn't want to share his secret with me. I looked around, assuring myself no one would hear what I was about to say, a force of habit, but here I was, about to tell the enemy's son what I could do. I took a deep breath. "You kind of guessed it before. I am good at willing things to happen. I try not to because it freaks out ordinaries like you."

He seemed eager to understand. "Ordinaries like me? Is that an insult?"

Did he not hear me? "Huh?"

"I've never thought of myself as ordinary, not that I shouldn't have when there are interesting girls like you going about."

He said it all so nonchalantly. Did it not bother him? "Can we not talk about this?"

"Why?"

"It's safer for me that way."

He looked puzzled. "Safer from what?" He touched his hand to my cheek to wipe off dirt, but his hand lingered for a moment longer than necessary, imparting his protective nature.

"Safer from your father and his Law Enforcement Organization. You already know they arrest girls like me for public mischief and breaking into your house certainly qualifies, if nothing else does. You have to promise to not say anything."

"There's nothing to tell. You're curious and good at making it rain flower petals and opening sealed windows. If that's all you can tell me, it's enough. But if you're afraid of him, don't be." His eyes relayed his determination to protect me.

"What if I told you I was a witch?"

"I would say you are the most beautiful witch I have ever met."

I nodded, feeling the heat color my cheeks. Beautiful? No one had ever called me that. My eyes widened in disbelief. "You know what I'm talking about, right?"

"Witch as in witch."

"That kind of thing doesn't bother you?"

"Of course not. In fact, I think trying to pretend to be ordinary when you aren't is what bothers me." He looked at me with acceptance. "I do have one question, though. Broomstick?"

I laughed. "No broomstick. They are a silly phallic symbol some artist gave them and the idea stuck."

"Do I want to know more?"

"Definitely not."

"Well, I like who you are." The warmth penetrated to my soul, causing me to shiver. I averted my eyes so he wouldn't see what I was thinking, but being near him was like being set free from a prison I didn't realize I was in.

"The moment I met you I knew you were different from all the simpering girls I'd met before." He leaned down ever so slowly, gripping his large hands around my waist. With just the slightest tug of his arms he enticed me toward him, the raw tension charging the air between us greater than ever. Every inch of my skin felt like he was touching it, electrifying it. My heart raced out of control. He slipped one hand under my chin and nestled his face into my hair, against the curve of my neck. I felt his warm breath and the roughness of his unshaved face on my skin. I rested my hands against the flexing muscles in his chest. The intensity between us rippled over me in pleasurable waves as flutters overtook my stomach. He wrapped his strong arms around me and breathed in again.

"I do not know what you have done to me, but having you here now in my arms, it only partly helps the loneliness I have suffered. Watching your heart shaped lips—the way they part and pout when you talk. How the intoxicating fragrance of your hair and skin drives me mad. And right now, you have no idea how pleasing the feel of your body against mine is."

He urged me closer to him if that was even possible, his hands against my back, pressing me into him. There were still secrets between us, but no boundaries. I wanted him. I slipped my hands around his neck, my fingers entwining in his hair.

I breathed in his scent; the floral, woodsy fragrance filled the emptiness in me I never knew existed until he arrived.

He leaned down. His lips brushed over my exposed throat, his shadow grazing the sensitive skin and drawing from me a soft, primal moan of ecstasy. He slowly dotted delicate kisses, each one potent and fiercely burning onto my tender, feverish skin. His mouth sweetly nuzzled under my jaw and trailed kisses over my cheek, pausing as if he were willing my lips to lock onto his. I glided my hands over his muscled shoulders and held tightly to his firm arms. He had to feel every quiet gasp I took as my chest expanded against his in rapid, shallow successions.

I shut my eyes, anticipating. My stomach tightened from the tension between us.

He paused, his body became still. He gently released my arms and stepped back. "I'm sorry. I can't do anything that will bring you harm," he said, his voice filled with regret and conflict.

Not wanting me to get scratched by hedges, he walked me to my front door in silence, but I was so numb from his conflict, deep cuts would have gone unnoticed. I watched him leave, his head hung low and his shoulders slumped with his hands by his sides curled into fists. Frustration flowed out of me like cotton bursting from the boll. As my fingers touched the knob, the door glided open with ease. I gasped. Reality cleared my numbness and left my heart racing—and not in the good way.

Inside, papers layered the floor like tiles and overturned furniture spilled into the hallway. Aunt Janie's freshly harvested angelica plants were strewn about the floor in small wilted heaps. I surveyed the chaos. My hands began to shake. "Aunt Janie?" I peered into the rainbow of colorful rooms on the main floor.

She hadn't returned from her late drop off of orders to the shop. I exhaled a whoosh of breath. Karma had taken twenty minutes to bite me back. Geez! I walked from room to room. Anxiety coiled around my nerves with each glance into the next room. Whoever had been here was searching for something, especially in my room where drawers dangled open and clothes draped across every inch of bright pink carpet.

Aunt Janie would freak if she found out. I glanced at my watch. She would be home soon. "Crud."

My cell buzzed in my pocket. I jumped. I pressed one hand to my forehead and pulled the phone out with the other, reading the name. "Macey, this isn't a good time."

"What happened to you? Did the Hottie-McTottie forgive you for breaking in?" she spoke at a speedy pace, her tone accelerated from the excitement of her escape.

"Uh, yeah."

"Natch. Because he likes you and…"

She had no idea. Neither did I. "I can't talk right now. I gotta go." I hung up and pressed another number in. "Hey Cal. I need your help. Can you come over, like right now?"

Five minutes later, Cal knocked on the door.

His eyes flashed wide. "Did you go postal on your house?"

As much as my spells had improved, my magic wouldn't work on the widespread mess fast enough and I'd be a dizzy mess before I finished the family room. "Ransacked by someone else, thank you. Don't know who. The house was empty when I walked in. I'm only glad Aunt Janie wasn't home when it happened."

"I'm glad you weren't home. Any idea what they were looking for?"

I shrugged, unsure. "Maybe my necklace. Nothing was taken, not even Aunt Janie's jewelry."

"Have you gotten that dumb thing checked out by the jeweler yet?"

I looked up at him, hurt by the unusual harshness in his tone. "I've been kinda busy."

He rolled his eyes and grabbed hold of the pendant. He eyed it suspiciously. "It's like red sea glass. Do you really think whoever made the mess was after this?"

I shook my head, thoroughly exhausted. "I don't know."

"You should call the police. What if you or Aunt Janie had been home? This person was crazy enough to break in and rummage through all your stuff. He might come back."

I stomped over the mess in the foyer. Who could do this? Instincts told me the hooded thief was responsible and, if so, he had no problem with boundaries, including door locks. "Can't call them. Aunt Janie will freak out and you know it. That's why I called you. She'll be home in twenty-five minutes and this place needs to look normal or she'll zone out for hours in the corner of her bedroom. I'm not even close to kidding."

I glanced at Callum who gave me the face that told me it wasn't a good idea to lie to her, but I knew her better than he did. "She will not freak out."

"Yes, she will. She's been fragile since...since my parents died." I started to choke up, thinking back to the judge's cruel revelation. The hate welled up like acid in my throat.

He nodded as if he were recalling some of our childhood memories with her in them, looking lost. He loved Aunt Janie, too, and he realized I was right. "Where do we start?"

"Family room." We both began stuffing papers back where they belonged and straightening the furniture. A few times when Cal wasn't looking I whispered, "*In Ordinem*," to straighten rows of Aunt Janie's English porcelain figurines and recipe books to speed things up. The spell worked perfectly, but only on a few small items at a time, otherwise lightheadedness would slow me down. We saved my bedroom for last since I could buy time, if needed, by closing the door, which is what I usually did anyway. We raced through each room.

Cal worked on Aunt Janie's and I worked on mine. As soon as I tossed the pillows back on my bed, Elizabeth's journal on my night table flipped open. The writing began without a spell. *I need you to find In Libro de Malo Incantationibus—The Book of Dark Spells.*

"Sophie, your aunt is out front talking to Mrs. Marbley across the street. Hurry up," Callum said from her room. My pulse sped up. "This isn't a good time, Elizabeth."

It is crucial that you do and as soon as possible.

"I want nothing to do with dark spells." There was no response and I didn't have time to ask any more questions. I shoved the book in the table drawer, ignoring the iron statuette. Callum and I met in the hallway, our panicked eyes locked on each other. Without a word, we both dashed downstairs and slammed our bodies into the sofa cushions. I grabbed my worn copy of Romeo and Juliet and Cal picked up a gardening book from the coffee table. Even though the seriousness of the break-in and the stress I was under, I had to pinch myself to keep from laughing at both of us.

Her keys jangled against the door. "Hi…Aunt Janie." I purposely slowed my words, feeling a tremble from the adrenaline. "We're in here."

"We?" She strolled in and crinkled her forehead, seeming suspicious.

"Hi, Ms. Janie. How are you?"

"Hi Callum. How's work?" She spied the book he was holding and smirked. I glanced at the cover. How to Grow Fields of Beautiful Buttercups. I pinched my leg to keep from laughing.

"Okay. Trying to save for a car."

"Sophie, the front door wasn't locked. You have to be careful. Don't want strangers getting in here."

I almost choked on her words. "Definitely. Won't happen again." I would have to do something to make sure it didn't.

Macey stood in the shop bathroom, stuffing bobby pins into her upswept hair. She glanced amusedly at me from the mirror. "If a quiz is a quizzical, then what's a test?"

"Oh my gosh. You told me that joke in seventh grade."

A laugh snorted out of her. "Okay, but seriously." She turned around to face me. "Here's a pop quizzical for you…if Alexavier wasn't mad about you breaking into their house, which doesn't surprise me at all, why did you sound all freaked out on the phone last night when I called?" She stuck one last bobby pin into her curly hair, taming the whole thing into place.

I yawned from sleep deprivation. "Macey, you have to promise to not say anything. Nothing. Not even to Daniel." She made a locking motion with her fingers against her lips and tossed the imaginary key into the toilet. "When I got back inside my home last night, it had been ransacked."

Her smile melted away. She grabbed my hands and pushed me all the way back into the store room. "Sit on the stepladder. Are you okay? Was the intruder still there? Did you call the police?"

I sat down and shook my head. My muscles tensed from anxiety as I recalled the sight of the mess. "He left before I got there and Aunt Janie wasn't home. She would crack like an egg if she knew."

"W—T—H!"

"I know. Callum came over and helped me clean up before she got there. She didn't suspect anything. I can't even believe it." I tried to dismiss the seriousness of the crime, but the stress of it was too much. I dropped my head into my hands.

She patted me on the back. "You're okay. That's all that matters." She hesitated.

I glanced up at her. "I'm not sure about that."

Her face squished into a grimace. "Why?"

I wiped my face with my hands, weariness and stress had taken their toll on me. "Nothing was missing. If the intruder didn't find what he was looking for, he could come back."

"Sophie, you're shaking. Hold your hands out."

I stuck them out in front of me and watched my fingers tremble like a Starbucks addict.

"I'm gonna tell Mrs. D to let you go home. You can't work like this. We'll manage without you."

I waved at her. "No. I don't want to go home. I want to be here. I feel safe here. Besides, we have a sale today and I'm fine."

She eyed me with concern.

"I'll take a walk on my lunch break. That will help."

At lunch, I grabbed up my sneakers in my hand and walked home. I needed to feel the ground beneath me and be surrounded by our blue rose bushes and boxwood hedges. I leaned back against the white Chippendale bench, feeling the dewy grass welcome my feet. I dug my toes into the cool, thick soil and my heavy eyelids closed. The sun warmed my face and the scents of summer and the buzz of winged bugs in search of pollen filled the humid air. I cleared my thoughts and surrendered my tired body to the firm wood of the bench.

"Stressed?" His deeply alluring voice was rich and smooth like warm English toffee.

The sun burned into my pupils as soon as I opened my eyes. "Ow." I shaded my face with my hand fanned out above me.

"Tired, actually."

"Yes. Breaking and entering can cause fatigue."

"I didn't break into your house, exactly. I knew the back door would be unlocked."

"How did you know that?"

I smiled. "I have eyes."

He feigned relief. "Promise you won't do that again. I don't want to worry about Zeke killing you."

"Should I be worried?" I asked, not needing anything more to deal with.

"It was a joke."

I wasn't sure about that. I wanted to ask him why was he holding back with me, but I couldn't. I feared the answer. Instead, I kept him there with inane questions. "Tell me why you don't dress like a normal seventeen-year-old?"

"Old habit from boarding school. Pressed shirt and pants. Everything neat, everyday. I'm trying to loosen up, though."

I was certain the boarding school was expensive and ultra exclusive. "What was it like living there?"

He wrinkled his brow. "I don't like to look back."

"I understand that. School was never a playground for me. I was the only preschooler asking for cookies in Latin. The grades came easily, but not the friends."

His lips curled into a lopsided grin. "And how exactly do you say cookie in Latin?"

I laughed. "*Crustulum* and I'm not ashamed I know that."

"You shouldn't be."

"When my friend, Macey, came along in fourth grade, she didn't care that I was different and she definitely didn't care what the other girls thought. She still doesn't."

He nodded. "Sounds like a good friend."

I still didn't know why they returned to Wethersfield and curiosity nipped away. "So your father wanted you back home?"

"Yes, he wants us to work for him. Zeke is fine with it. More than fine. But I have no desire to follow in those bitter footsteps."

I wasn't sure that was the whole truth. "What do you want to do?" I asked, ignoring the quickening of my pulse, which was now hammering in my ears.

"I'd like to finish my last year of secondary school here and go away to university. Far away. How about you?"

The far away part echoed in my ears until it faded to nothing. "I have two years of high school left and then I don't know." The fall would bring school during the day and, if things didn't go well at the Seeking, I would be living at Cross Manor and training after school and every weekend. Who knew what would happen after that?

"What about right now? Are you home for the rest of the day?"

I shook my head. "No. I have an errand to run." An important one—courtesy of Elizabeth—although I wasn't sure what I would find.

He narrowed his eyes. "Try to stay safe. If I could, I would go with you, but I have a meeting downtown with my father and Zeke." He rolled his eyes, not looking forward to it.

I nodded, always feeling dazed in his presence, even when I tried not to be. "There's still plenty of sunlight, so I should be fine," I joked.

He smiled a lopsided smile that made his face light up and I was dazzled by how handsome he was. "I'm not sure about that." I watched him disappear through the hedges. As his car roared to life and the sound of the engine grew fainter, I checked my watch. I slipped my feet back into my sneakers and ran upstairs to my room. From my night table drawer, I grabbed the two ancient Celtic coins before heading downtown. There was only one shop in town that might possess what Elizabeth needed me to find. The Rare Muse.

Muses were nymphs of memory and knowledge, so it wasn't hard to guess the owner might be able to help me with my quest. I walked past the display windows, which showcased a new arrival of Impressionist art books. Inside, the smell of dust, pipe tobacco, and old leather permeated the air, enhancing the shop's magical quality. I stared in awe at the literary scene. Not only were the walls lined with shelves and shelves of books from top to bottom, the ceiling was, too. Customers probably assumed the books were decorative and glued in tight for effect, but I suspected they weren't glued in at all. Large bright bulbs resembling round white lollipops stuck out over the main floor illuminating the shop. A short African-American gentleman popped up on a footstool behind the counter. "I am Mr. Oloy. May I help you, miss?"

I jumped back, startled. I pressed my hand over my pulsing heart. "I'm not sure." I glanced over him, thinking he definitely wasn't an ordinary. Maybe a leprechaun?

"Well, if you're not sure, then I'll be getting back..."

"No. Wait." I fiddled for the coins in my pocket. "I'm looking for a special book."

"Then you have come to the right place. How special?" he asked, doing a once over of my face in search of the answer.

"Special enough that it may not be on the main floor. Are there any other sections where I may search?"

"There is a special fee for entrance to the Muse's rare, rare book room." His bushy dark eyebrows arched upward as he waited for me to respond.

I slapped my hand on the counter and slid it away, exposing the two silver coins, crown sides up.

"Celtic currency." He picked up a coin and inspected the crown symbol on the head side. "You witches love to remind others of your royal connections, which is ironic as the king was the one who chased you out of England. However, that was before he bestowed many valuable gifts upon your kind." His eyes traveled the length of my silver chain to the inevitable pendant hidden beneath my shirt. "Very good." He looked outside the windows, searching. When he saw no one coming, he flipped the shop sign to "Closed."

"Follow me."

"Are you the shop owner?"

"You may think nothing of me as a lowly goblin, but I am more than that. I am a guardian goblin."

Sounded like a fancy way of saying he was a supernatural librarian, but his tone made me feel bad for him. "Why would I think nothing of you as a goblin?"

"That's the hierarchy around Wethersfield, with your kind topping it off." Sounded like he had dealt with the Mayapples recently. I wanted to make him feel better and tell him I was only a half-witch, but I didn't see the point in prolonging a polite conversation when he was already walking away from me.

The strange shop owner, in his small antiquated three-piece brown suit, led me through a short door. I was a hair over five-feet-tall and had to duck to get through. I followed him into a dim, candlelit hallway, which led to a sweeping, white marble staircase like something from an antebellum mansion. Up the stairs we marched, ascending into the rare, rare book room.

"What is this?" I spun around, taking in the vastness of the unusual space.

"This is my responsibility. The Otherworld Writers' Collection." The rare, rare book room resembled a grand nineteen-twenties theater with art deco columns supporting three terraces, each lit up with rows of light bulbs. Where the stage was, a large movie screen hung guarded on both sides by velvet red curtains fringed in gold on each side and crowned with a huge gold valance. Each illuminated balcony was overfilled with bookcases of rare, rare books where other goblins like Mr. Oloy pushed book carts and stacked the shelves.

"Where do I begin looking?" I had no idea and suddenly felt overwhelmed. This was going to take days.

He pointed to the front of the theater. "You need to follow the instructions on the movie screen. The main level is the Orchestra, followed by the Grand Tier, the Balcony, and at the very top, the Gallery. Good luck and may Fate be with you."

I frowned. Was that a goblin saying? "Instructions. Movie screen. Got it." I watched him disappear down the staircase and I turned my attention back to the enormous screen, wondering if I should say something to get it started. Suddenly, the lights dimmed. The red velvet curtains pulled farther to the sides and the clicking of an old-fashioned film projector started. In black and white like a silent film, the words appeared.

What do you seek?

In my best Latin I said, "*In Libro de Malo Incantationibus. The Book of Dark Spells.*"

Password, please.

Password? Elizabeth didn't give me a password. "Celtic coins?"

Password, please.

"Pretty please?"

Password, please.

The words reappeared for the third time. I was afraid if I messed up again I would get locked out like on my phone. I closed my eyes and searched my head for the right word. Who was the darkest spellcaster I knew who would use a book like that? Even Eldress Mayapple wasn't as dark as she hoped to be. Then the answer came to me clear as witch dew.

"Rebecca."

The projector began to roll.

Gallery, Section 7, Shelf G, Row 7.

Stairs ran along each side of the rare, rare book room, so I picked the left side and raced to the top. I spied Section 7 and scanned each tall mahogany shelf looking for the letters. G. One, two, five, seven. The books were old and cracked and covered in an array of dark colored leather. My fingers brushed along the spines until a chill blew across my face, followed by a whistling breeze. One of the shop assistants in the gallery section tried to shush me until I pointed to the troublemaker. He turned away, looking annoyed. I tugged the black book from its snug spot.

The lack of light made it difficult to see. I gulped a breath of dusty air and did what I had to do. Slowly. Reluctantly. I opened it.

The ancient book resembled Elizabeth's journal, except for the color, but these pages weren't blank. The yellowed paper fanned out before me, containing formal handwriting. The content reminded me of Aunt Janie's herbal recipe book because it contained tons of handwritten notes and measurements listed under unusual titles like Bewitch and Amalgamate. As I read on, I realized it was exactly like Janie's recipe book for plants, flowers, and herbs, only these combinations used mostly poisonous ingredients and came with spells to concoct something for more than a headache cure. I turned to the front page and saw the list of owners' names. Rebecca Greensmith was the last owner. It seemed appropriate that the little book was here, hidden away in the dark. I closed it and gently returned it to its dark hiding spot, wondering why Elizabeth wanted me to find this. She didn't practice black magic.

"What are you doing?" Mr. Oloy asked, appearing from out of nowhere.

"Where did you come from?" I looked beyond him, wondering if there were secret passages he was using to get around.

"I came to check on your progress and I am glad I did. The book is yours. You paid for it and you must take it now."

I drew back in dismay. "No, it's not mine."

"Yes, it is. Look at the front page again."

I glanced at the list of owners' names. Beneath Rebecca's, my name now appeared in the purplish black ink I had become familiar with over the last few weeks. "This...this is a huge mistake. I don't want it."

"These books do not contain errors. You must take it and go."

No good would come of the secrets held within the book, but I knew he wouldn't let me leave without it. I reluctantly took it. I left the shop, feeling like I weighed a hundred pounds more with that thing tucked into the back waist of my shorts. I took a backstreet to return to Scents and Scentsabilities so Macey could take her break, but as I walked along, I heard a twig crack behind me. I whipped around. "Stalk much?" I said without thinking.

Zeke's face flushed with color at the sight of me. His eyes grew dark and deadly with determination. "Just making sure you're alone."

My breath came in short, quick gasps. I pressed my body against the back wall of a business. "You should really think about getting a hobby. Golf, ax-sharpening, maybe?"

Spit coated his lips. "My brother is different since he met you and he won't listen to me. So I'm doing what I have to do."

A lump formed in my throat. I swallowed loudly. Cal's warning about Zeke and his distaste for the locals came back to me. I needed to be firm with him, but I wasn't feeling tough at all. "Alexavier doesn't need you to babysit him."

"We'll see about that." His shrewd eyes filled with hatred as he stared me down. I forced myself to maintain my glare, tapping into my anger to fuel it. He snarled then spit on the ground before huffing away.

As he disappeared around a building, a tremendous headache started behind my eyes and hammered its way to the back of my head. If anyone needed a heaping dose of Aunt Janie's valerian in his mocha frappuccino to calm down, he did.

After work, I headed home. As I walked, I reached into my front pocket and tapped a handful of orange Tic-Tacs into my palm. I popped them in my mouth. The wet, earthy scent of an impending storm tinged the air. The patter of my footsteps on the barely illuminated, tree-lined sidewalk reminded me I was alone, instilling a sense of urgency in me to walk quickly.

As I rounded a corner, a withered hand whipped out in front of me. My feet stopped, throwing my body forward while an unsettling scream caught in my throat. I threw my hands out to balance myself. My wide eyes traced the man's hand to the face it belonged to. No hood. No tattoo. No angry snarl of Zeke. I gulped hard, seeing the vagrant step out from behind the weeping willow. It took a few seconds to catch my breath, totally relieved he wasn't the thief or Zeke.

I shrugged my shoulders. "Sorry, don't have any money on me." I shook off the heebie jeebies and continued to walk home, but as I looked back, I realized the man seemed out of place when Main Street was bustling with crowds of generous tourists catching a late night lobster dinner.

As I continued to stare, he stepped away from the tree and followed slowly behind me. His footsteps were heavy and exaggerated. I just couldn't catch a break today. My heart began to race. I faced forward and walked faster, stunned and unsure what he was doing.

"You positive 'bout dat?" he snarled in a gruff accent.

I spun around, watching him slip something shiny onto his filthy hands. As he passed under the light of one of the lampposts, I could see more clearly. He was short with long arms and a barrel chest. The long, thin strands of hair on his head flapped in the wind and the sunken hollows of his cheeks accented his middle age and hard life. A creepy grin crawled across his craggy face.

I turned away and tucked my pendant beneath my shirt. My hand brushed against my throat, which was beginning to tighten. "I'm sure." If only I had a five-leafed clover on me. I rubbed my pendant, instead, thinking of a spell to make him go away.

"Where you headed?" he asked.

The hair on the back of my neck bristled. I picked up my pace and ignored his inane question. Where were the Leos when someone actually needed them?

"Hey! I'm talking to you," he shouted after me. His footsteps increased in pace with mine. "Didn't anyone ever tell you it's not safe to walk home alone?" he added with a wry chuckle as if this was a regular activity for him. He closed the distance between us.

I crossed the street to the other sidewalk, hoping someone might walk by so I didn't feel so horribly alone. I locked my eyes on the stop sign ahead. I wanted to sound calm, but I wasn't. My emotions whirled out of control. I wanted nothing more than to release them. I stopped dead in my tracks, turned around, and whirled my finger in his direction. The energy spun inside me, but stalled. "*Liberum!*" I shook my hand, trying to unleash it.

Nothing.

Standing there, I shook my finger, urging the magic to trickle out. "Leave…leave me alone." My voice quivered, but it was loud enough for him to hear.

He stepped closer. "If you ain't got no money, how 'bout a date tonight, sweetie?" His calloused hand suddenly gripped around my jaw and I knew what he had slipped onto his hand—iron knuckles. The heat from the hard metal radiated past my bound lips to my throat, paralyzing my vocal cords. With his other grimy hand, he inched toward my chain.

I kicked him hard in the shin and stomped on his foot. He cursed until his hold loosened. I finally managed to jump back, wiping his dirty touch from my face, disgusted. How did he know to use iron on someone like me? My fists flashed in his face as I coughed to get my voice back.

"Leave me alone." With a screech of the brakes, Alexavier's white Audi came to a halt on the street beside me. He jumped out of the car and stood between me and the man, towering over him as his strong arms reached back and wrapped around me, pressing my body against the back of his. Relief washed over me. I gripped my hands around his waist, the moist heat radiated through his shirt and under my fingertips, leaving me unsteady.

"Leave. Now," Alexavier growled, shielding me from the aggressive vagrant. Alexavier was capable of unleashing his own brand of danger upon the middle-aged stranger, iron knuckles or no iron knuckles. I had no doubt. I peeked over his shoulder at the homeless man, wanting to gauge his reaction. The man, noticing Alexavier's tensed muscles and fierce stance started to back away slowly, conceding his loss.

As he retreated, a stray dog trotted into our midst. The mangy-looking beast stopped in its tracks. The black and tan scruff on its shoulders thickened. It snarled and barked ferociously at us, rearing up on its hind legs and baring its sharp, wet teeth. Alexavier remained steady. However, seizing upon the distraction, the homeless man rushed him. The impact knocked me over. I landed on my wrist, the bones shifting under my weight. A jagged pain shot up the length of my arm. I ground my teeth together, muffling the scream.

Alexavier grabbed the man by the shoulder with one hand and landed a punch to the side of his face with the other. The two men violently engaged each other, throwing punches. I cringed, hearing the sound of bones cracking while the stray dog backed away.

Alexavier stepped back for a second, shaking his head and flaring his nostrils as if he were struggling to contain his anger.

Wanting to distract him from himself, I released the cry of pain I held in. "Ow!"

Alexavier glanced back at me. His scuffed up face flushed with hot-blooded heat. He returned his attention to the vagrant, tapping into his burgeoning strength and tossed the man to the curb. The vagrant wobbled to his feet and darted down the street faster than the hungry dog, but with a noticeable limp he didn't have before. Alexavier closed his eyes, calming his breathing; a conscious effort to regain control of himself. His muscles quivered from the rush of danger. He ran his fingers through his hair and knelt beside me. A crimson streak marred his lip and a fresh bruise swelled above his right eye.

Guilt rolled over me. This was my fault. "What are you doing here?" I asked, thankful, but completely confused at the same time.

"I stopped by the shop to give you a ride home, you know with it being nighttime and your luck when it's dark. Macey told me you already left. Are you all right?" he asked, pacing his words so he sounded calm.

"My wrist…I think I sprained it." I knew it was at least sprained, matching the pain to a memory of investigating a childhood mystery gone wrong. Aunt Janie had patched me up afterward, as usual.

He helped me to my feet, steadying me with his hand on my waist. His gentle touch blazed through my clothes, leaving me very aware of his masculinity. My head grew hazy from the feeling. I tried to stay in the moment, focusing on my wrist, which screamed for attention.

As he looked down at me and spoke, his voice vibrated with hushed emotion. "That vagrant seemed very determined to take me on to get to you. What do you think he was after?"

"A handout. I told him I didn't have any money on me."

"Do you really believe he wanted money or something else?"

I wasn't sure what he was getting at and I didn't want to think about it anymore. "He did ask for a date."

He exhaled his impatience. "Is there anything else of value on you?"

"Not that I know of," I said honestly. After all, I had no proof my necklace was worth anything and the book pressed against my back only held value to a witch.

He grimaced. "You need to be more careful."

"Nothing happened," I said, not wanting a lecture.

The muscles under his torn shirt shuddered. "There must be a reason so much trouble finds you."

I grasped my injured arm with my good hand. "Does trouble include you?"

He shoved his hands onto his hips and gritted his teeth. "Yes, regrettably."

I brushed my disheveled hair from my face. My lower jaw jutted out. "You can leave me here, you know. I mean, I appreciate what you did, but clearly you've got a secret you're letting get between us so I don't really see the point in whatever this is."

He pursed his lips, still marked with a trace line of moist blood, not wanting to say anything, but he finally did. He took a deep breath and closed his eyes.

"You're right. It's a secret that's going to stay secret."

I took a step away from him, letting the gusty evening breeze cool my blood-warmed cheeks.

He reached for me. "Let me see your wrist." His arrogance in full force grated on my nerves as he grabbed hold of my arm.

If I weren't in so much agony I would have yanked it right back. "Don't!"

"I don't have X-ray vision. I need to see it!" He gnashed his straight, white teeth.

"Leave me alone," I protested.

"I'm not going to hurt you!" he growled, releasing my arm back to me. He shook his hands in the air and exhaled with frustration. He paused before starting again. "Sophie." His edgy voice relaxed, melting into liquid honey. "Trust me."

I resisted, feeling the conflict between my heart and head. I knew how I felt when I was with him, but his stupid family secret wedged between us like a big, stinking corpse flower.

"Let me help you," he implored sweetly. His piercing, dark eyes imparted sincerity.

The breath rushed out of me.

"Sophie," he whispered again, his voice aching.

Butterflies flitted about in my stomach, immersing me in the moment, which was quickly heating up. I tried not to be dazed. I brushed my windblown hair from my eyes and extended my hand to him, desperate for his touch. His long fingers brushed against the tender surface of my arm, sending chills of pleasure across my skin where it didn't hurt. He examined my wrist, turning my hand over slowly, lifting it. He checked the rest of me for other injuries, seeming serious and methodical in his examination. I wondered if he felt the electric sensations, too.

"Ow!" I yelped again as he applied the slightest pressure to bend my wrist. "Were you a boy scout or something?"

He laughed out loud. "Hardly. I remember a few things from health class, that's all. I'm sure it's more than a sprain—it's starting to swell." He studied my scrunched up face as a piercing clap of thunder echoed above us. "Time to go." He nodded his head in the direction of his car.

"I-I can manage by myself," I stuttered in an obstinate attempt to persevere and not let Aunt Janie see him anywhere near our house. She didn't need anything more to add to her fragile state.

"Sophie, let me help you."

"I don't need help."

"Would you rather walk home alone after what just happened?"

"No, but…"

"Then there is no point in challenging me," he stated with determination that would not be questioned.

I locked my knees in a stubborn effort to not move. He observed me, shaking his head. Without another word he wrapped his lean muscular arm around my waist, this time crushing me firmly against him. He escorted me to the passenger side of his car. It did not escape my attention that as tough as he seemed, he was careful and unexpectedly tender in the way he held me to him, letting the bad boy take a break.

The streetlight sparkled off the white metallic paint and tinted glass of the German vehicle. He opened the door and carefully guided me into the seat. His arm barely brushed against my injured wrist. I winced from the minor shift, but as I opened my eyes, I noticed a very blonde girl walking toward us—Laney—paying careful attention to who I was with. As soon as our eyes locked, she turned and ran, too fast for me to erase her memory. She would be hissing in her mom's ear for sure, telling her I was with a forbidden Mather.

I turned to Alexavier, agitated with all the trouble. My irritation heated and rose to the surface. "Why do you always have to get your way?" I stated indignantly as he sat back in the driver's seat.

"Why do you have to be so difficult?"

"I'm not difficult!" I wrestled with the unyielding seatbelt.

He paused, looking straight ahead at nothing in particular, clenching his jaw.

I took another loud breath, this time to ease the sharp pain that throbbed in my wrist. My discomfort did not escape his attentive watch.

"Sophie, you need to go to the hospital." His brow creased, exasperation crossing his ivory face as he waited for my refusal.

"I'll be fine at home," I said, knowing Aunt Janie was there.

"I understand you think you know it all, but you need more than an ice pack for that."

"My aunt will take care of it."

He paused for a moment, considering my solution. "Is she able to make things happen, too?"

I nodded. "In a different way."

"Of course." He shook his head, seeming to understand, but he couldn't possibly without seeing her in action. He hit the ignition switch, sparking the engine and as he did the radio came on, blasting a classical song I recognized from Aunt Janie's shop playlist.

"Mozart?"

His finger tapped the mute button.

"You always surprise me. I had you pegged for a classic-rock-slash-British-invasion kind of guy."

"Perhaps I'm not as ordinary as you think."

I smiled, knowing he was definitely not the boring kind of ordinary. I breathed in the warm leather fragrance of his car that mixed with his subtle scent while I focused on the details of the car, including the crate in his back seat stamped "London."

"Is that your order from Goody's Market?" I asked, remembering Callum talking about the eccentric treats he and Zeke ordered from England.

"How do you…" he broke off mid-sentence and exhaled a laugh. "Criminal background research, illegal house searches, and now inquisitions into my store purchases? Did Mr. Geoffrey tell you?"

"No." I paused, not wanting to reveal how I knew, but it was too late. "Callum. He's my friend. Sorry."

"Don't be. I like that you're true to your curious nature. Do you know what's in the box?" Raindrops splattered against the windshield.

I crinkled my face, ignoring his insinuation. "Burned mistletoe?"

"Yes. What else?"

"I don't know. Why burned mistletoe?"

"I'm superstitious."

"I know what it's for."

He glanced at me, knowing I wouldn't let it go. "It's to protect my brother and me. After everything that has happened to my family, I figured it couldn't hurt." He paused. "And I do think you know what else I ordered. You're just trying to be polite. However, I think after breaking into my house, we've crossed beyond that line, don't you agree?"

I nodded, not feeling bad about it since he didn't. "How was the meeting with your father?"

The wipers squeaked across the windshield. "He wants me to spend the rest of the summer fundraising for him."

My mouth dropped open. My breath escaped in a gasp.

"I told him, no." The car came to a sudden halt in front of my house. He jumped out into the rain and a moment later opened my door. I fumbled with the seatbelt until he lifted my hand out of the way. His hand reached in and with one quick click I was free and standing with his arm wrapped around my waist again.

"Please let me walk in my house alone." I pulled at my shirt, which was beginning to cling to my skin from the rain.

"Your aunt won't approve?"

I looked up at him, puzzled. "Would your father?"

He stood there waiting for a better answer as the rain fell down around us.

"It's nothing personal against you."

"Well, maybe it's time to change our families' attitudes," he said, determined to take on more than three hundred years of bad blood.

I bit my lip. Nervousness made it difficult to think straight. A minor shift in my wrist brought the pain to the forefront. I blinked back the welling tears that pooled regardless of my effort and conceded to his request. As he escorted me into the house, I looked at how badly the bruise had swollen above his eye. I wanted to say something, but the pain in my wrist mounted to an unbearable level. "Owww."

Aumt Janie rushed to the foyer. She read my uneasy expression, which upset her. "What happened?"

"A homeless man followed me and…"

"A man?" she interrupted.

"Alexavier confronted him." She spied the tear in his shirt. "I got sidelined. They fought." I tried to downplay the details for her sake, but it was too late. I regretted it immediately.

"A fight!" She glared at Alexavier, restraining her anger.

"Aunt Janie, this is Alexavier. Alexavier, my Aunt Janie."

"A Mather?" she said, her voice quivering with a combo of anger and impatience at the mention of his name.

"Uh, nice…nice to meet you, Mrs…." The words stumbled out ungracefully in his British accent, very unlike Alexavier. He ran his hands through his wet hair, looking not so fierce.

"It's Ms., thank you very much," she replied tersely. "Why are you anywhere near my niece?" she demanded, sounding unnecessarily outraged. Embarrassment flooded my cheeks.

"Aunt Janie, if he hadn't been there, something bad could have happened," I argued, knowing he needed protecting from her.

Alexavier's temporary discomfort faded under his inflating arrogance. His posture straightened. "You don't need to defend me. I can see I'm upsetting your aunt and I'll be going now." He turned and left, shutting the front door behind him, a little too loudly.

I defied her warning glare and raced after him into the storm.

He spoke without looking back at me. "You're welcome."

"I told you not to come in and I didn't ask for your help," I shouted, hoping I sounded thoroughly ungrateful.

"Our families' feud is their problem and my concern for you is my problem." He kept walking to his car after dismissing me with that antagonizing sweeping hand motion that infuriated me like nothing else ever had. He was so…he was so…arrogant and wrong.

"Let your concern go. I'll take care of myself!" The sarcastic words flew out of me like a flash of lightning. Thunder rumbled above us. He stopped dead. He spun around and walked back to me, his eyes seized my full attention. I dug my feet in, ready for his reaction as if the force of it would knock me over.

"You want to know what your problem is? Take a look in the mirror," he said. His lips curled upward, setting my temper on fire.

My eyes wanted to burst from their sockets. He infuriated me. Being around him…he was like a wild wind igniting embers I never knew were smoldering in me. Every word, every action between us building heat until the inferno exploded.

I boiled. My right hand made a gathering motion to the trees around me. A whoosh of internal energy peaked at a dangerous level and rushed out of me through my fingers. "*Ceciderit!*" A crack of splitting bark and splintering hardwood shattered the quiet. A tall chestnut tree from Mrs. Marbley's property tipped over from its roots and the heavy trunk crashed to the street in front of his car. The Audi shook. I jumped back, startled at what I had done. But he didn't even look back at me. He jumped in, threw the car in reverse, and swerved around my mess.

I clasped my good hand to my forehead, dealing with the awful lightheadedness. At the moment, all I could think about was him and how he drove me crazy, but in a heart-pounding, red blooded, wild way that made me feel alive and strangely…exhilarated.

I stomped back into the kitchen where Janie waited with arms folded tightly across her chest.

"My clairvoyant fog is clearing. Everything I'm foreseeing is coming to fruition. You are on a dangerous path, my dear. You know our history. You know the Mathers are no good for us," she said. She mashed her soft lips tightly together.

"Maybe someone needs to bend before we all break. Maybe I'm the one who is going to bend." I grabbed a kitchen towel and awkwardly started blotting my hair dry with my right hand.

"You're going to break!"

I stopped breathing and stared at her face. She wasn't lying about what she had foreseen.

"He has their blood running through his veins. Remember that."

"What if that doesn't mean anything?"

Her eyes bulged. "He got in a fight on the street with you next to him!"

"He was protecting me!"

"Mathers don't protect our kind. They only bring death to us," she said, sounding strangely like Zeke. She pointed a finger at me. "Have you broken any of the rules?"

My lips tingled with the little spray of fireworks. "No."

"Are you sure?"

"Yes," I said with attitude.

She said nothing as her lips pressed firmly together, not appreciating my snarkiness. I rolled my eyes and turned my head away from her. "No banishing powder," I warned, knowing she was capable of taking care of her concerns on her own, gray area or not.

Her lips puckered. "We have more pressing matters to contend with. The Council will be here any minute. What do we say about the tree in the road?"

"Tell the old crones lightning took it down."

"Brilliant," she said sarcastically. "Let me see your wrist."

"Fine." I sat in the chair, extending my left arm to her.

She pulled up a chair beside me and felt the bones in my wrist with her delicate fingers.

"Ow!" I cried, flashing my eyes open in pain.

She kept shaking her head like she was totally disappointed in me for hanging around Alexavier. "The bones are fine. Probably a ligament strain." While she walked out to the garden I slipped into the Flower Library, extracting The Book of Dark Spells from my shorts and hiding it among the other books. A minute later she returned, slightly wet, holding three apple blossoms in her hand. She plucked the fragrant petals from their glossy green stems and reached up in the cupboard for her antique copper mortar. She grasped the pestle and gently ground them up into a fragrant, pink pulp, adding a fine sprinkle of white powder from a golden vial into the mix. "Witches wort," she explained. She spread the magenta-colored pulp in a bandage she pulled from the first aid kit under the sink and wrapped the moist concoction around my wrist, whispering an old Latin rhyme I had heard her say before when applying a remedy.

"I've never seen you use apple blossoms."

She sat down again, placing her hands on her knees. "The petals reduce swelling."

"The injury feels like more than a strain."

"Should be better by morning." She glanced nervously at her watch. "I wish we had time to do a tea leaf reading, but we don't."

"What do you mean?"

"I read the Tic-Tac box you left behind this morning. The Council is coming here. Laney told her mother she saw you with the Mather boy." She lifted her hands in the air. "I couldn't believe it when I foresaw it."

"His name is Alexavier and he can't stand the Mathers any more than we can."

"Blood is thicker than water, my dear. And ordinary men have no problem saying something meaningless to get what they want."

"I don't believe that. He's been nothing but helpful to me without asking for anything in return."

"Why can't you fall for a nice warlock? The Badeaux boy is friendly enough."

"Ugh. They want nothing to do with a half-witch and Montel stinks."

She rolled her eyes like I was a jerk for saying that. The doorbell ominously chimed three times. "Tread carefully, Sophie, and try to control your emotions for the next thirty minutes."

Janie showed them in. They quietly entered the kitchen where I waited. Except for Lana, they all wore the witch uniform paired with black pearls, including hunched over Mistress Deedee, while Eldress Mayapple draped a thin, silk, blood-red scarf around her neck. Lana, looking like a linebacker, preferred the comfort of black pants and a loose fitting white shirt. I was sure she was here in case her services were needed in hauling me off against my will to Cross Manor for a lesson in our histories. I was beginning to think their punishments weren't much different from Judge Mather and his conversion tactics.

Mistress Isobel faced Aunt Janie, purposely making herself a barrier between us. She was known as the blinder, talented with creating a psychic fog to prevent interference. This trick proved helpful to the eldress as she tried to cloak me in her truth spell. "Please, Mistress Jane, let us step out into your garden. A tour would be lovely right now." The Council thought they were so clever with what they assumed was their unannounced surprise visit, not realizing how acute Aunt Janie's clairvoyance skills really were. She spent the day in the garden, moving and disguising any plants which would reveal our specific talents, like covering the absinthium, its cuttings used to boost her clairvoyance, in delicate white blooms so it appeared to be nothing more than winter tarragon. A tour would leave Mistress Isobel unimpressed, reaffirming their assumptions of our low level magical abilities.

Eldress Mayapple wasted no time getting to work. She rolled her sleeves up and began flapping her hands in the air as if she were massaging an invisible man in front of her. I tried not to laugh.

Immediately a tingling sensation prickled on my tongue. With a nod from the eldress, Mistress Deedee began questioning me. Lana tried conversing with her mother, who obliged her, knowing Deedee would alert her as soon as she discovered an ounce of troubling truth from me.

"Have you met the Mather boys?"

"Yes." I tried to speak very matter-of-fact, not wanting to upset Aunt Janie any more than I had.

"How much time have you spent with them?"

My concentration faltered for a moment, as I thought of Alexavier. I watched Deedee's eyebrows turn in curiously as she asked me suggestive questions. My heart skipped a beat. "They've been to the shop. The older one, Zeke, is exactly like his father. Being near him makes me angry." I took a breath and tried to drown out Lana's idiotic voice. Aunt Janie made sure I tasted the devil's bit nectar earlier, knowing what was coming, but there had been no time to mix up a calming confection.

Lana continued in the background. "Laney said the Dayo boy is not lacking in the looks department. Any chance he might like me?"

Callum, I thought. A bout of laughter nearly choked out of me. I pinched my leg.

"I'm afraid he's an ordinary and, even if he weren't, you're just too big," her mother replied.

"Exceptions have been made in the past and you can make one for me. Besides, Laney said he is really tall. I can wear flat shoes or you can cast a spell on him."

"You know I don't do spells. That is Mistress Belladonna's department, and no exceptions will be made for you."

I pinched myself harder, picturing her pinning Callum down for a kiss.

"You need to focus on your obligations to the witches of Wethersfield because no daughter of mine will be involved with an ordinary."

Mistress Deedee cleared her throat. "And what of the younger Mather?" Her question slipped in. My concentration shattered like a crystal goblet exploding in my hands. "I love him." I flashed my eyes to Deedee's. Her mouth dropped open. Her eyes bulged with awareness.

"Eldress Mayapple, Eldress Mayapple!"

"*Deleto*," I whispered, focusing on her beady brown eyes and pointing my finger ever so subtly in her direction. The familiar dizziness crept in from the effort. Then I coughed so loudly my lungs hurt.

"Yes? What is it? What did you find?" There was immediacy in her voice. Her eyes tainted with condemnation.

"I, uh...uh." A vexed expression fell over her face like a shadow. "I need you and Lana to stop talking. You're breaking my concentration. How can I do my job, if I can't have quiet?"

The eldress's lips curled into a sneer of disapproval. Her foot tapped against the kitchen floor. "Well, if you haven't found anything by now, you're not going to. Whatever Laney thought she saw, she was wrong." The eldress glared at her oafish daughter with contempt for interrupting the test with her nonsense. "Let me check with Mistress Isobel out back. I'm ready to go. I knew this would be a waste of time. The Greensmith descendants, talented or not, have always been the most loyal of witches. The idea of one of them befriending a Mather or worse is unimaginable."

"All clear. Do you know they are actually growing soup and soap ingredients out there?"

"Probably a precaution to keep Judge Mather and his defense league unaware. We all have to take safety measures or he'll imprison each and every one of us. When I think of all our girls already in his detention center, it makes me want to act on the terrible things I dream of."

My fingers brushed against my own neck, listening to the anger in her boil over. She really was absorbed by the darkness.

"Sophie, what are those strange little moonflowers that resisted my plucking?"

They didn't need plucking. They were slowly dying on their own. An obvious reminder to me of my time left. "A hybrid accident." Sort of like me, I thought.

"Fascinating. You should have more accidents like that. I can't wait to see your herbalist talent at the Seeking."

"Be careful what you ask for," I said under my breath.

"Did you say something, Sophie?"

My lips tingled. "No."

The eldress chimed in. "I'm looking forward to the Seeking. It will truly be a surprise to see who are the most talented of our young witches." Her eyes rolled to Aunt Janie and me, sending goose bumps over my skin. "We're not expecting much from this household, but at least we can rule out disloyalty. That counts for something," she said, followed by a hearty laugh.

The devil's bit had done its job as well as could be expected under the eldress's pitiful truth spell, but my lack of focus had almost proved detrimental. The Council would have charged me with betrayal for my association with a Mather. It seemed no matter what I did, I was damned. I wondered if I truly belonged with the witches of Wethersfield under Eldress Mayapple's leadership. She was destroying all the good we could do for the community. I glanced at my watch. Aunt Janie needed me at the shop on time this morning.

I followed a group of tweens around, helping them sample Aunt Janie's new lip glosses. Forbidden Fruit was my favorite, containing flavors of pomegranate and quince, but the younger girls enjoyed the less intense glosses. As I glanced out the shop window, I saw Alexavier walking down the street in dark jeans and a black shirt, heading right for me. I tried to look away, but I couldn't resist. Even with the dark blue bruise above his eye and his lips slightly marred by the cut, he looked unfairly and devastatingly handsome. His square jaw, shadowed in just the right amount of black scruff, tensed. "Girls, help yourselves to the free samples of peppermints by the register. They're organic and made locally."

Why couldn't he leave me alone? Why couldn't I stop thinking about him? He pointed at me and curled his finger, suggesting I join him outside.

From behind the counter Macey winked, signaling me to go. I slammed out the door and grabbed the crook of his arm, dragging him behind the shop.

We stood there silent, facing each other as the words struggled to form on my tongue. He lifted a hand and grazed the skin on my forearm with one finger, igniting little tingly sparks along the way. I pressed on my stomach, calming the flutters while trying to remember to breathe. "It would appear your wrist is feeling better today."

I rolled my wrist around in a circular motion. Janie was right about the apple blossoms and witcheswort. My wrist felt good as new. "Uh-huh."

"Your aunt is an herbalist?"

"Uh-huh," was the most I could utter. The edginess between us vibrated like the wings of a honey bee, making it difficult to think about anything other than the pleasant, sweet tension. I gazed up into his eyes. "I want to know the secret you're holding so tightly to."

"You really want to know?" He circled behind me, not touching me, but I could feel him there, just an inch away. He stepped closer, his body heat warming my exposed neck.

I tried to ignore the trembles and craving his alluring voice provoked. Heat and tension continued to roll off him. My breathing quickened. "Secrets never stay secret in Wethersfield. It's going to slip out eventually."

He circled around to face me again and nodded. "Your curiosity is inexhaustible."

I pressed my hand to my forehead, trying to regroup, which was harder than it should have been. "Look. It doesn't matter. I can handle whatever it is."

"Zeke will be thrilled if he finds out what I'm about to tell you."
He shook his head, probably imagining the ugly scenario. "I come
from a long line of Mathers who have been more than unlucky in
love. A staggering number of them, so many that one cannot blame
it on misfortune or bad luck. For years, my father thought it was a
genetic fluke until he had our ancestor's DNA tested and, like his
own, it showed nothing." He rolled his sleeve up enough to show
me the pinkish birthmark on his wrist. It resembled a small heart
broken in two, exactly like Zeke's. "You see, from my father's
research, every Mather heir for centuries has carried this mark in
this spot. It is something passed down in our family, inherited, but
not genetic. That leaves only one explanation. Our bloodline is
cursed."

"Are you sure it's not Karma or bad luck?" We knew Francis had
been cursed for his father's hand in the hangings. But all of them? I
didn't think a generational curse was really possible.

"I don't believe in bad luck, but I do believe in the power of this
curse. It has haunted us through time."

"How many of you?"

"After they fell in love? Since Francis Mather, the one buried
under the tree next to your ancestor, all of them. Not at first. Some
of them were able to bear a child or two before their love deepened
and the curse took hold of one or both of them. It is why my father
used a surrogate rather than risk a relationship. He, Zeke, and I are
the last of Rev. Mather's direct descendants. It's too many to make
sense so all we are left with is the fact that we are cursed to live a
life without love or die from it."

I staggered backward, staring at the trees lining the path, in
shock. Elizabeth warned me about a curse living on. The judge even
sputtered on about a problem caused by the witches. Did they both
mean a generational curse on the Mathers? Generational curses were
only heard of in myths because they required great power and a dark
heart. Did Rebecca have that much power? "Let's say that's even
possible." I could barely grasp the possibility for the irony got in the
way. A curse cast by my ancestor meant to punish the Mathers was
now threatening not only my happiness, but my life.

"It is."

"Let's say it is." I swallowed hard. "Curses, even generational
ones, are meant to be broken. Has your dad not tried to remedy it?"

He looked to the sky, the frustration showing in his beautiful face. "We have tried all kinds of soothsayers, Hoodoo priestesses, and medicine men, believe it or not. Most of them were con artists, swindlers who lied to my father, frauds. The bad experiences only enraged his hate for all mystical beings."

Including my parents, I thought. My hands trembled. The hatred and pain mingled together, causing a stabbing sensation in my heart.

"A few weeks ago, he decided to bring us back from London when he realized the change in geography did nothing to affect it. That's the other big secret. You see, while we were there, my oldest brother, Marcus, professed his love to a British girl he had fallen for. A few weeks later, they were involved in a car accident." He looked away, his face pained with grief. "They both died."

I clasped my hand over my mouth. Aunt Janie had rightly remembered there were three boys. I had no idea. "So that's why you moved back."

"The tragedy left Zeke bitter and me with the realization that being a Mather was my cross to bear. Our only hope of living, is to live without love. There is no other remedy."

"That's not a remedy. That's the curse. So this is why you've been so conflicted about us? Why you won't kiss me again?"

He stared at me, the seriousness weighing heavy like lead. "I shouldn't have kissed you in the first place. I lost control of myself. I can't afford to do that anymore. For both our sakes."

"I lost control, too."

His pink lips pressed thin. He shook his head. "It was reckless. You have a life to live, a real life with someone who can love you and not condemn you to an early death. I won't take your life from you."

"What about me? Don't I get a say in this?"

He looked at me like I was crazy. "No."

"Yes, I do."

"I can keep you safe from the danger you seem to attract. That's easy," he said like it was nothing. "But there's nothing I can do to keep you safe from the inevitable death that comes with loving a Mather." He looked at me with his beautiful eyes as if to remind me he was danger. I didn't need a reminder. He exuded rebel. From his black as midnight hair to his sultry gray eyes, to his addiction to fire and his fast car. It was the reason he went out in rainstorms looking for fights.

"Keep me safe? I don't want safety. I want to be with you. Can't you see that?"

"Of course I can. God knows I've tried to keep my distance because of it." He paused and looked into my eyes. "What am I going to do with you, the way you're looking at me?"

"Kiss me."

His shoulders tensed along with his resolve to stay away from me. He held one hand up before turning away. "Please understand. I can't."

Frustrated and tired from a long day of selling flower-scented soaps and perfume pencils to tweens who didn't care about the judge's warnings on our products, I took my shoes off and walked home. As I approached my house, I saw a small crowd gathered out front. The front door opened. Three men led Aunt Janie out the door. My heart raced. Adrenaline filled my muscles. I dropped the objects in my hand and raced toward her, wanting to pummel the men stealing her away. Mistress Phoebe, in her Edwardian tea party finest, caught sight of me rushing toward the scene. As my foot landed with my next step, I faltered. A rough and unyielding rope grasped my ankle and pulled me backward behind the trunk of a thick weeping willow. I scraped at the binding around my ankle, but the bark surface of the tree root wouldn't budge. "Phoebe!" I eked out under my breath. Her spells on trees never failed. I glanced up, desperate. My breathing raced out of control. She calmly nodded and placed a cool finger to her lip, warning me to stay quiet.

Judge Mather marched toward Aunt Janie with a crooked police officer following behind. With one hand he gripped her slender arm while the officer faced her. "Jane Carrington, you are under arrest for public mischief."

Aunt Janie resisted with her small fists. "What are you talking about? I'm a law abiding citizen. I own a business and pay taxes."

"You are going to Kingshill where you will await trial."

"A trial that will never come," Mistress Phoebe whispered.

He turned his laser focus on Janie, shaking papers in his hand. "It is a shame there are women like you who pretend to be purveyors of organic, wholesome products when in reality you grow poisonous plants to put in your products with the intent to cause illness around our town."

He found the wolfsbane plants in the garden, I thought. In small, processed doses, it was a natural anesthetic, but Janie would never allow it to be used for anything more. They wouldn't believe that. My stomach sank.

"I don't use poison in my shop products. Those test results are false and you know it."

The judge, in his dark power suit, elbowed the officer in the arm. "Cuff her."

The blankness washed over her face and her eyes drifted away to her quiet place. Magic and hate surged and spun inside me, the fierce energy unyielding. There was no restraining it. The force thundered like horses racing to escape. Again, the liquid black ice began to course through the veins of my hands, the black magic tempting me. I raised my slender arm and pointed my index finger in his direction.

Then I saw him. My fiery heart turned cold. The whirl of emotions fizzled to a whimper. Everything went numb. The boy exited my house, catching up to his father and the other men participating in Janie's arrest.

Alexavier.

My face dropped into the grass. The rest of my body curled into a ball. I wanted to die.

I trusted him with our secrets when history told me I shouldn't. I was a fool and worse, a traitor. My numb hands clenched fistfuls of earth and uncontrollable weeping ensued.

As the adrenaline subsided, I loosened the binding root with a simple retracting spell and ran. I lost her and it was all my fault. I ignored the dizziness and ran as far as I could to the only place I could think of. Once inside the back room of the shop, I texted Macey and told her where to meet me. I was going to need backup.

Two hours later and several missed calls from him, I found myself leaning against the side of Judge Mather's house. A cold rage had replaced my devastation. I glanced at my watch. I couldn't wait any longer for her. I rushed to the front of the house, not caring which of the three opened the door. My hands quivered with an unbiased need to inflict my rage on someone.

My fist pounded on the door. Alexavier swept it open. "Sophie! Where have you been?"

I paused in disbelief as his cool mood raked over me. My gut twisted in a frenzy of emotion. How did he have the nerve to stand there and talk to me as if he weren't the reason for my worst nightmare? My bare feet twitched, ready to lunge my body at him. My fingers curled, prepared to grip his flesh.

His face froze. I looked beyond him. Everything froze in an odd, paused DVR kind of way. I nearly fell over, unsteady on my shifting feet. I wavered to balance myself. I stared at Alexavier again. He stood stiff. His expression still. I glanced around, looking for something to move.

"Don't do it, Sophie."

"Macey?"

She stepped from around the side of the house. "I heard what happened to your aunt, but this isn't the answer." She spoke with calm in her voice and slowly approached me.

My jaw clenched. "Don't tell me what to do. I'm here to let them know this whole Mather-witch thing is over. They are going down and I don't care if I go down with them. Do you hear me?"

She nodded. "I hear you. I know you're upset. But we need to focus on getting your Aunt Janie out of the detention center. And you don't even know Alexavier's side of the story. I don't know him that well, but I can't believe he had anything to do with it."

I stomped my foot on the ground. "You're wrong. I saw him with my own eyes."

"Then you don't see what I see."

"He followed his lunatic father out the door with my poor aunt in cuffs. In cuffs! He is guilty like every other bitter Mather who came before him, preying on powerful women."

"Sounding a little judge-and-mental there, huh? That's not like you, Sophie."

My temper softened as the venting I intended to unleash on the Mathers vented on Macey. I wiped a tear away, thinking of Aunt Janie, frail and stressed, zoned out in a wretched little cell with an iron lock. I shook myself out of the thought. "What's going on here? Why is he not moving and we are?"

She winked. "I can work a little magic of my own," she said, revealing why she never seemed ordinary.

My eyes widened as it hit me. "You're a time suspender." I remembered the French magic symbol for time on her tote. All those times she seemed to suddenly appear behind me—it made sense now. Manipulating time was a gift of her bloodline. It was how someone who liked to sleep in was never late to work.

Macey's eyes met mine with satisfaction. "My grandmother is a French sorceress. Now fix this," she said to me, stepping back so she was concealed behind a bush. With a snap of her fingers, Alexavier unfroze like a statue coming to life. He grabbed my hand and yanked me into the house, shutting the door behind us.

"Tell me why you were there today." My anger leveled off, but my stern tone imparted impatience.

Hurt shadowed his eyes. "You don't think I helped my father, do you?"

"Tell me. Now." My hands trembled.

"I didn't have time to warn you. I barely had time to get there myself."

"Why were you there at all?" The outrage vibrated in my voice.

"I couldn't stop him, but I figured if I knew where she was going, I could help you break her out. That's why I've been calling you."

The anger seeped out of me. My shoulders relaxed and I sighed. "How do I know you're telling the truth and this isn't a trap for me?"

He shook his head and held his hands out. "You have to trust me."

"But... But...I thought you told your..."

"Sophie, you know me. You know I would never do anything to intentionally hurt you." His eyes pleaded for understanding. "She's in cell D19. I can get you inside, but we're going to need more help once we're in there. Any ideas?" he asked, suggesting I might have some talented friends.

Tears of joy filled my eyes, veiling my vision. I leaned forward and kissed him on the lips. "Thank you. I will find some way to pay you back."

"Doing the right thing does not require payback."

It did in my book. Within minutes I dragged Macey into Alexavier's house and placed calls to those who could help us. Macey and I forged a plan before Riada and Adair arrived at the judge's house while Alexavier waited patiently. Riada gleefully brought me a pair of sandals for the mission, already suspecting I wasn't wearing anything on my feet. We were all risking something by attempting a breakout, but maybe Alexavier more than anyone. I would never forget that.

Alexavier and I drove in his car while the twins rode with Macey in her little red VW bug. We headed toward Kingshill Detention Center. The country roads were dark, illuminated only by our headlights. Silence engulfed the car interior as we waited to arrive in the back parking lot. Without a word, we crept through the overgrown grounds to the main door, ignoring the screech owls in the trees above and the rustling of field mice around our feet. Each of us knew our part to perform. Macey and I hid in the bushes next to the entrance. Alexavier rang the night bell, alerting the guard at the front desk.

Riada and Adair stood behind him holding their hands so it looked like they were handcuffed. "Good evening."

"Good evening, Mr. Mather. What do you have there?" the guard asked, looking around him at the twins.

"Two more to be detained. My father is on a roll."

"Yes, he certainly is. We're almost full up, at least three girls to a cell as it is now. It'll sure be nice when he breaks ground on the new addition." He paused, seeming to sense something was off, but he wasn't going to question a Mather. "Bring the detainees in."

With a snap of her fingers, Macey suspended the guard. The two of us snuck in around him while Alexavier and the twins watched in awe. He told us the night shift had the least amount of guards on duty. Once inside, we would be able to locate Aunt Janie's cell without interference, but he wanted us to maintain caution, and we needed to hurry because we didn't know how long Macey's magic would hold.

The overwhelming sterile smell of rubbing alcohol and lemony ammonia followed us as we found the stairway to the second floor. We raced up. The eerie sound of submissive moans and collective whimpers filled the hall beyond the door. I cracked it open and peeked.

"All clear," I whispered. We dashed through the white tiled corridor under the dim flickering fluorescent lights. A chill washed over me. I stopped in my tracks, sensing we were in the presence of a spirit.

"Who are you?"

Get out while you can. Terrible things happen here. Ungodly. Get out, he moaned. Despair drenched his young voice.

"Who are you?"

My name is Jefferson. My parents brought me here before the war. Terrible things they did to me. Drilled a hole right in my head. Terrible things they still do.

"Before the war?" The psych hospital opened before World War II. He must have been young when he died. "Jefferson, I'll get out as fast as I can, but I need to find D19."

Macey nudged me. "Who are you talking…?" An ethereal form materialized in front of us, glowing as if he had swallowed a star and it illuminated from within him. Macey gripped my hand hard and stepped behind me. "You can conjure spirits, too?"

"I'm definitely not a conjurer. More of a magnet, since they seem to find me." He was a young African-American boy, looked to be around ten with a sad misty expression. He lifted his hand and pointed to a cell seven doors down.

"You should get of here, too, Jefferson. And thanks." He smiled ever so slightly and disappeared into a wall.

We reached the door and looked above. Printed in black was D19. It was my turn. I pointed my index finger at the iron lock.

"Aperi."

The lock clanked and rotated within. I turned the iron knob, feeling the heat tingle against my cool palm, but it wouldn't budge. I should have expected the metal to be unyielding. Please, I thought. I closed my eyes and concentrated.

"Aperi," I commanded, demanding it open. The energy in my voice swelled as I pictured Janie behind the door. Magic tickled my finger as it released. I gripped the knob again. This time it twisted with ease. I pushed and slipped in with Macey behind me, ignoring the lightheadedness.

I spied Aunt Janie lying in her tiny cot. Two other cots were jammed into the cell, the girls asleep.

"Aunt Janie. Aunt Janie!" I gently shook her by the shoulder, desperate to wake her. What if she fell into the blankness? What if I was too late?

She moaned. "Sophie?"

"Yes. It's me, Aunt Janie. Are you okay? Can you stand up?"

She mustered enough strength to roll on her side.

"I saw you coming to break me out. I held onto that."

I leaned down and hugged her like it had been ten years since we were apart, ignoring the rough feel of the polyester orange detention center uniform gaping around her frail frame.

She sensed my deep distress. "It's okay, dear. I'm okay."

"Good." I glanced anxiously at the sleeping girls. "What about them?"

"They won't make it tonight. Too drugged up. I stuffed my pills in the hollow of my cheeks."

Tears welled up in my eyes. My fists tightened. "When it's time, I'll make sure they get out, but we don't have much time right now." I clasped her hand, which felt weak, but warm and steady. Macey checked the hallway.

"All clear."

I slid her arm over my shoulders to support some of her weight and Macey took her other arm. We retraced our steps back to the stairwell and crept down and out to the first floor hall where we stopped in our tracks. The guard was moving. Macey, about to snap her fingers again, hesitated. We stared, our mouths wide open.

Riada and Adair entertained themselves as they flicked their fingers at the poor guard, taking turns reading his mind and imparting a new memory as if they were flipping through the channels on a television. Alexavier must have trusted the girls to handle the guard. He stood outside, waiting and keeping watch.

"Aunt Janie, I'm going to help you outside and then Alexavier will take you to his car. He'll keep you safe."

Instincts and history told her to argue, or maybe she already saw him driving the getaway car. She gave a slight nod. Alexavier met us at the main door and lifted her in his capable arms. "I've got her. Grab the twins and let's go."

"We need a few minutes. Macey and I need to take care of something first." I hurried back to the twins. "Psst." Riada looked up, a big smile on her face. "Are you good with him?"

She waved us on. We still needed to clear the computer memory of Janie's record. We stepped into the guard's office and Macey tapped away on the keyboard. With a few clicks of the mouse, Janie's record was deleted. "Thank you," I said.

"What are friends for?"

We approached the twins. "Finish up with him. We'll meet you outside."

"We're going to make him think the two of us were selling cookies," the girls said together. They laughed melodically.

After checking on Aunt Janie, I threw on a shirt and flannel shorts and slipped between the soft cotton sheets. I left my light on, hoping Elizabeth would pay me a visit through the journal tonight. The book sat there, silent. My head sunk into the down pillow and a song hummed in my throat.

The tumultuous gray clouds heaved and moaned above the house. Rain streaked across the upstairs window panes in jagged paths as the wind gusted. I shuddered and rubbed my arms, suddenly feeling silk beneath my fingertips. My hands pressed down along the cool, blue silk skirt of the formal gown. Nervousness wrapped around me. I began to hyperventilate, but my ribcage couldn't expand against the binding corset-like stay. I tried to walk, but my toes felt pinched. I tugged the hem of the gown up and stuck my foot out only to see the most beautiful, hand sewn, white leather slippers with silver buckles. I rubbed my hands together, feeling something new. I looked, spying the bride's ring on my finger. The ruby gemstone seemed familiar as I stared solemnly at it, feeling the gold grip my finger like an iron claw.

A scratch at the window caught my attention. I spun around. A tree branch clawed at the window like a determined skeletal hand wanting in. My heart pulsed loudly in my ears, drowning out the harpsichord playing from downstairs. I stumbled into the hallway. Candlelight glowed from the wall sconces, casting eerie shadows around my feet. The girl hummed her haunting melody.

My journal regards both of us. Open your eyes and see, she whispered.

I lifted my head warily and glanced up from beneath my eyelashes to see the reflection in the gold gilt hallway mirror. Eldress Mayapple grasped a small object in her hand. With a flash of her wrist, she revealed the iron figurine with its nearly severed head and its resemblance to me was undeniable.

I shot up. "No!"

My agonized scream pierced the air. I kicked and wrestled the sheets off me, gasping for breath. I wrapped my hands around my sides, searching for the iron statuette then I glanced down, searching for the ring. Neither was there. What did it mean?

The foreboding dream left me uneasy. I crept downstairs and out the back door. From the garden I plucked a handful of red corn poppies, inhaling the hazy floral fragrance until sleep drew me back to bed.

In the morning, I checked on Aunt Janie again. She rested soundly in her bed. I tiptoed downstairs, recalling the details of the dream: the mirror's horrifying reflection, me in the dress, the raging storm, and the ring. After the detention center breakout and the foreboding dream, I couldn't handle work, so for the first time in my life, I called in sick and delved my restless mind into my old copy of Romeo and Juliet. The play seemed suddenly like an enlightening glimpse into my life, a how-to for dealing with warring families and ill-fated love. I had read the play a dozen times before, but it suddenly seemed as if I were viewing it through fresh eyes.

I sat up, realizing the answers I needed weren't in the play. Alexavier shared his family secret with me, but I refused to accept the finality of it. Aunt Janie would be asleep for another hour after the amount of valerian I put in her tea. I grabbed the phone and called the one person who might be able to help me. Fifteen minutes later, I stood on her porch, which jutted out from her small home that was built around the largest and oldest tree in Wethersfield.

My godmother, Mistress Phoebe, greeted me in a long, Victorian-style dress with a high collar and a dainty tiara with diamonds shaped like dewdrops she liked to wear indoors for whimsy's sake. Her usual gold key brooch glimmered on her dress. She peered behind me to make sure I came alone.

"Thank you for calling and letting me know your aunt is home safe. Now, come in. I know you have questions and I'll try to help you, but you must promise to keep this between us."

"Promise."

She led me to her blue parlor and gestured to take a seat on the blue Edwardian settee next to her. She summoned Marleigh, her wood sprite who wore a clingy green dress of moss. "Cornflower tea, please, Marleigh." Little Marleigh nodded and took off to the kitchen, her green lacy wings flapping wildly behind her. Phoebe properly folded her hands together and rested them on her lap, her posture impeccable. "Now, what do you want to know?"

I rubbed my hands together, wanting to appear calm, but now that I knew what I needed to do, I wanted to know how to do it yesterday. "I owe a debt. I need to know how to break a spell."

"You never ask for anything, now you're asking for something so difficult?"

"If you don't know how to break a spell, tell me what you do know."

Her lips pressed together as she considered my request. "Open your eyes, dear Sophie," she said. She gestured to my pendant, which had slipped out on the run over to her house.

"What do you mean?"

"Didn't your aunt tell you about your mother's charm?"

"Not much," I said, not wanting her to think Aunt Janie wouldn't approve.

She looked upward and shook her head, seeming concerned. "Did you know that our witch ancestors were given pieces of special jewelry by the English king as a thank you for our clairvoyant gifts and healing cure-alls?"

"I'd heard something like that recently."

"Our foremothers enchanted these pieces and they have been passed down through each family along with the responsibilities that come with them."

I shook my head. "I had no idea about that."

"You see," she said, gesturing toward her gold key brooch. "This is a real key to a very important door. I am the keeper of an enchanted portal, just as my mother was during her lifetime here in Wethersfield. The door is the entrance to a secret passageway to Essex in England. Your family heirloom is the stone in your pendant, which was previously set in your mother's ring. It was her bloodcharm, passed down through generations of witches in your family and now, to you."

"Passageway? Aunt Janie told me nothing about that. I mean, she may have hinted that you could travel to England without a plane or a boat, but I had no idea."

Her lips puckered. "And what of the ring? What has she told you?"

"She's too fragile to talk about my mother for any length of time. I think she's scared."

She frowned. "Yes. She knows you were destined to be a very talented spellcaster, more talented than your mother. She feared the power from the bloodcharm paired with your gift would make you a target, a pawn for the black witches and with her visions of the future…"

"But I'm not that talented. I make mistakes all the time."

She tilted her head back and forth as she weighed the pros and cons of telling me more. "From what I've seen, I have to agree with you. It may be too early to tell, but your spells have been less than expected, probably because of your father's ordinary bloodline." She tilted her head, weighing the consequences. "I suppose I don't see the harm in telling you what you should know since you are the keeper of the Greensmith charm."

My godmother was unaware of the recent improvement in my gift and I wanted to keep it that way for as long as possible. "Telling me what?"

"First, you must understand your aunt would never do anything to hurt you or deceive you if she didn't think it was for your own safety."

Her intentions were always good when it came to me. I wasn't angry, but I was old enough for the truth. "Tell me of the blood charm."

"You mean, can a blood charm break a spell?"

I nodded.

"Naturally, but I'm not sure how powerful a spell you're looking to break. You see, a blood charm's power depends on two things: the power of the witch and the type of stone. The rarer, the better. Whose spell are you trying to break?" Marleigh buzzed back into the parlor with a large silver tea tray, which looked like it weighed more than she did. She set the tray down on the table between us and began pouring the dark blue tea into two porcelain cups. Beside the cups, a small porcelain plate was filled with sugared purple pansy petals. The steam swirling above the cups smelled of cornflowers and hibiscus. She drizzled honeysuckle nectar into one of the teacups and handed it to Phoebe before buzzing out of the room.

She plucked a petal and let it dissolve on her tongue, her eyes closed for a moment as she savored the sweetness.

"I think the spell belongs to an old eldress. Rebecca."

She sipped from her delicate cup. "Uh-huh, and it lives on? A perpetual one?"

I nodded. "Generational."

She pinched her chin with her thumb and forefinger, pensive. "I don't think you are up to breaking a former eldress's spell. Generational, too. That requires some doing. But if we are speaking hypothetically, if her magic was strong enough to last through time and the blood charm and the power of the witch canceling it was rare and strong, all you would need is to be up to the test and the proper spell to break it, of course." She took another sip of the blue tea.

I had a good idea where to get the spell. "That's it?"

She gauged my contemplative expression and set her cup onto its saucer. She wagged a finger at me. "No. No. No. You can't think about doing that. Even a strong witch would have to know from deep in her bones that she could harness the blood charm's energy. Channel it through her touch. Feel its power merge with her own. Once the cohesive bond is made, it enhances the witch's abilities by tenfold. But that tenfold power would have to at least match the power of the witch who cast the generational spell. If she is not strong enough, breaking that kind of spell could kill her. It's like swallowing another's magic with heaven knows what kind of poison is in it. A strong witch has to know how to take the curse's power, nullify it with her own energy, and spit it out as harmless waste, so to speak. That kind of expertise takes years."

I rubbed my face with my hands. "Why can't anything ever be easy?"

She pursed her lips. "The greater the challenge, the greater the rewards. Now tell me of this debt you owe." She plucked another sugared petal with its glistening sweet crystals and plopped it on her tongue. She paused as it melted and washed it down with a sip of tea.

How could I explain to her I owed a Mather my life? I couldn't. She would never understand and she was obligated as my witch godmother to protect me. "That's not important. I need practice. Can you curse something and I'll try to undo it using the blood charm?"

Her lips formed a frown. "Oh, my dear. Cursing is only possible through black magic. I don't practice that. No one in our families has." The corners of her eyes crinkled. Her posture went rigid. "Except Eldress Rebecca. Are you telling me she cast a generational curse, a curse, and you're thinking about breaking it?"

I nodded.

She slid her teacup onto the tray, sloshing blue liquid over the rim. Her finger wagged at me. "No. Out of the question. Impossible."

"Why? What if it's my responsibility to do that with the Greensmith charm?"

"Out of the question! Your responsibility? She was a powerful, dark eldress. The only way you can break her black magic curse is with equal power. And that means embracing black magic, which still wouldn't be enough in your case. Besides that, I forbid it. So does every one of your ancestors and witch sisters."

I closed my eyes and sighed. I didn't need her to tell me I couldn't do it when she already said it was possible. "What if I did take that path? Would I be able…?"

"Sophie Goodchild!" Her face drained whiter than it already was. "You would never survive the reconversion and, even if you did, the blackness never goes away. Not really. A piece of it stains your soul forever. Forever. Tempting you back. Forever. This curse is not worth your precious soul I have sworn to protect as your godmother."

I left her house with my lips tingling from promises to never consider that course of action. Then I dashed home, ready to practice with the charm, now that I understood what it could do.

By dusk, my stomach grumbled, reminding me I had spent my afternoon practicing simple spells paired with the power of the blood charm. The magic came out wobbly and lopsided at first, draining me dizzy, but I persevered with some minor success As I entered the kitchen, needing to make a sandwich, the doorbell rang. I cautiously unlocked the door.

As I peered at the visitor, a happy dance ensued. "Callum!" He stood there with his hands in his cargo short pockets. "What are you doing here?" I asked, thrilled to see him. Callum may have been big for his age, but he reminded me of a playful puppy with big paws and lots of determination to have fun.

"Hey. I was bored and thought maybe we could rent *Zombie Apocalypse Four*."

I wanted to tell him how glad I was that he was here, but he usually preferred sarcasm over sentiment. "You make me feel so special," I said wryly.

"Is this a bad time?"

"Nah. Come on in." I opened the door fully and watched him fill the opening.

He eyed my head suspiciously. "What's up with your hair?"

I touched my hands to the dark chestnut strands, the texture resembling a wavy mop. "Rough day." My appearance was the least of my concerns.

He laughed his warm laugh. "Too worn out to see me?"

I looked up at him with a grouchy expression. "Not possible."

"So what's for dinner?"

I stretched my soft, worn T-shirt out on both sides. "Do I look like I'm cooking?"

"No, more like a worn out ghost, but I'm a growing boy and I'm starving." He touched his hand to the top of his head to emphasize his height.

"I think you're done growing." He didn't need to get any taller.

He smiled with anticipation, ignoring my comment.

"I think we have stuff for cheese sandwiches or granola bars. You game?"

"Mmm. Sandwich." He patted his stomach.

I rolled my eyes at him, trying to stifle the inevitable laugh he always inspired. I curled my finger and gestured to him. "Follow me." I pulled a chair out for him at the kitchen table. I layered arugula and cucumber on my bread, and slapped circles of provolone cheese between two slices of wheat bread for him. I poured two glasses of orange thyme iced tea and set the plates on the table. "So what's up?"

"I didn't have anything else to do so I figured we could kill some time together."

My lips twisted into a smirk. "Huh. Being bored and wanting me to entertain you doesn't sound like much of a compliment."

His nose crinkled and his lips flattened. "Since when do you need compliments?"

"I guess I don't."

"Good!" he said, munching into the soft sandwich. He talked with his mouth full, letting a few crumbs fall onto his plate. "I have a secret to tell."

I frowned as I swallowed a chunk of cucumber. I washed it down with a swig of cold tea. I wasn't the kind of witch that liked gossip, and secrets were a whole lot worse. "The trouble with secrets is that we keep the ones we should be telling. If you're getting ready to share yours, it's probably not worth sharing."

His mouth full of sandwich hung open, feigning offense. "That's harsh, but I swear this is a good one. Someone likes you," he mumbled and then gulped.

My heart jumped. I hadn't heard from Alexavier since the Kingshill breakout and it had everything to do with his family's secret curse. Even though I entertained Cal at the moment, my mind worked on the problem. "Go on?" I watched each subtle movement of his lips, waiting for the name to form. I sipped my tea.

"D—rew."

I choked. Iced tea spewed from my nostrils. My eyebrows furrowed as surprise settled in. "Drew? Daniel's brother?"

"You don't remember him from the boat? That's harsh." He slapped his hand on the table, amused with the situation.

I wiped my face with a napkin. "No. No. I remember. He was wearing skinny jeans. I just...never mind." He was the boy going through an awkward growth spurt with the unruly mop of brown hair that matched the mottled stubble on his lower face. "I was right. Not worth sharing."

"Not worth sharing because there is someone else?"

I smiled and tossed the balled up paper napkin at him. We finished our sandwiches and Callum decided that because of my pale complexion I required fresh air instead of the zombie movie. I finger combed my hair and dragged him out back. A pair of orioles nipping at the feeder flitted above us and scattered. "Have a seat." I pointed to the bench under the arbor.

"How about having some fun?"

A smile engaged my cheeks. "I always have fun with you. See, that's a compliment." He smiled a big wide grin in return. He eyed the garden and its elemental terraces. "Ha! Here's a deal. If I can teach you something about your garden that you don't know, then you have to have fun with me." He reached up to touch the crimson wisteria.

It seemed like an offer I couldn't refuse. What could Callum possibly know about gardening that a Greensmith descendant didn't? "Deal!"

"Hmmm. Let's see what your Aunt Janie's got here." He summoned me toward him. He knelt down beside a small bed of plants.

"You don't know anything about this!" I scoffed.

His eyes sharpened as I challenged him. "My mom taught me a lot. She's really into herbs."

"I guessed that about her since she always seems thrilled when a shipment of exotic and hybrid plant ingredients show up for Aunt Janie's products."

"Follow along." He glanced at the array of plants growing, sniffing a few different blossoms, including my poppies.

"Uh, you should be careful with those."

He shook a finger at me, irked with my interference. "You have all kinds of interesting stuff here."

I chuckled at him. "Of course, we do. The women in my family all had green thumbs, including me."

He waved his hands over a leafy plant bed like a celebrity chef slathering his attention on the fresh herbs for a recipe. "See here..." He pointed to a thriving row of leaves. "That's California dandelion lined up in front of the black rose bushes."

Their small yellow blooms reminded me of a tiny lion's head with a full mane of fur around it. "Do you know what that kind of dandelion is used for?"

I thought back to my childhood lessons. "California dandelion root makes you pee, cures liver problems, and the leaves can be used in salads." Most of Janie's perpetual teachings had stuck.

"Fine, smarty pants. Over here, these velvety spikes—that's Twickel lavender. Lavender is useful for achy muscles, soothing burns, and when added to tea, helps you sleep."

"Twickel, impressive."

"Did I stump you?"

"I had forgotten about the achy muscles, but I did know it was Twickel and about the sleep part, although Parisian lavender is better for sleep. I have a pillow filled with it, but the summery scent doesn't always help me."

"Scary dreams of Alexavier waking you up?"

I sighed. "A weird dream and neither you nor Alexavier were in it."

He scratched his head as he looked at me. I waited for the snarky reply. My hand readied to punch him in the arm.

"You really do have the craziest blue eyes—uh, crazy as in pretty, not cuckoo," he clarified.

An awkward silence fell between us as he continued to stare at my eyes. We had been friends forever, but this felt different...and uncomfortable. I turned my face away from him. "Come on, Callum."

"That was a compliment, by the way," he said. His cheeks took on a rosy glow as if he were embarrassed, too. An evening breeze whipped up around us scented with the strong, sweet perfume of the white-flowering nicotiana. He returned his attention to the plants. "Your aunt is a specific kind of gardener, huh?"

"What do you mean?"

"I mean that everything in this garden is used by the Tribe of Yoruba. Ever heard of them?"

I shook my head no. I didn't know anything about these tribesman, but after seeing Macey suspend time, I wondered how many people were out there pretending to be ordinary.

"My mom and I practice the tribe's white magic, which is based on nature. That's how I know so much. Even this dwarf golden apple tree is familiar to me." He touched the leaves on the tree, examining their color and shape. "You know, if you cut the apple in half around its equator..."

"You see a five-pointed star." I wasn't trying to show off. The answer rolled off my tongue before I could stop it. "White magic, huh?"

"Yup."

"My aunt is simply an enthusiastic gardener and herbalist."

He winked. "Uh-huh. Sure she is."

My nose crinkled. "What does that mean?"

"It means she's growing the same kind of plants my mom is growing."

Witches were so concerned with maintaining our secrecy that we never looked around to see if there were others, like Mr. Oloy from the rare book shop, and Macey, practicing their own kind of magic. I wondered how he would react if he knew what I was. I laughed to myself, already knowing. It wouldn't faze him a bit. "How does she use plants in her magic?"

"Holistic medicines and cure-alls, sort of like your aunt, but not as fancy."

I nudged his shoulder with my fingers. "You're a mess, Cal."

"Yeah, like your hair." He burst into a laugh. I didn't join him. "Okay, seriously. See over there," he said, pointing to the tree in front of the stone wall, at the end of our property. "See the ivy clinging to the weeping willow?" he stood tall, his white T-shirt, damp from sweating, clung to his broad chest. "The ivy brings good luck. Something tells me you need that."

"I'll be sure to drape myself in it." I swallowed hard, recalling the iron figurine in the eldress's hands from my dream.

Callum playfully imitated the ivy with his arms dangling over my head, his fingers entangling in my hair. He laughed again, a deep hearty laugh.

"Cal, do you believe in ghosts?"

"Nope."

I thought of Elizabeth and her diary and poor Jefferson stuck at Kingshill. "Maybe you should." He smirked at my childlike notion, but the seriousness in his eyes made me think he really did believe. "If they could communicate with us, why would they do it?"

"That's it. No more horror movies for you."

"Seriously."

He smirked. "I don't know. To scare us. Maybe to warn us."

"Maybe to keep us from repeating the past?"

"Hey—I don't want to talk about ghosts anymore. You're giving me the creeps." He mockingly rubbed his arms, pretending to be scared.

My face tensed. "It's not all about you."

He stepped back, looking appalled. "Said no one ever!" We broke into a fit of laughter. I could never stay irritated with Cal. "I'll tell you what I really think." He lowered his voice to a whisper as if someone was listening. "I think you're talking crazy."

I unintentionally matched his whisper. "That's why we get along so well…cuckoo birds of a feather."

He pressed his finger into my shoulder and nudged me back. "Forget about that," he said, rubbing his hands together like he was getting ready for something. It was easy to forget about stressful things when I was with him. He exuded a nothing-will-happen-to-you kind of air that was like a cushion. His voice returned to its booming volume. "Time for fun."

"Nope!" I teased.

He grabbed me by the shoulders and eyed my slender legs sticking out from the flannel shorts. "A deal is a deal." He contemplated his next move. "Hey—that tree?" He pointed to the ancient weeping willow again, growing tall and wild.

"What about it?"

"How fast can you run?"

"I'm so not racing you. Your legs are a mile long!"

He nudged my shoulder again and whispered, "Fun…"

"Stop it. I'm not racing you."

"That's because you know you'll lose. That's all right. I understand." Condescension saturated his tone.

My lips formed a pout. I crinkled my forehead irritably. I knew what he was doing, but I took the bait anyway, curiosity not letting me ignore it. "Understand what?"

"You're just a girl. What if I give you a head start?" he provoked as he ignored my stubbornness.

I rolled my eyes. "You're an idiot."

"Oh—that's so not a compliment!" he scoffed.

My temper heated. "Fine. You want to race, I'll race. I'll show you," I snapped as I launched forward into a run before he could start to count. The wind rushed through my hair. Before I knew it, I was sprinting over the terraces, my stride as long as my legs could stretch, like a wild rabbit, extending its entire sinuous body. All I could hear were my feet pounding the earth beneath me and a whoosh of motion behind me as he worked to catch up.

Callum's longer, stronger legs stretched farther and he passed me in no time, staring back at me with an easy, confident smile. I stared straight ahead paying him no attention, but my efforts were useless. He slapped his hand against the bark of the willow and pumped his arms up and down in the air victoriously. He leaned against the trunk with a carefree expression as if racing me hadn't even been a challenge.

I panted, putting my hands on my thighs and leaning over to catch my breath. My hair draped all around my face in loose, messy waves. "That wasn't fun."

"Yes, it was. Winning is always fun and I'm the winner," he childishly bragged, doing a Rocky dance with his fists in the air.

I flipped my head up and lunged angrily at him. He grabbed my arms to thwart my attack, but it was too late. He lost his balance, taking me with him. We tumbled onto the grass, breathless. He threw his arms over me to brace himself against the ground so we wouldn't collide.

"Whew! You sure can run fast when you're pushed. For a moment, I didn't think I was going to win."

"You are an idiot," I muttered again as I wiped the hair from my eyes and caught my breath. "You did all that just to get a reaction out of me, didn't you?"

"You needed someone to. You look half asleep and all that talk about ghosts…"

His sweaty body hovered only inches above mine. He slightly pressed his weight against my hips and tilted his head, listening to my erratic breathing. His eyes focused on my lips, causing a strange tension between us. He gazed into my eyes.

I didn't want to see what I knew was there. I shuffled out from under him, shoving him off me. When he got to his feet, I pushed him away, although he barely budged from my efforts.

"Callum...don't," I stated seriously.

At that moment, the quiet of the property shattered. A loud, peeling crack echoed, followed by the loud clanging of a large metallic object being ripped from whatever it was attached to. The sound came from the Mather's property. Our heads snapped in that direction. Callum's eyes widened.

"Probably construction noise," I assured him, who, for a big tough guy, now seemed anxious.

"There's no construction going on around here," he replied, jumping up to look over the fence.

"Maybe it was a ghost," I whispered. "Since I'm just a girl, why don't you go look around? Don't forget to take some ivy with you."

His amber eyes stayed focused, his body alert. He exhaled loudly. "No. Maybe you're right. Construction. I'm good and it's time for me to go."

"It's not that late," I complained, tugging on his arm.

"Sophie, it's dark and I have to get home. See you tomorrow and don't do anything stupid like going out there to investigate by yourself. Okay?"

"Are you afraid for me?" I asked.

His eyes nearly popped out. "Maybe."

He pressed his lips tight and shook his head as if saying the words would make something bad happen. His eyes flickered to the left and the right. "Don't go looking, Sophie."

"Fine," I sighed, disappointed in his lack of action, but I wasn't afraid. Besides, the noise didn't seem to come from too far away.

I followed him back to the front gate and watched him leave. Then I raced back and slid through the hedges. I stepped lightly onto the Mather's property and searched in the direction of the clatter. As I walked around, I tumbled over an object, long and clangy.

"Ow!" I yelled. I landed hard, hands first. I stared back at it. A six-foot-long piece of metal gutter with jagged edges and loose screws all around it. I stood up and ran my hands over the delicate skin on my legs, wiping away the grass and debris. Who would do this? I glanced around. There were no workers in sight. No one at all. I thought I heard footsteps growing fainter, but darkness blanketed their yard.

17.

Sunlight crept through my window, reminding me I had been awake for hours, trying to get Elizabeth's enchanted journal to reveal more. Finally, the pages began rustling and blowing. A familiar cool shiver went through me as I touched my hand to the book.

Before I passed, I shared my visions of what was to come with my sister Evie, the spellcaster. She granted me a dying wish that I might one day be able to change that vision. She enchanted this journal and when I passed, my ring became hers, then in time, became yours. Our shared bloodcharm.

"Wait a minute."

Sophie, I have waited a long time for your arrival. And I am so pleased the statuette, regardless of the darkness it represents, brought awareness to you as I hoped it would. Awareness of our connection, of our shared destiny, of our hidden enemies.

"So her spell allowed you to come to me in a vision?"

Yes.

"How did you make the journal and iron statuette appear, and the Celtic coins?" The scratching sound of the invisible quill pen filled my ears.

Part of her gift to me was to be able to get the objects to you when the time was right.

"I have so many questions. Like why does the bloodcharm hum?"

The stone reacts to the magic in our bloodline and when the magic surges, the stone vibrates.

My brow crinkled as I considered what she was telling me. "Why did it grow hot when Alexavier Mather returned it to me?"

The last time the stone was touched by both a Mather and a witch was when Francis declared his love for me, holding my left hand where the stone rested. This, along with the intensity of your mutual love, caused the stone to heat, a magnification of your feelings. You are meant to be together, but it will not be without difficulty. I was not strong enough to fight against Rebecca's black magic and her curse on the Mathers, but you are. You are the one.

"That's impossible. I can't be the one. I'm only a half-witch. It makes me an outsider with my own kind and the ordinaries, too. And I make so many mistakes. I'm impetuous and..."

You are different. Being different make you stronger and your impetuous nature is a sign of your passion for living. These traits, as well as the bloodcharm, and the book to undo Rebecca's spell, will serve you if you dare, but it will require something more. Something you must find on your own, within yourself, which you locked away long ago.

I grabbed hold of my pendant. The only way to break Rebecca's curse was to use the same magic she did to make it, plus find this missing thing within me, whatever that was. My fear was that no white witch had ever changed back after choosing black magic, and if I did, I would be changed forever, a part of me tainted by the darkness, forever tempting me to return as Phoebe warned. I considered the decision I had to make because I would also be betraying my aunt, my godmother, my bloodline, and everything I held sacred. I thought of Alexavier. I could see no other way to free him from Rebecca's curse of a life lived without love. Then I thought of the judge and what he had done to my parents. Vengeance would come easily once my heart was blackened.

I ran downstairs to the Flower Library where I had hidden Rebecca's Book of Dark Spells. I opened it and leafed through, hoping something would catch my eye. I saw it. The spell she cast to curse the Mathers. On the opposite page was another. Blank spaces within the spell indicated words were cloaked. I closed my eyes and hummed the haunting melody I heard during my dream. As I recalled each note that should have been lost through time, the tune radiated from my throat, and the missing words appeared, filling in the blanks. Rebecca did not want anyone using this spell. It was the last entry and the only one partially cloaked—the spell to undo her true love curse. I studied and memorized each word. A few lines were difficult to read. As I read the recipe list below the spell, I noticed a special ingredient was needed. All the items but one were things I could scrounge up at the shop. I grimaced and returned the book to its hiding spot. All I could think about was how it was my turn to take care of Alexavier.

I quickly dressed, plucking a shirt and shorts from my dresser drawers. I dashed to the garden and pressed a devil's bit blossom to my lips. I grabbed the key to the shop and a small black duffel bag before shutting the door behind me.

As I walked through the town toward Scents and Scentsabilities, I tried to squelch the nausea, afraid the hydrangeas, which lined the front of the store, would get splattered with the worst of my stress. I pressed my hands to my head as dizziness overwhelmed me. I glanced around. There were people milling about in front of the eateries and shopping in the boutiques.

Inside the store, I left the lights off, not wanting to alert anyone to my presence. I quietly stepped to the back room and flipped on the single dangling lightbulb. The light was enough to help me see what I needed.

On tippy toes I reached for the wide-mouthed glass jar up high, gently tugging it from its hiding spot. I set it on a lower shelf, lifted the lid, and scooped a handful of dried black rose petals into my palm. I grabbed a small glass vial and a large sachet bag and dropped the petals into the sachet. The drawstring tightened with a tug. I shimmied the jar back to its spot and searched for the twigs I would need for the binding; birch for mystical energy, golden dwarf apple for love and family, and willow for death—Rebecca's spirit and the curse. I took a few strands of dried sacred sweet grass for peace and wrapped them tightly around the three twelve inch twigs. I stuffed everything, including a small knife from the shelf, in the duffel bag and zipped it up, committed to what I was going to do, what I had to do.

Wouldn't the Council be surprised when I showed them my herbalist trick, I thought. I locked the door and stuffed the key back in my pocket.

Later that day, I listened to Mrs. Dayo whistle a song as she tidied up around the shop. I walked past the front window only to see a familiar, but unexpected face outside approaching. I did a double take. Laney strolled through the door wearing all black, her white blonde hair adding an extreme in contrasts. She had to be in the wrong place. I summoned the most polite greeting I could muster for her. "Can I help you, Laney?"

She eyed me up and down as she ran a red, forked-tongue nail across her lower lip. "Nice apron you got there, Martha Stewart," she snickered. "Have you heard the good news?"

"What's that, G-Reaper?" I took a whiff and realized the smell of stale cigarette smoke was wafting off her. The muscles in my hand tightened around the bottle of Innocent Hyacinth perfume, resisting the urge to spritz her.

"Ha. Good one. Not. Several of our sisters have been released from Kingshill. The therapists released them." She uncapped a bottle of white willow bark ointment, the hemorrhoid reliever, and rubbed a dab on her hand and her neck before recapping it. I bit my lip to keep from laughing. "Said the girls didn't need converting."

"Huh?" I tried to focus on what she was saying.

"I don't know why I bother with you. I only came down here to meet someone."

I set the perfume bottle down and tried not to breathe in the mix of white willow and cigarettes. "No. Go on. I want to know."

She rolled her eyes up to the ceiling like she was totally doing me a favor. "My mother is keeping them at Cross Manor for safekeeping and the judge is totally pissed off, sent out a search party for them. He'll never find them, and it was his therapists who set them loose. Mistress Isobel has cast a psychic fog around our house that the ordinaries' eyes will never be able to penetrate."

Before I could even ask how, I realized I already knew. Riada and Adair returned to Kingshill to free the other girls, working their magic on the therapists' minds. The released girls were a promising group filled with charm makers, mind readers, and conjurers. "That is good news. I'm sure your mother is pleased to have them back." *And under her roof*, I thought. *Safekeeping, my butt.* Tensions were escalating and she was padding her team. "So did you come here to shop, because that perfume you just dabbed on is on sale?"

"Of course, not," she hissed, instantly turning on me. "I told you. I came down here to meet someone. And I was curious what kind of crap your aunt sells to the ordinaries." Her coldness made my skin crawl. She would have no trouble when she was ready to embrace the darkness.

"Okay. Time to go, Laney."

Her lips thinned into a straight line and her eyes narrowed. She laughed. "I really get you riled up, don't I?"

I crossed my arms over my chest and tapped my foot, hoping my spells would stay under control. I didn't want to set the shop on fire in front of her. My fingers tingled. I tried to maintain an emotionless expression, but there was no way the anger in me was not showing up in the creased muscles of my face.

She rolled her icy blue eyes. "Don't strain yourself. I'm leaving."

"Perfect."

She flipped her blonde hair over her bony shoulder and slithered out the door. The nails of my hands dug into the tender skin of my palms. Various spells popped and fizzled on my tongue. I needed to cool down. She wasn't worth losing it in front of the ordinaries. I tried to erase her from my memory before I greeted the customers.

"You look stressed," Macey said, resting a hand on my shoulder. "Take a break. I've got the shop."

"Thanks."

I hung my apron on its hook then slammed out the back room door onto the deserted path. I breathed in the calm and walked toward Main Street. Before I got too far, I heard Laney's fake cackle. I followed it around the next corner. I stopped dead in my tracks, catching sight of her as she traced her finger down the front of Alexavier's light blue button down shirt. Right there on the sidewalk, in front of the world. She pressed herself to his lips. I couldn't breathe, stunned from witnessing the intimate gesture.

I glared in her direction. Was he the one she was meeting? I must have gasped out loud, because she whipped her head in my direction and as soon as her eyes set on my shocked expression, she glared like a competitor before a race, threatening to win at all costs, and Alexavier was the prize, regardless of the fact that he was a forbidden ordinary and a Mather.

"Time to go, Sophie!" Laney's shout cracked through my pitiable daze. Anger set in, heating my blood to a cold boil. A dark, frigid shiver ran through me. The temptation of the black magic returned. Thoughts of ruining Laney danced in my mind. Hatred tingled in my index finger. My breathing accelerated. I closed my eyes and curled my fists, resisting as much as possible. No. Not yet. A fraction of my anger seeped out.

"*Ictus,*" I eked out, pointing my finger at a tall oak on the sidewalk ahead.

Immediately, the tree cracked and fell, the top of it landing at her feet. I shook myself out of the anger.

Her eyes flashed wide, wild with surprise. "You tried to hurt me, you dirty little half-breed," Laney yelled, staring wide-eyed at the tree. "I'm telling my mother what you can do."

The inside of my head spun, but I didn't care. My pendant vibrated, reacting to what was going on inside me. "*Deleto*," I whispered, staring into her icy eyes and pointing in her direction. The glazed-over look appeared. As I turned on my heels, I didn't even bother to look at Alexavier, whose silence was indefensible. I raced home, my cheeks flushed and my eyes wet with hot tears. Why would he let her touch him? Was he playing some kind of head game with me?

I took the path and slipped through the opening in the stone wall. I fell to the ground, wallowing in pity and self-loathing until I heard a noise coming from behind me. A crunch in the brush. A footstep.

I flung my head around, hoping to unleash on him. Zeke jumped in front of me. I leapt to my feet, stunned. I balled my hands into fists as if I stood a chance against him, physically, but I had had enough for the day.

His complexion phased to crimson and his eyes narrowed to bitter slits. "I warned you to leave him alone." He pounced with a fury—one hand grabbing both my wrists and binding them together while the other hand squeezed my throat. We landed on the grass. My head pressed into the earth beneath me and my lips trembled with fear. Pressure on my neck drained my clarity, leaving me dizzy as I writhed desperately beneath him. He yelled and foamed at the mouth, but his angry words were incomprehensible.

The pressure on my neck loosened enough for me to grab a breath. "You're a monster. Just like your father!" As I said it, I wondered if Zeke would kill me just as his father killed my parents and their ancestor killed my ancestor. Was I going to die right here on the ground? My blood boiled. I fought against him even harder.

He snarled and held me firmly beneath his weight. "You're the monster and you're wasting your time. Alexavier loves someone else."

My heart pounded like a hammer against my ribcage. "That's a lie!"

"It's true."

As I realized my legs were free, although feeling like rubber, I found the strength to knock him off me. I scrambled to my feet, unsteady, and kicked him in the shin before he grabbed my ankle and knocked me down again. Words escaped me when I needed them most. Tears filled the corners of my eyes. I scraped at the grass and dirt to get free.

"Zeke! What are you doing?" Alexavier rushed him, slamming him down. He gripped his hair and pounded his head into the ground, over and over, until Zeke, blood streaming from his nose, passed out.

I scrambled to my feet and ran, dashing back through the crack in the wall. I was unsteady at first, then stable and quick. My lungs burned as they expanded with each breath that wasn't enough to feed my leg muscles. I wiped the stinging tears from my cheeks. His feet, smacking against the ground behind me warned me he was drawing closer. My heart sped up. The pencil in my hair fell out, releasing long, wavy strands, falling into the wind behind me. Instantly, I felt the faintest touch of his fingers brushing against my shoulder blades. A second later he gripped onto me. His hand slipped down around my arm and yanked me to a stop. He tugged me around to face him. Anger and confusion trembled through me as I resisted and emotion rushed to my lips.

"Leave me alone!" I screamed, searching for an escape from him. How could I have ever trusted him? I hated myself for being so stupid.

Alexavier wrapped his other hand over my mouth, muffling my pleas for release. I twisted and writhed under his strength, kicking him as hard as I could. He spoke into my ear, his voice warm and hushed. "Sophie. Let me explain. Please. It's not what it seems."

Contempt filled me as I gnashed my teeth, refusing to listen. "Let me go!"

"No. Not until you hear me out." He was firm in his course of action, but so was I.

"Let me go. Let me go and I'll listen," I lied easily. My heart thundered in my chest. My breath came in short, quick gasps.

"If I do, will you let me explain?" he asked, exhaustion etching lines into his face.

I shook my head.

"Let me explain."

"Fine," I lied again. He slowly dropped his hands. I took a step back. And another. I glanced to my left, spying the other end of the path that led to a busy street, my goal.

"Sophie, don't…"

I darted. My knees wobbled, but I pushed hard into a sprint.

He ran behind me, this time clasping one arm around my waist and the other around my flailing wrist. My feet kicked in the air.

He turned me around to face him. "I am not letting you go again, until you hear what I have to say. Please, Sophie," he begged.

I inhaled a deep breath and stared into his eyes that pleaded for understanding. "How dare you? You kissed her! I am so stupid; I refused to listen when you said you were trouble. You were right. You were trouble from the moment you set foot in this town." I wriggled back and forth, trying to break free. "Take your hands off me!" I seethed.

Two men in dark business suits walked past the path. Alexavier pressed his warm mouth to mine to stifle my scream. I chomped down and bit his lip hard. He stifled his groan. Neither man looked our way, wrongly assuming we were sharing an intimate moment. Alexavier pulled back. Blood trickled from the curved gash on his lower lip. He wiped it away with the back of his hand. "We are going to my house."

I wriggled and fought him as he walked next to me, holding me firmly to his side with one arm around my waist. My feet barely touched the ground under his strength. He nudged me through the back door and locked it. I ran, but he quickly cornered me in the kitchen. On the stone counter next to a pile of mail, I grabbed a knife from its block.

My fingers flushed white from gripping the blade tightly. I blew a strand of hair from my eyes, trying to stay focused on him. "Get back!"

He slowly walked toward me, unafraid. "Sophie, you don't scare me."

I waved the knife to and fro, glancing at a pile of letters on the counter. "*Incendium*," I commanded, not needing my finger to direct my energy. The power was rolling off me. Dizziness didn't dare interfere. Flames burst from the stack of mail, heaving and growing with my accelerated breathing. His eyes never strayed from the distraction, as if he had seen this happen before. As if he understood it was an extension of my temper. "I'm still not afraid. Let me talk before you stab me through or set me on fire. Please. I am begging you to listen." He pleaded with me. His hands remained in the air.

Cornered without an escape, I had to listen. The knife shook in my trembling hands while the letters burned and sizzled behind me on the stone countertop. I exhaled loudly as if that would relieve me of the frustration, but it didn't. My head finally began to throb. "How could you?" I cried under my breath.

"What you saw back there was all Laney. She touched her fingers to my lips and I couldn't talk. I literally could not move my lips," he assured me calmly. "When she kissed me, it was unexpected and one-sided. Sophie, forgive me."

I dropped the knife to the floor and lunged at him. My hands gripped his bloodstained blue shirt, the crisp cotton crinkling under my anger. "Is this some kind of perverted head game?"

"No. It's the truth. Whatever she gave me tasted bitter."

My jaw tensed. I released his shirt. "Snake venom. Her specialty. It causes temporary paralysis of whatever muscle she applies it to."

"Think, Sophie. How could I like her when I love you?" He absorbed my anger without resistance.

I wiped my eyes with my palms. "What?"

He inhaled through his nose. "I'm crazy in love with you. Do you not see that?"

"No, I don't see that. You won't even come near me."

His eyes ached for understanding, but the ever present conflict was still there. Still between us.

"Because I love you, because you'll die if I do."

I huffed in disbelief.

"It doesn't matter anyway. You see, I'm leaving."

My knees went weak. I gripped the counter to steady myself. "What? But you just said…"

"I decided it would be best for everyone concerned if I left, and after seeing Zeke hurt you, I know I'm right. I need you to understand." His voice ached.

My heart accelerated. A shaky panic set in. I reached for his hand and held on tightly. "You can't leave. You love me."

"Yes. I love you enough to let you go. I don't see how else I can protect you."

"I don't need your protection. I need you here."

"I'll only end up hurting you and destroying us. I can't stay around and let that happen."

My heart hammered in my ears. "What if I told you I can break the curse?"

Optimism flickered to life in his beautiful eyes, calming the panic in me. "We've already tried everything."

I shook my head vehemently. "No. You don't understand. I can disenchant your family."

His eyes narrowed. "How?"

"I think I have a way. I'm missing one piece and once I have it, I can lift the curse that was put on your family centuries ago."

"I've seen how gifted you are, but a family curse which has plagued us for so long…"

"I know it sounds impossible, but my magic is growing stronger." I turned to the stack of fiery letters. "*Desine*." The flames extinguished themselves. A thin column of smoke floated above the mess. "If anyone can, it's me." I leaned forward and looked at him. His optimistic expression paired with hope in his eyes. The sight overwhelmed me. It felt like a dozen butterflies' wings fluttering inside me. The pleasurable tension between us loosened my inhibitions. He gently took my hand and pulled me closer to him. His fingers, warm and soothing, glided under my jaw. He looked deep into my eyes.

He shook his head. "It won't hurt you, will it?"

"It won't hurt." That part wasn't a lie.

"Because if I thought you were in danger in any way I would want nothing to do with it. Do you understand?"

I nodded, looking up at him with longing.

"How can I deny you anything when you look at me like that?"

"You can't." My lips parted ever so slightly.

"Can you forgive me for all the trouble I've caused you?" he asked, sounding truly unsure what my answer would be.

"You mean for letting Laney kiss you?"

He grimaced. "For everything."

A slight smile tugged at my cheeks. "On one condition."

"Anything." His eyes melted into mine.

"I will need something from you in a few days and I need you not to ask any questions."

"Anything," he promised.

Disenchanted

With Zeke keeping Alexavier as busy as he could with their father's issues, wanting nothing more than to keep us apart, I found myself at Goody's Market, scanning the produce section. Fruit skins of crisp crimson, royal purple, granny green, and sunny orange glistened under the morning sunlight streaming through the large front window and the colors reminded me of the inside walls of my house.

I played with my pendant, thinking about Alexavier and the curse. I questioned my hatred for his father and wondered if the intense feelings would interfere with what I wanted to do for Alexavier. I owed him so much, even if I didn't survive the curse breaking or the reconversion. He deserved a chance at a life filled with love. Feeling the stone in my hand, I thought back to Phoebe's warning about the stone needing to be rare. The rarer the better. I realized if I was going to disenchant the Mathers, I would need the bloodcharm to be powerful, but what was it exactly?

Callum snuck up behind me and tapped my shoulder.

"I'm too tired for pranks this morning, Cal. Sorry."

"What's on your mind?"

"My pendant."

And Alexavier, I thought.

He held a cardboard box of Golden Crisp apples he needed to unpack. "You haven't shown that thing to the jeweler, yet?" He stood next to me, stacking the fresh apples in their bin.

"I don't know him and you said you would introduce me. I'm not going to ask a stranger for an appraisal. He'll think I'm an idiot."

"Are you kidding me?"

I sighed. "No."

"Well, if you want to meet him, he's in the back of the store strolling the sandwich bar." He nodded in that direction.

I searched in the back and saw a few customers milling about as they clutched their baskets. "Which one?"

"Tall, older gentleman in the pin striped suit." Callum cupped his hand to his mouth and yelled, "Mr. Sam! Come here. I want you to meet someone."

The jeweler made his way to the produce section. He was taller than average with pleasant dark brown eyes and graying hair. His smile was warm and kind.

He immediately introduced himself to me as Cal walked away to help a customer. The next thing Mr. Sam did was remark on my pendant. "Where did you get this unique piece?"

I held it up in my palm, pleased he thought it was unique. "It belonged to my mom. It's been in the family for a while, but I don't think much about it." I hesitated to say anything more, wanting him to fill in what he could without me getting in the way.

His eyes remained glued on it. "May I?" he asked, gesturing that he wanted a closer look at the rock. I leaned forward. "I don't have my loupe on me..." he said, pinching the squarish stone between his index finger and thumb, tilting it back and forth so it caught the light and lit up on the inside. "I'd say that is definitely not a ruby." His brow crinkled with surprise.

"What, then? Sea glass?"

"No. It's quite a rare stone. Large, easily twenty carats or more. A primitive cushion cut. I've never seen anything like it and I've been in this business for thirty years."

"But it's not a ruby?"

"No. What you have there is a very rare red diamond. You should be careful walking around with that on. Red is the rarest diamond. And one that size—could be worth millions. Maybe a million per carat."

My eyes bugged out. My knees quivered and almost buckled. I grabbed onto the produce stand. A rare diamond would make the bloodcharm extremely powerful. "I...I don't come from money. Did you say, 'diamond' and 'millions' with an 's'?"

"You must come from a royal bloodline or something," he said, offering me a hand to steady myself.

Phoebe said the English king bestowed jewelry on our kind a long time ago. How else could my family acquire a red diamond? I shook my head, calculating the value if it was around twenty carats. Twenty-million dollars.

"I guess today is your lucky day. Happy to be the bearer of good news. If you ever consider parting with it, I'd be happy to help you with that." I had a feeling other people would be happy to help with that, too, including the hooded attacker and the Mather he worked for.

He smiled and left to pay for his sandwich. I stroked my neck, feeling like the pendant suddenly weighed twenty pounds instead of twenty carats. I didn't feel lucky. I felt like a target.

Cal returned to me holding another box of apples. "Why are you so freaked out?"

"Huh?"

"You're gripping the fruit bin like a granny walker. What's wrong with you? You got an answer, right?"

I breathed in, hoping the air would clear my head. "Do you mind if I go in the back to make a call on my cell? It's kind of loud out here." Feeling self-conscious, I tucked the pendant away.

He held a price scanner up to me like a gun. "You have the right to a phone call. You have the right to ask me to lunch."

"I'm serious, Cal."

"You're no fun today. Sure. Help yourself."

I wound my way into the cluttered back office. There were boxes everywhere, including the desk chair, so I paced back and forth as I waited for Aunt Janie to answer her phone. I busied my free hand, tapping on the tops of the crates and cardboard boxes. I walked back and forth in the confined space until I noticed something sticking out of the desk. A clump of black fabric wedged out of the large overcrowded bottom drawer. I tugged on the drawer until it opened with a whoosh. I packed the fabric down to make it fit, but suddenly, I noticed drawstrings on the garment. I set my phone on the desk and lifted it up.

Black hoodie.

I swallowed loudly. My fingers released the jacket back into its hiding spot. My knee slammed the drawer shut. The judge had allies everywhere, including Goody's Market.

"Hello?" Aunt Janie said from my phone.

I grabbed it up. "Never mind, Aunt Janie. I've got to go." I clicked off and shoved the phone in my pocket as I stood stiff and wide-eyed. My thoughts raced as I pieced it together. It couldn't be Mr. Geoffrey's. He always liked me, didn't he? I ran out the office door to the front of the store so I could get out of there, but it was too late. Mr. Geoffrey arrived. Sweat formed on my brow. I tensed my hands and kept walking, trying to control my pace, but all I wanted to do was get the hell away from him. There were too many truths coming at me too fast. My head and body filled with panic.

"Hi, Sophie. How are you?" His eyes immediately went to my chest, but it was the outline of the pendant that had drawn—and continued to draw his—attention. I glanced at his wrists. He wore a long sleeve shirt, which lifted enough to reveal the bottom of the lion in the circle tattoo. I surveyed his average height and size. At that moment, I realized he knew what my pendant was worth and so did the judge.

"Fine." I hesitated nervously. "I, uh, have to get back to work. 'Bye." I feigned a half-smile and walked as slowly out the door as I could. Seconds seemed to last as long as minutes. I controlled my gait past two store windows before breaking into a mad run.

The next afternoon, my nerves still frayed and a foreboding feeling weighing heavily on me, I tried to shake off the uncontrollable quiver in my fingers. I managed to pull it together enough to help a few customers.

"What's wrong with you?" Macey asked, noticing my lack of enthusiasm.

I closed my eyes, feeling freaked out. I wanted to tell her about Mr. Geoffrey working for the judge and how my mom's pendant was a twenty-million dollar diamond blood charm and how I was going to break Alexavier's family curse with it, which could be deadly, but I couldn't tell her anything. She would try to talk me out of it, but I wasn't changing my mind.

"Nothing."

"You're more of a mess today than usual. Let me fix your hair. Looks like a squirrel got in there.

She grabbed me by my shoulders and pinned my hair up. I stared at Rebecca's painting on the wall, wondering what I was up against. "Thanks."

"When are you and Alexavier going to see each other again?"

"This evening." I needed him at my house to collect the one last item on the recipe list.

"How about going on a double date with me and Daniel next week?"

"Next week?" Would I be alive next week to break coven law for Macey? Would I be the same, look the same, if my soul and heart turned dark? "I'll let you know."

"Why wait? You can tell me now." She grabbed me by my shoulders again and turned me around as he entered the shop. "He looks amazing in that white T-shirt. Alexavier!" she shouted. "Sophie has something she wants to ask you."

I elbowed her in the side. "Shut up."

She cupped her hand to my ear. "Go for it," she whispered and hurried to the back room as he approached, looking as handsome as ever.

His smile, slightly marred from my bite, was filled with concern. "How are you?"

"I'm not sure." I was upset and out of sorts about everything. My world was chaotic and changing all around me. I honestly didn't know how I felt. "Numb."

"What's wrong? Has Callum been bothering you?"

I scrunched my face up. "Callum? No. Never. Why would you ask that?"

"I saw the two of you together the other evening and it looked like he was taking advantage of your friendship."

That was code for getting too friendly. My shoulders shifted down and I locked onto his eyes. "The other night? In my garden? You were spying on me?"

"Watching over you."

That sounded like a stalker's way to describe what he was doing. "From a distance?"

"You know that's how it has to be until…"

My lower lip jutted out. "And what exactly did you see?"

He seemed stressed by the question. Sensing my objection, he stretched his hands out in front of him, the muscles straining under the ivory skin that bore the broken heart mark as he asked for a moment to explain. "I'm sorry. You spend a lot of time with him. I couldn't help to question his motives."

"He's my friend. Of course I spend time with him." My thoughts shifted back to Callum's childish antics and how we ended up wrestling on the ground like children.

"Yes. However, he behaves inappropriately around you," he snorted brusquely, sounding possessive of me. It made sense now. Callum did have a way of bringing out a person's primal emotions.

"That noise we heard—the gutter ripping off your house…that was you, wasn't it?"

He said nothing, his silence an admission of guilt.

"I don't think of Callum like that. He really is more like an exasperating brother."

"He doesn't see you as a sister. I assure you." His terse tone grew more agitated. "What I am trying to say is that he is not worthy of your attention. He is careless and I don't trust him around you," his voice boomed under his breath. An older customer in the back peered over at us. He closed his eyes, reining in his anger.

His concern stirred me deeply, but I found his appall to be hypocritical. "Callum never intentionally disabled a boat and never tore a gutter off a house," I responded firmly, not backing down.

He remained stiff, frozen in his insecure state. "I repaired all the damages."

My voice dropped to a whisper. "Why are you even worried about Callum? You and I have bigger obstacles to worry about than Callum."

He sighed. "You're right. I'm sorry."

I glanced back at the painting. "How much money does your dad need to build his addition to Kingshill?"

"Don't worry about that. He's struggling to secure a bank loan, so it might never get built."

"How much?"

"Twenty-million dollars. Why?"

I closed my eyes. A breath escaped through my lips. The last puzzle piece. "Not important. I don't have time to argue about Callum or anything else." Thunder rumbled outside, rattling the windows.

His shadowed eyes disconnected, not wanting to say goodbye, but knowing he wouldn't give himself any other choice.

From the other end of the call, a Vivaldi mash-up played in the background as the phone burned hot against my face. "Aunt Janie, when will you be home?"

"I'm running late, dear. I'm taking a blue anchusa tincture from the shop to Mistress Revel. She isn't feeling well. It's complicated."

I wanted to say the same thing about my life, but I resisted. My lips tingled. "I'm heading directly to the fairgrounds with Adair. I'll meet you there."

"That's fine. Oh, and I almost forgot. Before you go out, I made a special concoction I want you to drink. To calm you before the Seeking." She paused and I wondered if she was tucking her hair behind her ear. "You've been on edge lately and I thought it would help, so drink the iced white cocoa in the short glass. Okay?"

"The good cocoa from Nicaragua?"

"Yes."

"Sure. See you tonight." She sounded stressed and preoccupied, but steady. That's all I could hope for.

Next to the pitcher of my orange thyme iced tea, I spotted the short glass filled with a creamy white liquid and covered with plastic wrap. I lifted the wrap and sniffed. The drink smelled delicious, like toasted hazelnuts, fresh cream, melted chocolate, and parsley. The glass met my lips, but my fingers lost their grip from the condensation on the outside of the glass. With a smash, a mess of white cream and tiny glass shards surrounded my feet. Crud. I didn't have time for this. I quickly cleaned up the mess and spied the time on my watch.

Upstairs, from my bedroom window, I gazed out to the horizon. A brilliant waxing moon began to rise as the fiery sun blazed. My gaze drifted down to the garden where the last lonely moonflower simultaneously bloomed and withered in the dark, moist soil. I turned away. The long, hooded black robe hanging on my closet door next to my coven uniform waited for me. I pushed the consequences that gnawed at my insecurities away. Thoughts of Alexavier and the memory of our first kiss rushed in like warm ocean waves on a sunny day at the beach.

In the bathroom mirror, I sighed at my reflection. I brushed and pinned my hair into the best messy knot I could manage, needing it out of the way tonight. I dabbed Forbidden Fruit lip gloss to my lips for a touch of luck and picked up a small jar of powder. In the mirror, my wide blue eyes stared back at me.

A white flash like silent lightning exploded in my head. When the whiteness cleared, I made out the angry face of a woman, dressed in seventeenth century clothing. She yelled bitterly, shaking a small statue in her hand. The figure with painted dark hair and a blue dress was the same as the one Elizabeth left for me on the shop counter, the same one I had dreamed of Eldress Mayapple holding that resembled Elizabeth and me. I gasped for breath, listening to Rebecca rant to Elizabeth about betraying the witches of Wethersfield and how her love for the Mather heir was vile and that her purpose as a clairvoyant was to serve her, the eldress, and not to fall in love with an ordinary. She pointed to the figure's nearly severed neck and cursed. "As a traitor, you have earned your death and the reverend has earned his son's death along with a slew of Mathers' deaths to come."

As the vision wore off, the glass jar tumbled from my fingers and smashed into tiny shards against the porcelain of the sink. I crumpled to the bathroom floor. The vision of Elizabeth's last night was her final message. I cradled my face in my hands. My hatred for the judge was no different from Rebecca's in its depth and darkness. I hated that it was, but I was going to need it. It would carry me through the ritual necessary to save Alexavier. I gripped the edge of the vanity and pulled myself to standing.

I touched my hand to my blood charm and dressed in the uniform then took a deep breath as I slid the ceremonial black robe off its hanger and tied the satin belt around my waist. I smoothed my hands against the front panels of fabric, feeling the cold silk against my fingertips. An icy trickle of darkness, the same liquid black ice I felt before listening to Judge Mather and Laney, traveled the length of my arm.

This time, I invited it in. I felt the darkness tame my impetuous nature, allowing me to feed slowly on the hatred and control it. The coldness flowed through my veins and to the lengths of each limb. The icy darkness pooled in my chest and chilled my heart.

The change was beginning. "Elizabeth, I hope you're right about the magic in me being able to change black hearts 'cause I'm going to need it for my own."

The doorbell chimed, startling me to a more alert state. "Hold on," I shouted. I opened the duffel bag and removed the knife and vial before tossing the robe in. I stuffed the small items in my skirt pocket and carried the bag with me downstairs, setting it in the foyer. I clenched my hands tightly together before opening the door. "Cal? What are you doing here?" I asked, shocked to see him on my doorstep.

"I was worried about you," he said abruptly, entering the house and grabbing me by the hand.

"I don't have time for this right now. I have a meeting with my aunt tonight," I implored impatiently.

"A meeting?" He noticed the gray skirt and white shirt. "Not yet." He led me to the kitchen and pulled a chair out for me.

He studied me and grimaced. "Sophie, I don't know what's going on, but I get the feeling you're in trouble." Perhaps it was his connection to tribal magic, but beyond his tough guy exterior, he was surprisingly intuitive.

"Cal, I'll be fine. I'm a little stressed and tired, that's all." I blinked, feeling a strange weight on my lashes. I glanced at my hands, turning them over. My skin looked luminescent. Flawless. I smacked my lips together, feeling their plumpness.

He scrunched his face up as he eyed me. "Tired? You don't look tired. Are you wearing makeup?"

The physical enhancement was beginning. I raced to the foyer mirror, out of Cal's view. My heart-shaped lips bloomed a blood red, my lashes thickened and bowed upward like the arms of a goddess, a dewy glow radiated from my flawless ivory complexion, and as I watched, the messy knot unrolled down the length of my back into a wavy sea of glossy sable hair. My mouth fell open.

"I wasn't finished." Cal marched toward me. "Whoa. What is going on?"

I turned to him, having to act like I normally did. "Nothing."

His eyebrows arched. "Something. Did you get a makeover in the last thirty-seconds?"

I gathered my silky hair and draped the long smooth tresses over one shoulder. "I'm trying something new. Don't make fun."

He shook his head, stupefied. "Whatever. I came here to give you something." He took a breath as if to say something else, but he stopped. Our friendship had evolved and deepened into a mutual love for each other; a love between friends, but nonetheless sacred and forever.

I shook my hands at him. "Cal, don't. It's not…"

He reached into the pocket of his jeans and extracted a tangle of black leather string. Angst crossed his bronzed brow. "I want you to wear this."

I glanced at the object resting in his open palm; a small wood carving attached to leather strands. The amulet was the size of a postage stamp.

"It's a talisman carved from eucalyptus wood. It wards off evil spirits and will protect you."

"Is this a white magic token?"

He smiled without explanation.

"Cal, it's incredibly thoughtful of you. I love it. But I can't take that." I didn't deserve to wear it at the moment, not as the darkness spread through me like the poison Romeo drank, silencing the warmth in my heart. My lips tingled. "Your mom wouldn't like it."

His lips twisted to the side and his expression was one of rejection. "I think she would be okay if she saw it on you." He smiled, a hint of sadness seeped into the corners of his mouth. "Here..." He took my hand and looped the leather around so the talisman dangled delicately from my wrist. I could feel his gentle touch on my skin as he secured it. He placed his large hands on my shoulders and looked at me. "Promise you'll be okay?"

A laugh cracked through my stress. "Promise." Cal's sentiment was deeply appreciated. He never failed to make me laugh, even as the temperature of my heart dropped.

He leaned in and kissed my cheek as a small tear escaped from my eyes.

"You better be."

The doorbell rang again.

It was too late to stop him. In one long stride, Cal turned the knob before I could move.

Alexavier stood in the doorway, glaring at Callum with disapproval and irritation. "Callum, what a surprise to find you here," he said gruffly, sarcasm saturating his voice.

"I'm trying to take care of my girl."

I didn't want Cal to mess this up. I still needed one thing from Alexavier. Alexavier spoke directly to him. "Callum, I know you care about Sophie, but I can take care of her. She doesn't need you." He kept his voice low, but his tone was protective and threatening.

Callum stepped closer to him.

"Callum, this will not end well for you if you insist on challenging me," Alexavier warned. His voice remained even, but his body was poised to fight if Callum insisted.

I wiped my cheek and stomped toward them. "Please, stop this. Please! I care about you both, but Callum, you need to go," I pleaded, fearing Cal would snap. I pulled on Alexavier's arm roughly to break the defensive eye contact he maintained with Callum.

"I'm not afraid, Mather. I also don't need my fists to prove I'm the better man. Sophie will see that one day," he snarled ferociously.

I flashed my eyes wide. My jaw jutted out. I couldn't believe what I was hearing. This was the last thing I wanted to deal with or could deal with and I feared what I would do under the influence of my choice. "Callum...*leave now!*" I didn't care about hurting anyone's feelings at the moment. My emotions were shifting beyond that.

He pushed past Alexavier in a huff to leave. Alexavier ignored the action, focusing his attention on me. I was relieved he didn't engage Callum in a fight. He stood before me, astoundingly handsome in a blue button down shirt. He grasped my hands and looked deeply into my eyes. "What was that all about?"

My blackening heart skipped a beat. "I'm sorry about Callum. I don't know what got into him."

"Jealousy, I would say. I warned you."

"I don't want to believe that's it."

His fingers gently pressed against my hand and wrist, lifting them to inspect the talisman. "Did he give you this?" A combination of regret and jealousy lined his voice.

"It's to keep evil spirits away," I replied as I touched the wood carving with my fingertips.

He sighed. Our future was under a black cloud from the past where Rebecca's curse and his father's mistakes affected us in the present. And after tonight, even if the ritual went according to plan, there was no guarantee things would be the same or better for us. I was risking my life and my soul. Even if I survived breaking the curse and the reconversion, I would be different, changed, tainted from the black magic I had already invited into my heart and it might all be for nothing.

"Alexavier, it's just a symbol of friendship, that's all."

He fell silent. "Enough about him. I need to know what you're up to tonight."

I glanced up at him, falling into the pools of gray. "I need to ask you for that one thing you promised you would give me without question." I forced a smile, but worry creased in his brow.

"What's going on with you? You look different. Your clothes, your lips, your hair."

"Nothing is going on and is different a bad thing?" I batted my long eyelashes at him, playing at flirtatious.

"No. It's just different."

I touched my hand to the side of his face, the stubble teased the sensitive skin of my palm. "Look at me." His brooding eyes lifted to meet mine. A halfhearted smile appeared. "It will be fine. After tonight, we will be better than fine."

He pressed his perfect lips into a straight line. "Sophie, no. I have a bad feeling and I don't want you doing anything stupid or risky. Do you understand?" He grabbed my hand and pressed it to his chest. "Do you feel that?"

I nodded.

"My heart belongs to you. It beats because of you. If anything happened…I-I don't even want to think about that, about what I would do."

His heart pounded beneath my fingers, strong and rhythmic. I took my hand back, trying to stave off the emotion that was hitting me in waves. I swallowed hard. "That's why it's more important than ever that I take care of this."

"Sophie, no. When you said you could break the curse, I don't think you were telling me everything. It's not worth any kind of risk. We can see each other from a distance. I can love you from a distance and maybe it won't kill us. Because if you die breaking this curse, I will die, too, and then what was it all for? The curse still wins." His voice broke off.

"Love you from a distance? I can't do that," I snapped, not meaning to. He ignored my tone and clasped my hand again, staring at our entwined fingers. My stomach ached from the foreboding feeling. "You would do anything to protect me, wouldn't you?"

He laughed softly, his shielded eyes looking forlorn. "I don't mean to be so obvious about it." The words sounded so pleasant in his accent.

"Yes, you do." I swallowed hard, feeling the dryness take over my mouth. Lying required no devil's bit nectar. It came easily now. "Nothing is going to happen tonight. Stop worrying." I looked up at him, his chiseled features and his brooding eyes. His closeness, the warmth rolling off him, and his intoxicating scent combined to loosen my inhibitions. His hand gently touched to my cheek. I leaned into it, drawing my face closer to his. The anticipation affected me as waves of flutters left me breathless. I closed my eyes, my body trembling. The stubble on his cheeks grazed lightly against my skin, affirming his undeniable masculinity. He kissed me tenderly as my heart thumped out of control. My fingers slipped into his thick, black hair and held tightly. He paused, not wanting to pull away. I didn't let him. I was going to say goodbye properly. I held tightly, pressing my lips to his, soft at first then hard with desire.

His eyes flashed open as he pulled back. "What was that?"

My lips pursed. "What was what?"

"That kiss. That wasn't like you."

I leaned closer, whispering in his ear. "Was it bad?"

He pulled away from me. "No. Just...different. Are you sure you're okay?"

"Fine. I'm fine. Give me your hand. I need that something from you." There was no time to waste. My hand held onto his arm, making sure he didn't break free when the pain hit. I kept my eyes on him while I pulled the small knife from my pocket. With laser precision, I sliced his palm, barely scratching the surface, but enough to collect the most crucial item.

"What are you doing?" He tried to pull back, but I held firm, my hand gripping hard into his flesh. "No, Sophie."

"I'm doing this for us." I replaced the knife with the small vial and held it up to the scratch, exerting pressure on the wound. A few drops of Mather blood trickled into the vial like a tiny ribbon of crimson. I shoved the rubber stopper in.

"Adair. I'm ready."

From the purple family room, Adair stepped out. I knew he would try to stop me tonight and I couldn't let him. "Erase his memory and send him home."

She looked at me, knowing I could easily to do it myself, but I couldn't. Not on him. Being around him interfered with my spells and I didn't need anything going wrong tonight. "Just do it."

Alexavier shot me a look of confusion, but it was over in an instant.

Adair and I walked together to the old fairgrounds, a public green space, which was closed decades ago by the judge for being a green space. I looked up at the evening sky, seeing the full moon rising as the summer sun hung low. My gait matched hers until a sudden jolt brought me to a stop. I regained my composure, holding tight to the duffel bag and glaring at the stranger who bumped into me. Her blonde curls and blue eyes were unmistakable—Bess Johnson. Her face no longer possessed the luster of youth and innocence. She eyed us both with a shocked expression that phased to steely-eyed determination to report us for whatever she could conjure.

I took hold of her forearm, desperate to stop her. "Bess, it's me—Sophie. Don't you remember? We used to play together on the school playground. You would push me on the swing like a big sister."

"I know who you are. Sophie Goodchild." Her voice purred when she spoke, part of her alluring charm that was very effective on men. She turned her cold eyes on Adair, who stood tensed, but ready to change her memory. "Where are you two headed?"

"Goody's Market. And you?"

Her hand flew up, pointing to the horizon as the full moon and blazing sun drew closer together. Then she looked down at my gray skirt and gray patent leather shoes. "Liars!"

I shifted the bag behind my legs to protect it, knowing the damage was done. "Goodbye, Bess. I'm sorry it has to be this way." I squeezed Adair's hand, hoping she understood what I wanted her to do.

As soon as Bess was out of sight, I stopped. "Tell me you changed her memory."

"I'm sorry. I couldn't break through her head. I tried, I swear."

This was bad. She was going to report us to the judge. It was a matter of time before they came searching and I considered what I would do to him if he came near me while I was like this. "It's fine, but we have to hurry," I urged. We broke into a run. I led her to the old fairgrounds and we entered the vast property before anyone else arrived.

The wildness of nature and the isolation lent the grounds a tempestuous edge. The property was surrounded by the tallest oak trees and the scent of summer grass and wildflowers permeated the air around us. Beyond the crooked funhouse, the rickety merry-go-round, and dilapidated Ferris wheel, stood a circle of tall white marble columns, which had been saved from a demolished historic building, and had provided a romantic picnic area. But tonight they would serve a different purpose, overseeing our ritual. Within the circle sat a rounded decorative stone basin already filled with ceremonial kindling courtesy of Mistress Phoebe.

I set my duffel bag down near the basin and we slipped into our black robes. I positioned myself in front of the basin and looked around. The combined light from the moon and sun touched upon my face, feeling like a cold fire chilling my already cool blood and igniting my senses. The energy in me swelled. My pendant buzzed against my chest. "Do you feel your powers surging, too?" I asked her.

"It amazing."

I pointed to the kindling, "Blaze," I commanded. A whoosh of wind rushed out of my finger. Immediately, the kindling exploded into huge flames without the lightheaded side effect I usually experienced.

Soon, scores of black hooded robes encircled the growing fire. The eldress approached me. "Mistress Sophie." Her claw gripped onto my chin. "What a shame you have not turned out to be as promising as was expected—an herbalist like your frail aunt, minus her cloudy clairvoyance. One day, after honing your gardening skills to an acceptable level, you may be fortunate enough to serve my Laney, who will no doubt take over my position when the time is right."

Her presumptuous attitude forced my teeth to catch onto my tongue. The part of me growing darker wanted to spit on the ground at her feet and unleash the truth, explaining how Aunt Janie and I had fooled her so easily, but instead, my lips moved without thought. "You will see everything I can do tonight and decide for yourself where I will best serve you...and Laney."

She nodded with approval, not seeming to notice the change in my appearance. I cringed beneath my cold smile, tasting the acid of my words. I glanced around. From the faces not obscured by hoods, I could see Riada making her way toward us, and Mistresses Aster, Leta, and Phoebe with Aunt Janie following behind. On the other side of the columns, I spied Lana lumbering toward the Glitterati, who were sparkling brighter than ever under Josie's glitter charm.

Movement from near the merry-go-round caught my attention. Alexavier stood behind a white carousel horse, watching me. He looked ready to grab me from the ceremony and run us out the front gate. I flashed my eyes to Adair, who caught sight of him, too. She shrugged her shoulders and shook her head, unsure what happened with the memory altering. She elbowed her sister and the two turned their attention in his direction. Within a second, his body floated just barely above the white horse, leaving him writhing and fighting their levitation trick. I swallowed hard. My heart, growing blacker, still belonged to him and it pulsed against the choice I had made. I took a deep breath and shook my head ever so slightly. *Don't fight it*, I thought.

The outer circle of witches joined hands, creating a divide between the physical world outside and the spiritual world within the circle. We all began chanting our gratitude to the sun and moon as both astral bodies began to merge. A stronger surge of energy filled me. My fingers tingled, ready to dispel the power.

"Will the young witches step forward into the maidens' circle?"

One by one we marched forward in our hooded robes, hoods up. Mistress Deedee anointed each of our foreheads with a dot of sacred omega oil. She poured the remaining oil onto the fire, causing the flames to grow taller. The wood crackled and popped.

Mistress Belladonna approached, holding a small silver bowl. She tossed handfuls of tree resin into the flame. The incense, smelling of pine and cedar, encircled us in a cloud of white smoke that spiritually cleansed those within the inner circle. "Hail the maiden witches."

Mistress Catnip carried an ornate silver goblet filled with ritual wine and offered it to each of us. "May the fruit of your work sustain and keep us." I took a sip of the sweet fermented cherry juice and passed the heavy sterling cup to Riada.

Mistress Winsome stepped delicately to the center and tossed a handful of herbs into the fire. Scents of mugwort, lavender, and dittany radiated from the blaze to welcome the spirits. "I call upon the presence of our foremothers, Mistresses Leela, Angelica, and Gabrielle to please join us. Watch over our ceremony and guide our coven in the ancient ways." She dropped a small pellet into the fire causing an explosion within the blaze. As the smoke cleared, three female shapes appeared, their fiery forms undulating with the flames. A roar of applause broke out among us.

Finally, Eldress Mayapple stepped forward. Her voice boomed as she raised the sacred book of histories above her head. "May the witches who have come before us, watch over and guide us through our Seeking, that we may place our young sisters where they will best serve and sustain our continuity. These times are troubled, have no doubt. However, we are strong. Even as tensions mount, as witches continue to be locked away at Kingshill, and our shops are closed, we have hope. We have you, our young sisters and your emerging talents." She turned to Mistress Deedee. "Let the Seeking begin."

Adair and Riada stepped before the discerner. Together they levitated a pink lily Adair pulled from her robe pocket. As it floated down, Adair handed the flower to Mistress Deedee. Their gift of levitation was equally as strong as their mind powers and they were able to focus their energy on one talent over the other.

"Levitators! Fantastic. Join your sisters under the leadership of Mistress Winsome."

Laney pushed ahead of Misty and Josie, eager to be placed. She shoved her hands out in front of her, and instantly an anaconda slithered between her and Mistress Deedee. She applauded Laney's efforts. "Conjur..."

"No," Laney interrupted with a disappointed scowl. "I can do better."

"No. Allow me." Deedee closed her eyes and strained to read the blonde-haired daughter of the eldress. "Conjurer. I sense nothing more. Nothing less. You should not be disappointed. Now, take your place by Mistress Winsome."

Her lips mashed together. "I want to study under my mother."

Mistress Winsome glided over to Laney and grabbed her by the arm. "This way, Mistress Laney."

Mistress Deedee nodded at me. I gulped loudly, weighing the consequences of what I was about to do. "Begin."

My gift, coinciding with the eclipse, was at its peak and the pansy seed trick I had practiced to pass as an herbalist would easily be seen as fraudulent by Mistress Deedee. There was no turning back.

My hand lifted with the seed in my palm. My finger aimed at the logs in the fire. From the corner of my eye I could see Aunt Janie being held back by Mistress Phoebe. Phoebe nodded at me, knowing there was a reason for what I was about to do. Her face filled with understanding and imparted her promise to take care of Janie for me. That was all I needed.

My voice vibrated low in my throat as the spell came to me, slow and deep, then faster and higher as the energy of the words whipped up the fire. The flames licked as high as the columns.

The curse breaking ritual required not only the sacred ingredients, but perfection in technique and order, the way Rebecca detailed in her book. I closed my eyes and readied myself. All of the hatred in me, provoked by the judge and what he did to my parents, stoked the black magic that yearned for release. The ceremonial fire roared. I dropped to my knees, releasing the seed to the ground and from the duffel bag I removed the binding twigs and sachet, setting them by my feet. The red diamond trembled against my chest like a mini-earthquake, energized even more from the moon and sun's combined forces.

I chanted the summoning words and called upon the presence of Eldress Rebecca. My vocal cords vibrated, my lips parted and the magic in me burst out like a controlled nuclear reaction. An explosion within the fire produced another willowy form of a woman, distorted by the flames. Intense heat rolled off the growing fire. Rebecca's spirit rose from her hellhole, taking form within the flames above the foremothers, her hands and fingers undulating in a dance. From the corner of my eyes, I could see the coven gathering around me, curious, and in the distance, Alexavier watching midair, his face gripped with great apprehension.

The blackness trickled through my veins like liquid ice and rather than feeling trepidation, I delighted in what I was about to do. I scooped up the sacred bundle, swiftly removed the talisman from my wrist and secured it to the bundle. With a swift toss, the twigs landed square in the center of the fire. Rebecca's form began to writhe. An agonizing screech pierced the air around us as the fire consumed the sacred sticks, binding her and her curse to hell. The echoing scream filled my ears and her hellish pain sent me into a frenzy.

"Stop her!" Eldress Mayapple screamed, aware of what I was and what I was doing to the former eldress. Mistress Deedee held her back, entertained by my new talent.

The necessary dark spell raced to the tip of my tongue, clear as witch dew. With my free hand, I held tight to the diamond bloodcharm. Power pulsed to my vocal cords as the words rose up from deep within. With my free hand I tossed the vial of Mather blood into the fire while the spell flowed.

Summon spirits in flames from hell
Sacred trees and blood dispel
From my heart I chant the spell
To bid thy true love curse farewell.

The eclipse peaked. My voice grew stronger. My hand gripped the diamond pendant harder, its rough edges cutting into my palm as I drew on its power to break Rebecca's curse. There was no restraining the energy that thundered within me like a thousand well-muscled Arabian horses. I repeated the powerful words, over and over, knowing it was half of the ritual that would release the Mather family from the true love curse cast upon them nearly four centuries ago by the blackhearted eldress. The fire grew more intense. I grabbed the sachet of black rose petals and felt my shoulder muscles twitch, latching onto the energy pouring out of me. I stepped forward, approaching the hot flames.

Power jolted through me like a bolt of lightning. Finally, I tossed the petals into the fire with the last bit of hatred I felt to seal the magic and permanently undo the curse.

A growling explosion cut through the air as the earth sucked the fire and Rebecca's form down into it.

Thick, gray clouds surrounded us. The smell of smoke filled my nostrils. I coughed and shook my head, trying to steady myself. The black icy feeling continued to consume my head. My muscles, suddenly drained of every ounce of energy, gave out. I collapsed on my knees.

Aunt Janie rushed toward me, grabbed hold of my wrist, touching her hand to my watch to fully understand the events that lead up to the Seeking. She closed her eyes, waiting for the answers I wasn't giving her. Her eyes flashed open. "No! Sophie!" Her grip held firm.

At that moment, men's voices broke through clearing smoke. Our eyes shot in their direction. Judge Mather, wearing a dark power suit, along with a mob of men and Bess, invaded the fairgrounds, rushing toward us like a threatening menace. Mistress Leta whipped her hands in a circular motion and a dilapidated shed from across the field lifted from its foundation, hovered through the air, and dropped on the judge's entourage. Within several minutes, they busted through the rotted wood. Misty quickly spun a huge orange gas cloud above her head and tossed it in their direction to slow them. Gasps and coughs sputtered out of the ambitious group, but they stormed forward again. The small group, looking slightly disheveled from the gas, stopped outside the columns, waiting for the judge to speak. "Your evil tricks are futile. Cease and desist! In the name of the law," he yelled, breaking through the throng of black robes. He paused and glanced around, noticing several of the young witches, including Aunt Janie's two former cellmates, all of whom had been detained at his center before Riada and Adair forced the therapists to free them.

His long arm made a sweeping motion. "You don't think I know what you are? That you live under a blanket of anonymity? Bess has been very helpful in pulling the blanket away. You are all under arrest for trespassing, mischief-making, and gathering to imperil the peace of Wethersfield." He glared at Eldress Mayapple. "I'm half tempted to bring a return to the Wethersfield Witch Trials and throw a noose over a branch from that huge oak over there." Before she could speak, he turned his laser focus on me. "It would be a shame to let it go to waste when there are young women like you, Mistress Goodchild, causing so much public mischief." His sunken cheeks puffed with hot air as he pointed a wagging finger in my direction. He marched toward me with his henchmen and Bess Johnson following behind.

Aunt Janie's hand gripped tighter on my arm, not willing to let go of me, but she had nothing to fear. Black magic swelled and spun inside me, the energy of it fierce and unyielding, urging my muscles to react. Iciness flowed into my heart. I clasped onto the diamond. I pointed a finger in the judge's direction and with all the power I could muster, I yelled, "*Retro.*" The magic trickled off my lips like a roar of water bursting through a huge, cracked dam. Immediately, the judge flipped upside down in the air, my magic shaking him up and down like a rag doll. He whimpered and whined as I whirled him around with my fingers. I could taste his imminent death. I hungered for it, but a small part of me, still untouched by the blackness, strained to keep the rest of me from shaking him lifeless.

His mob stood in awe, eyes glued to his situation. Ashleigh seized on the moment and morphed into one of the mob men. She jumped into the group as if it were a mosh pit and began throwing punches at the judge's henchmen. Other young witches began throwing their talents at the mob while the stunned Council observed all of our skills, unconcerned with the judge's numbers.

Mistress Deedee broke into fits of giggles. "Wee! Impressive!" She nodded approvingly at Eldress Mayapple who scowled, aware she had been fooled by me and most likely worried for her own position.

Mistress Deedee offered her a suggestive look. "The war is all but won with Mistress Sophie on our side."

"If she can be tamed." The eldress's scowl turned smug as she considered how I could serve her.

Mistress Deedee nudged her. "Can you feel it? She has already embraced the darkness. This could prove very beneficial."

Aunt Janie released me and pressed her face into Mistress Phoebe's shoulder. I had no regrets for what I had done and she would be safe.

"Mistress Sophie, leave the judge suspended and take your place beside Eldress Mayapple. She will be your guide for the next two years. As a spellcaster you will hone your skills under her roof at Cross Manor."

My black-hearted temper flared with contempt and ambition. "No."

Eldress Mayapple stepped forward, her expression of displeasure apparent. "I am going to ignore the rules you have broken and leave your aunt unharmed as long as I know your devotion to the witches is about those who work together for the good of the whole, serving its leadership. However, if you choose to challenge me, there will be consequences." She clasped her large hands together and paused. "Together we are united and strong. Divided, we fall."

"United and strong," the coven replied in unison while I stood silent.

"Should we continue?" Mistress Deedee asked.

"The ordinaries are not going anywhere and they will not impede our ceremony." Mistress Deedee relit the fire. The eldress whipped her hand in the air and signaled to Mistress Isobel to summon one of her psychic fogs. A cloud of confusion washed over their faces as they were blinded to our ceremony. With a snap of a finger, the other young witches shuffled to the center, awaiting their placement, completely ignoring the outside chaos and oblivious to my internal nightmare. If I challenged her now, Aunt Janie would suffer the consequences. I mashed my red lips together and marched next to the eldress. Above us, the astral discs began to separate and, at that moment, the judge dropped to the ground, free of my spell. I scanned the crowd of hazy faces and caught Bess manipulating the air with her hands.

I kicked my shoes off and broke into a run, knowing hell was about to break loose with her on their side. I shoved my way through rows of black robes and ran toward the slanted funhouse. Judge Mather raced behind me. He wanted more than to arrest me and his hatred of everything related to the witches rolled off him in tidal waves, coming right at me. I was fine with that. His hatred couldn't match mine, and mine was as fresh as the day he told me he killed my parents.

My breathing quickened. I glanced all around, searching for a loose board or broken mirror. I searched every crevice, but what was left in the building was useless. Then it hit me. I didn't need a weapon.

I was one.

I whipped around, facing him. "What do you want?" I sneered, contempt articulated in each syllable.

Anger flickered in his narrow eyes. He spied my necklace and stepped closer.

With a flash of his hand, he extracted a gun from his jacket. He shoved it in my face. "What do I want? The same thing I've wanted for a long time."

"The same thing you paid Mr. Geoffrey to steal?"

He laughed. "Smart girl. And the vagrant, too."

"Why not take it yourself?"

"I'm a pillar of justice in this community. So when you're dead and the diamond goes missing, who would ever suspect me?"

My breathing grew slow and exaggerated. I closed my mouth and tried to breathe through my nose. My hatred flowed, yearning for vengeance. As my hand touched to the diamond, magic vibrated against my fingertips, waiting for me to tap into it again. I wasn't sure I could. My muscles ached to recoup. "You will regret taking anything of mine."

He laughed wryly and ran his free hand across his sweaty forehead. "Take satisfaction in knowing that it's for a good cause."

"Oh right. The rock to build the addition to Kingshill on, right?" His eyes grew wild as he handled the gun. "I'm not making any donations today," I said. My one hand clasped onto the diamond while the other aimed at the bitter man. The spell began to tumble off my lips as a hint of lilac perfume floated on the air. A second later, a woman's arms locked around mine, yanking my hand away from the pendant. I fought against her.

"Judge, we can arrest her and keep her at Kingshill," Bess said.

He scoffed at the idea. "I don't plan to arrest her." He paused with a wicked grin on his narrow face. "There's only one way to save my foolish son who has been under her spell and take what I need without complications," he said coldly. He turned his intense stare on me. "Once this is all over, Zeke plans to beat some common sense into him. Remind him of our limitations."

"You don't understand," I wrestled against Bess. "I have removed your limitations."

"Keep that liar's tongue in your mouth. You and your kind are the cause of our misery. It is why I must have the diamond, why I must build the addition, and lock the lot of you up. If I can't have love, I can profit from your misery."

Fury raged within me like a volcanic fire, consuming everything it touched. My cold heart began to pound as three goons rushed in. I struggled to reach the diamond, but my fingers weren't long enough and they weren't free enough to point at my assailants. I closed my eyes and summoned the remainder of my magic. My vocal cords vibrated with tension. "*Desine.*"

Instantly, the judge went rigid, his gun dropped to the ground. Bess' body froze in place, her eyes, the only things moving, shifted with panic. I grabbed hold of my pendant and focused on every face I could see. The small piece of me, untouched by blackness, fought against the hate, it fought for their lives. I bit my lip, tasting the iron-tinged flavor of blood as the conflict waged in me. The stone pulsed with energy.

A strange calm swept over me. "*Semper memoriam tui delebo Diamond.*" I locked onto the judge, commanding him to forget about the diamond forever, rather than killing him. "*Deleto, Deleto, Deleto, Deleto.*" As soon as their eyes glazed over with the dazed look, I knew I was done. My heart slowed to an unusual pace. Dark desires, rather than dizziness consumed my head as I dropped to the floor on my hands and knees, the silk robe cascading around me like a black waterfall.

Aunt Janie stumbled into the building, throwing fistfuls of banishing powder on the men and Bess. Phoebe, following on her heels and realizing what I had done, escorted the mob out the door, as if she were done giving a tour. Janie closed her eyes, looking exasperated. She dropped to her knees beside me. "You didn't drink my concoction, did you?"

My eyelids fluttered, thinking back. I sat back against a distorted mirror. "What exactly was in it?"

"Something to keep you out of trouble." She examined me closer, looking drained. "Tell me you didn't do what I saw you doing?" she asked, staring into my eyes.

"Of course I did, and I was successful with what I had to do. Now, I need you to go to Alexavier. He's here at the fairgrounds. Tell him he's free."

"And what of you?"

"I can undo this."

She shook her head, her eyes distraught. "No. You can't undo this forever choice. What's done is done. There's no coming back."

I shook my head as I fought to think through the dark, selfish thoughts. "It's not true. Elizabeth said there was magic in me to heal black hearts and change lives."

"I don't know what you're talking about. I have never heard of such a thing. You don't know what you've done. I've lost you forever. You have invited black magic into your white witch's heart. I can't undo what you've done. No one can. Unless..." Silence deadened the air. A shadow fell over her face.

Mistress Phoebe rushed in. She eyed us both and placed a hand on Aunt Janie's shoulder, knowing. "She won't be the same, it's true, but if we try the reconversion maybe she'll be close to it. I brought the English white truffle like you asked."

"Thank our departed witches that you are the keeper of the key to the portal of Essex."

"Retrieving the truffle would have been impossible otherwise."

"Did the Grand Coven's Council give you grief?"

"No, but they are curious how our local coven gets on. They asked me many questions. It was difficult to not tell them of the Eldress's ambitions."

Aunt Janie sighed. "They'll be wanting a visit soon, I'm sure of that, but it is another battle to be fought another day. For now, we must focus on the task at hand. Let us begin. Phoebe, grab that lantern and seal the doors."

With a sucking sound, the room darkened, then the crackling of a flame brought with it a dim light reflected off the curvy funhouse mirrors. "We are going to attempt a reconversion. Are you ready, Sophie?"

Part of me was growing fond of the power I felt, the surge in confidence that accompanied my increased knowledge and the energy from the diamond. The darkness in me pitied these frail women who spent their days either harvesting plants for half-effective cure-alls for ordinaries who didn't deserve them, or talking to wood sprites. I could even have the eldress position, if I wanted it. I was stronger now. She wouldn't be able to fight me. "I...I don't know."

"Think Sophie! I know the goodness is still in you. Think of your mother, think of your friends and the Mather boy."

Who I had been began to seem pointless. A cloud of dizziness filled my head. It was difficult to think and remember. "My parents. Macey. Alexavier."

"Yes. What do you feel for Alexavier?"

A wave of warmth washed over me and a tingling sensation began in my chest and radiated toward my limbs. "I love him." Sadness drenched my tone. Aunt Janie eyed Phoebe with a pitiful look.

"Can you hold onto that feeling of love, Sophie?" Phoebe asked, emptying the contents of her pocket onto the floor and setting it afire.

I nodded. "Yes." Outside the sealed doors, a man hollered and pounded with his fists.

"There's nothing for you here. Go away!" Aunt Janie shouted, gripping my hand with a fierce intensity.

"Hold onto that love, my dear," she said, as she wafted the smoke under my nose. Aromas of fennel and burned mistletoe wrapped in a smoky cloud of burning mushroom filled my chest. She repeated a rhyme over and over while Janie anointed my pressure points with sacred oil. She took my pulse.

"It's not working. She's lost forever," Aunt Janie cried out loud.

With her words, the pounding on the door subsided. The somber silence pressed on my chest. Warm, salty tears streamed down the sides of my face. "He won't want me like this. I have nothing to return for."

"That's not true," Phoebe said. "You have the power in you to undo the darkness. Look what you did outside. You broke a centuries-old black magic curse. You are strong, Sophie. Hold onto hope and love."

"Do it with your whole heart, my dear," Janie said.

I closed my eyes. I thought of all the damage hatred had caused, all the lives it had taken; Rebecca, Elizabeth, a long line of Mathers, and my loving parents. I didn't want to be like Rebecca or the judge. With a deep breath, I released the hatred and replaced the gaping hole with hope, with dreams. "I love him." The blackness, which gripped firmly to my insides, began to tear loose like Velcro peeling away from my fingers, and then my arms and legs, and finally from deep within my chest and head. Lightness filled every corner. Exhausted of my energy, I let go.

My body shook under someone else's power. "Sophie, wake up!" Riada's voice urged. Something was wrong. "Get her up. It's a matter of life or death."

"What's wrong?" Aunt Janie asked.

"It's Alexavier Mather. I can sense something is wrong. He's losing consciousness. I'm struggling to read his thoughts. I think he's dying," she said, panic ringing in her voice.

No! I screamed inside, battling to get to the surface. I swam in a sea of dark water, pushing the water beneath me with my flailing arms and legs. Fingers of sleep tugged at my ankles, urging me to succumb. *No.* I opened my mouth, gulping air. My ribcage begrudgingly expanded. "Hit me."

"What did she say?"

"She said, 'hit me,'" Riada replied. A jolt of energy twisted my head to the side. My cheeks stung as if a thousand jellyfish tentacles brushed across my skin. I shook my head and forced my unwilling eyelids to open. "Help me. Help me to my feet."

"Sophie, no. You have to rest." Aunt Janie frantically checked my eyes and appearance to see if the black magic and its physical attributes were fading.

I brushed her hands away and clasped Riada's arm. "I have to go to him."

Riada read my mind. "He's lying under the tree in front of your house. It's not that far, but can you make it?"

I nodded.

We found Alexavier collapsed under the mulberry tree. His lips and cheeks grew paler by the second. I dropped on my knees, wrapping my warm hands around his cooler ones. "Alexavier, what have you done?"

Riada placed a comforting hand on my shoulder. "What do you need to fix this? I can get it for you."

"I'm not Aunt Janie. I don't need botanicals, only the right spell." My thoughts raced through the fog in my head. *Think, dammit. Think!* The second hand of an imaginary clock boomed in my brain with every passing moment, and with it, Alexavier drifted farther away from me. I leaned down to his ear, cradling his face in my hands. "Come back to me, Alexavier. *Reditum.*" His breathing grew more shallow. "Riada, what did he take?"

She pointed to the thin pointed green leaves scattered by his hand. "Those."

I pressed my lips to his and tasted to be certain.

"No!" Riada screamed, worried for me.

I raised a hand to calm her, but my own heart raced with panic. "Wolfsbane. Deadly and quick. Riada, I don't…I don't." My lips trembled. Tears trickled down my cheeks as helplessness took over. For the first time in my life, real fear gripped me and shook hard.

"You can do this, Sophie. Will yourself to fix this."

I took a breath and bit my lip. "Maybe. Okay. Um."

Elizabeth's words came back to me and I finally understood what she meant. The power within me that was greater than magic—I had wondered all this time what it was and now I understood. Love, the force burning bright in my heart, healing me. Alexavier's love for me saved me from the darkness and now, I needed love to save him. I gathered my senses and closed my eyes. I pressed my hand to his chest where the poison was working to slow his breathing and heart rate. I inhaled a deep breath, my exhausted muscles filled with power.

"*Relego!*" I commanded, desperate. I pressed my hand against his neck, checking his pulse. It was weaker. I closed my eyes and summoned the magic again. The power felt like a wave leveling off. "No! Please, no."

I peered up at Riada. "Help me."

She leaned over him. "Sophie, I don't know what to do."

I couldn't think of anything else. "Take my hand. Say the spell with me."

"I'm not strong like you, Sophie, and I'm not a spellcaster. It won't work."

"Dammit!"

"Try the spell again. Concentrate on Alexavier."

Staving off the exhaustion that wanted to pull me under, I closed my eyes. The lightness in my heart expanded, pushing through my veins and pulsing to every corner of my body where the blackness had clung. The blood charm started to hum, soft at first, then buzzing with a vibration that matched my racing heartbeat. I clutched the red diamond with one hand and kept my other hand hovering above his heart. "*Relego!*"

A gurgling sound broke through the quiet, growing louder from within him. I moved my hand to his neck. A weak pulse sputtered erratically. I held my breath.

Seconds seemed like hours as his circulation slowly increased, coloring his ashen cheeks and lips with the warm glow of blood. With a sudden cough and gag, he rolled to his side and spewed the poison onto the grass beneath the tree. He rolled back and looked at me. "Sophie."

"Why did you do this?" I asked.

"I saw you collapse by the fire and then my father chased you. I fought so hard to get free. When I did, I raced toward you. I heard your aunt say you were gone." He reached for me, touching my cheek. "How are you here?"

"What else do you remember?"

"I was at your house earlier tonight. Then everything turned foggy. I woke up at my house, but I hadn't been sleeping. That sounds crazy, doesn't it?"

"Not really." What else could I say?

"I followed your aunt to the fairgrounds. I wasn't sure what was happening. I was floating above the carousel horses and you were wearing a black robe. When I saw my father go after you, I knew what he was going to do. That's when I managed to break free of the floating." His voice quivered. "My God, I can't live without you, Sophie. I won't."

The aching subsided as his hand pressed firmly against the side of my face, reassuring him I was fine. I took his other hand searching, wondering. The broken heart mark was gone. I pulled his hand from my cheek and checked his other wrist, in case I was losing my mind. No marks. The spell had worked. I collapsed on top of him and buried my head in his shoulder in a tangled and tired heap of arms and legs, our hearts beating together.

Disenchanted

A twirling sensation encompassed my whole body and a warm hand pressed on mine. Aunt Janie's eyes looked upon me in a somber way, sending my heart into a panicked race.

I sat up. "What happened?" I blurted out. I wondered how Alexavier was doing and when I would have to leave to move into Cross Manor. She said nothing, as if she were afraid to tell me. My hand touched the diamond. It vibrated against my fingers. I threw the blanket off and raced to the bathroom mirror. My previously crimson-colored lips were almost back to their natural pink and my skin was not as dewy. Ironically, it was a good sign; however, my eyelashes and hair were still longer. Definitely not a dream. I went back to my room and plunked on the bed, staring hard at her.

Aunt Janie rubbed her hands together. "Are you okay?"

I nodded; a dull ache in my chest grew sharper as I struggled to calm the hyperventilating.

"You broke your promise to me," she said, playing nervously with her black pearls.

"I'm sorry, but I need to know what's going on. What happened at the Seeking?"

"You chose black magic..." She brushed her hand along my hair that draped loosely around my shoulders, the strands straighter than they had been. "Somehow you came through the reconversion, but there will always be a part of you tinged black. Tempting you to return."

"I don't regret what I did. It had to be done."

"I understand why you did it. You are a white witch. It is innate in us to want to help the ordinaries. Just promise me, you won't ever go back to the darkness."

I shook my head. "I can't promise that." I wiped my forehead, wanting to change the subject. "Tell me about the Seeking."

She exhaled a sigh and studied my anxious face. "The Seeking? As far as everyone else remembers, you forced the pansy seed to grow. The Council placed you with me for your herbalist training."

With that news, a bit of relief settled in. I wouldn't have to leave to live at Cross Manor with the eldress. A sigh wheezed out of me. "How? Pansy seed? But that's not what really happened."

Her voice dropped to a whisper. "No. That's not what happened, exactly. What you did has never been done before. You broke Rebecca's dark spell on the Mathers and with it, you changed their lives, their history." She paused. "And ours, too."

"Their history? You mean, the whole line of Mathers survived finding true love?"

She nodded

"So Alexavier is fine?"

"Yes, but..."

I sat up taller, my eyes wide. If the judge no longer hated us and married Alexavier's mother, was it possible? "And my parents?"

"Sophie stop right there." She placed a concerned hand on my leg.

"You said our past changed, too? So that means..."

"Do not imagine it, child. They are not here."

"Mom and Dad?" I jumped out of the bed again, desperate to find them.

Her expression clouded over with grief and sadness. Her voice cracked. "Sophie, that has not changed."

My feet froze to the carpet. "Why not?"

"I do not know."

I searched for clues all around the room. I grabbed for my night table drawer and yanked. The iron girl was gone. Gone. Was she ever crafted? "Where is she?"

"Who?"

"The iron statuette, from the shop."

"History has changed. It's likely that thing was never made."

My hard breathing filled my ears. "How is it you know what really happened at the Seeking?"

"I consumed an awareness concoction before the Seeking so I could protect you, and it seems to have done its job, keeping me aware of what really happened. Your spell changed the past, starting with the present and working its way back in time. It took hours before Rebecca's wrongs were righted, changing the Mathers' lives and altering Alexavier's present."

My heart sputtered. "What of Alexavier and me?"

Her agonized pause told me before she spoke it. "He doesn't know you. You've never met."

Sorrow gripped my body. I dropped to the floor, sobbing.

Two weeks later, still heartbroken, I held on to the positive of what had happened. From a portrait of a silver-haired couple that appeared above our fireplace in the family room one day after the Seeking, I learned that Elizabeth and Francis had gotten their happy ending. And Janie told me how all the parking lots the judge had commissioned in the past were once again beautiful green parks and gardens, thriving in the Connecticut summers. Aunt Janie also told me that Kingshill was nothing more than a dilapidated old building, rotting away on the outskirts of town. The judge had changed. Alexavier had his mom back. The witches' relationship with the ordinaries was mended.

I had been trying to avoid him, not wanting to see the disconnect in his eyes. We had never met. I locked the shop door behind me and headed home, trying to outrace the looming storm.

Lightning flashed and the summer rain broke all around me. My wet sneakers splashed through fresh puddles. As soon as I reached the spot where the thief once caught me, I paused. My eyes closed and my head tilted upward, feeling the splatter of each heavy raindrop on my warm skin.

"Are you lost?"

The familiar voice, although lacking the British accent, sent butterflies to my stomach. I kept my eyes closed, not wanting the fantasy moment to end. *Say something else*, I thought. *Tell me you love me.*

"Miss?"

My brow crinkled. I wiped the water from my eyes and looked over at the beautiful face that eyed me with curiosity. "H-Hi," I stammered. "I'm Sophie." I didn't know what else to say.

"I'm Alexavier. Can I help you find your way?" He stood there, drenched in his white T-shirt and dark jeans that accentuated his height. His hair was as dark as midnight and his stubbled jaw was the same as it had always been, sexy and masculine.

"I...I think I know where I live." I pursed my lips, tasting the rain.

"Yes. You look familiar. I think you live next door to me." He looked up at the intersecting street signs and laughed. "You said your name is Sophie?"

I nodded, enthusiastically. Too enthusiastically. What was wrong with me? He didn't remember. He wouldn't and this was stupid.

"Well, Sophie. It looks as if our meeting was destined by the street signs. See?" His long arm pointed. "We're standing at the intersection of Alix and Sofie Streets."

"Ha. Funny coincidence." I stared at the ground nervously.

"Is it? This sounds weird, but meeting you out here, in the rain, it feels like déjà vu."

A crack of thunder pealed through the air. I jumped, suddenly very aware of all my senses. His fragrance whirled around me, intoxicating as ever. "Doesn't sound weird at all." I scrounged up enough courage to glance at him.

"I should walk you home," he said, looking concerned for me.

"You don't have to." As the rain pelted us, I felt something slip from my neck. Plop. Alexavier and I bent down at the same time to pick up the pendant. Our fingers clasped around the stone and as it heated, we both dropped it back to the street.

"Did that just heat up or was it my imagination?"

I waited a second and plucked it from the puddle by my feet. I couldn't do this again. "I'm sorry. I have to go."

"No. Wait. This isn't déjà vu, is it?" His gray eyes pierced me with a knowing look. My fingers trembled. My breathing picked up.

"No," I said, my voice barely above a whisper. My lips quivered.

"I've been dreaming of you," he whispered into my ear. He drew back slightly and lifted my chin with one finger. I shut my eyes. His lips met mine, kissing me with intention. His hands explored, tender at first then hungrily touching. His mouth created a feverish blaze of pleasure within me. I could not get enough, the ache growing…the delicious temptation begging. Pleasant shivers tingled through me as we paused, connected momentarily by the slightest touch of our lips. Then I stepped back, trying to regain my scattered sensibilities.

"Sophie? Are you okay?" he asked.

I wasn't sure how to answer. He smiled upon me, and I knew I was where I belonged, although I was going to have to get used to his American accent. "I've been dreaming of you, too.

Disenchanted

Acknowledgements

This book is the beginning of a dream and would not have been possible without support, love, and faith from my family and friends. I want to thank everyone who expressed encouragement and enthusiasm along my journey to publication, as well as, joy and happiness for my success. You will never know how much that continues to touch my heart.

My sincere appreciation goes to Mirror World Publishing. Their exceptional team has been a joy to work with and their vision has exceeded my expectations.

To my sister, Bernadette, thank you for filling my childhood with fantastic fun and laughter.

Most importantly, I want to thank my husband, Brian. Without your love, support, and unshakable faith in my abilities and determination, I could not have dreamed so big. For loving me, for encouraging me to live life when I'd rather curl up with a book, for making me laugh, and for your bigger than life supply of joie de vivre. You are truly one of a kind.

About the Author

Leigh Goff grew up in Maryland where she resides today. Her writing is inspired by an eclectic childhood, a vivid imagination, and compelling historical events. After taking several writing courses in college and attending professional writing workshops after she graduated from the University of Maryland, she joined the Maryland Writers' Association and Romance Writers of America. She is also an approved artist with the Maryland State Arts Council.

If you liked this book, you may like some of our other titles.

To learn more about our authors and our current projects visit:
www.mirrorworldpublishing.com or follow @MirrorWorldPub or
like us at www.facebook.com/mirrorworldpublishing

 mirror world publishing

*We appreciate every like, tweet, facebook post and review and we
love to hear from you. Please consider leaving us a review online
or sending your thoughts and comments to
info@mirrorworldpublishing.com
Thank you.*

CPSIA information can be obtained
at www.ICGtesting.com
Printed in the USA
FFOW04n1722200515
13439FF

9 780992 049096